Pet Shop Girls

ANJA SNELLMAN

Translated by

Scott Kaukonen and Helena Halmari

IceCold
Crime

Disclaimer: This is a work of fiction. All characters, names, incidents, and situations depicted in this work are wholly the creation of the author's imagination or are used fictitiously. Any resemblance to actual events, organizations, places, or persons, living or dead, is entirely coincidental and beyond the intent of the author, the translator, or the publisher.

Published by
Ice Cold Crime LLC
5780 Providence Curve
Independence, MN 55359

Printed in the United States of America

Cover by Ella Tontti

Published in agreement with Stilton Literary Agency, Finland.

Originally published in Finnish

Library of Congress Control Number: 2013936895

ISBN-13: 978-0-9824449-6-2
ISBN-10: 0-9824449-6-6

Pet Shop Girls

For Alma, Elsa, Jukka

Part one

for whither thou goest, I will go;
and where thou lodgest, I will lodge;
thy people shall be my people,
and thy god my god;
where thou diest, will I die,
and there will I be buried.

the book of ruth

Part two

what remains is
clearness, sinking, depth

göran sonnevi

Part three

It is not knowledge that we lack.
We lack the courage
to understand what we know and the courage
to make conclusions.

sven lindqvist

A Girl Who Looks Like Me

1.

I disappeared twelve years ago during the first week of December in the city of O. The last eyewitness sighting of me and my girlfriend, who disappeared along with me, was made in the stairwell of her apartment building on Friday, the first day of December, around 6:30 p.m. The police regarded this account as highly reliable.

It said that most likely I was wearing blue jeans, faded in the thighs; a white T-shirt that fell all the way to my hips; and a hooded pink sweatshirt with the face of a laughing black monkey on the back. Around my hips, I wore a wide, brown, studded leather belt with a big buckle. I had a long pink scarf around my neck over silver-colored chains. In my ears, pearl earrings and silver hoops. Possibly, I was also carrying a turquoise satin backpack and a small, blue-and-white Nike duffel bag. My height at that time was five feet six-and-a-half inches, and according to my mother's informed assessment, I was of slender build and my hair was blonde and straight, falling a little below my shoulders. My eyes were bluish gray. A quintessential Scandinavian. Literally. The policeman who filled out the forms typed up everything, as usual. Later, it was also reported that my hair had looked somewhat dirty, and there had been a large red spot on my left cheek, possibly an inflamed zit. Well, I had never really doubted the snooping skills of Linda's neighbors.

The police considered another observation from December third, Sunday night, a bit vague, but nonetheless recorded it. In cases like mine, there are always lots of "tips," two-thirds of which come from the "usual informants," those who call the police whether the missing is a girl, a car, or a parrot.

The Sunday night observation came from a midtown kiosk owner, who once had been suspected of robbing his own kiosk. The allegation was never proven, but suspicion always persisted. The neighborhood thought he was gay; the residents of the nearby buildings had complained about him often and had told their children to buy their candy and tram tickets from somewhere else. The man kept his little kiosk, which resembled a railroad car, open from early morning till late into the night. During the night, he sold snacks, french fries, hot dogs, and meat pasties from another window in the other end of the kiosk. After the bars closed, residents of the nearby buildings found that the traffic around the kiosk consisted mostly of loud swarms of restless, young men.

A girl who looked like me had come to the kiosk late in the evening of December third, a little bit before midnight, with a middle-aged man. The girl who looked like me had worn the man's camel-colored overcoat on her shoulders and had a bunny, or possibly a chinchilla, in her arms. The kiosk owner had not been able to remember anything else about my clothing, except that I wasn't wearing a hat and my hair had been a mess. The man who had been with me wore a dark suit, a brown-checkered scarf, and a broad-brimmed hat that shadowed his face. Under the hat, his hair was longish, wavy, and light brown; and, in one hand, he carried an expensive-looking black briefcase. The kiosk owner remembered that the girl who looked like me had appeared tearful and somewhat out of sorts, and she had a sore on her left temple and a bruise under one of her eyes.

The kiosk owner's story irritated my mother, and she vehemently denied that it could have been me. Strangely, she ignored the part about the chinchilla, although she had heard from Linda's mother that Linda and I had been dragging such a thing around with us. Mother let out a laugh when the police called her about the Sunday night account. Absurd, incredulous, impossible—that's what she responded to many of the police's comments and questions. Back then, Mother was not her usual deliberative, analytic self. She cried a lot and laughed a lot, mostly at the same time.

When the "Jasmin Task Force" was established, the head of the investigation bluntly told Mother that if nothing happened within the next six months, we should amend her wish list. After the police found Linda's body, he personally visited Mother and told her that now the team had even less of that famous eternal hope. Mother told him to give it to her straight; she preferred to hear just the cold facts. And what followed were cold facts: a case, he said, about the murder of two girls, or the murder of one and a ruthless kidnapping of the other. Either way, it was difficult to solve; a stroke of luck was needed.

Mother grew to like the detective, who wore a black ski cap and always talked about my case in the "we"-form. He liked to use his wife's bright red reading glasses, and when he was young, he had been one of the country's best hockey players. Within police ranks, the man was known as Penalty Box, and my mother began to call him that too. Mother wondered about Penalty Box's beard. Never before had she seen a policeman with facial hair, let alone one like his. Penalty Box promised her he would shave his goatee as soon as Jasmin was found.

Over the years, the police occasionally received reports about a girl who looked like me. A classmate had seen me in the amusement park with a small child. My former riding teacher had nearly bumped into me in a department store elevator. A family on vacation in Malaysia reported that I had stayed in the same hotel. A few times, Penalty Box received bogus calls as well; someone posing as my kidnapper demanded a six-figure ransom. Penalty Box told my mother about the first call. He had already warned her that sooner or later opportunists of all sorts would try their luck. Despite the warnings, Mother was horrified and insisted that the police agree to the caller's demands. Mother would sell her apartment, her mother and father would liquidate their stock portfolio, and so on. Penalty Box was familiar with the constant mood swings of kidnapping victims' families, and so, after the first time, he didn't burden my mother with such calls. Penalty Box could smell fraud, and even busted a few of them.

The Jasmin Task Force was reconvened every now and then. From time to time they received calls about a possible location of my body, but any connection to my case was soon ruled out. My disappearance—a presumed homicide—was, however, revisited in these contexts, and the police routinely checked out all the details. Chains of events, lines of investigations. Would something new turn up? Or, could some connection be made to another cold case? Could the fire at an industrial building have had some connection to Linda and me? Could something have been missed? They interviewed the motorcycle gangs, who had their meeting places near the industrial building. They asked key figures about recent rave parties at the industrial halls, and sought out the homeless who had been sleeping in the vicinity. A few arsonists who were active in the area at that time were interviewed. Recent police academy graduates eagerly read through the files, searched the internet, bookmarked new links, and added exclamation points and question marks in the margins of the reports. A chinchilla bunny in her arms? Oh well.

The kiosk owner's observation was precisely correct. It had been me. In his hurry, the Baptist took a risk and dragged me out from the car with him to buy his favorite pipe tobacco, the kind that smelled of dates, which he had run out of or which had fallen from his pocket in the blazing rush. Oh yeah, and then he had to have his coconut chocolate. Bounty. Those two smells were always around him. Then, too.

I remember well the look in that bald kiosk owner's eyes. He had some kind of nerve problem in one of his eyes, and I thought he winked at me. I was freezing and nauseous. I don't remember exactly what I was wearing under the Baptist's overcoat, a top and small glittery shorts, I imagine. The drinks mixed with the pills had made me both sluggish and given me sensory overload.

By then, Linda was already dead. She died on Sunday, in early evening. Her body wouldn't be found until a few months later. It's strange that the sharp-eyed kiosk owner didn't mention to the police the bitter stench of smoke in our clothes. It stayed in my hair and in Miss Frank's fur for days. Perhaps the man's sense of smell was poor, or maybe the odors from the grill masqueraded the scent of smoke. In any case, had he mentioned it, Penalty Box might have caught that small detail, might have put two and two together, and perhaps might have taken up our trail.

Somewhere in there, in the cold case archives of the police department in the city of O., are the broken pieces of my last weekend in my hometown.

Since that night, I have not touched snow. I haven't stood in a blizzard, tasting the snowflakes falling on my tongue. I haven't skied, nor have I ridden a sled down a snow-covered hill. How I did wish during those first years that there would be snowdrifts outside so deep I could jump from the window and flee. I haven't even thought about snow and ice for years now. Nor jumping. I haven't thought about escaping or leaving, even though it would be easy now, when there is no hope of the Baptist getting better. I know where he keeps the keys, and I know the code for the gate. With only the two of us in the house, he's at my mercy.

Could I still skate? I don't know. Could I knit a mitten? I don't think so. But I can do all kinds of other things. I can take dictation in shorthand—in the Baptist's native language, of course; I can list all the species of roses in our garden, and cut and fertilize them; I can find the right kind of sponges from the bottom of the sea; I can clean them and press away the gray mucus, cutting the stem into a beautiful shape. In addition to all these things, I can do unmentionable acts about which no guidebooks have ever been written, and won't be. Or—who knows? Maybe you'll one day read *Jasmin Martin's Guide to Lap Dancing* or *Introduction to Pole Dancing*.

I don't miss back home; my home is here. When my home country is mentioned in some news broadcast or when I read a newspaper clipping to the Baptist about a movie or concert review or a visiting opera, I say to him, How could I leave you now? And he smiles, looks me in the eye, and pats my arm with his frail, unsteady hand, so timidly and clumsily that it pains me. The formerly muscular wrist is now thin, filled with gray spots, like a branch on a eucalyptus tree. And then we talk about something else, or I ask if he'd like me to wash him. We use a really big sponge, a honey-yellow one. That's what he likes most. That, and the sound of my giggle. It's true, he says, that for years my giggle has been too old; the sound he adored died a long time ago. That's what happens to all girls—with the giggle and other things. To please him, I've tried to practice a child's giggle. In the evenings, I watch TV ads, and there is always a cute little girl in a dress softened by a flower-scented fabric softener letting out just the right kind of giggle.

In the beginning—when I was trying to escape at least once a week—the Baptist reprimanded me with all kinds of threats. The yard is full of mines. The gate and the fence on top of the wall are electrified. Your mother and little brother will suffer. Without a passport, you'll be in trouble and eventually fall into the hands of ruthless criminals.

There will always be tomorrow and the day after tomorrow, I answered. That was his favorite saying. I stole it from him, threw it back in his face. But he just laughed. Little Ruth, I like you just like that.

At the time I didn't even know his real name. I called him Jim Thompson, since I knew he didn't like that name. When he asked me to organize the bookshelves in his study, I learned that his real name is Bruno Max Huber. Several books written by him stood on the shelves.

Recently, I was declared dead. Mother could have done it much sooner. After the tsunami in Thailand, my home country, too, eased its laws for declaring persons dead. They wanted to alleviate the suffering of the families, the hopeless life-suffocating waiting. But had I been among those washed away by the waves, I believe my mother would have waited for me anyway, all these twelve years.

I became a cold case, just as Penalty Box had warned my mother.

No body, no suspect.

Vanished like ashes into the wind. Proverbs in my native language come to mind, and I hear them in my Grandmother Muma's voice.

In my heart I know that my mother is still waiting for me, even though she's been informed of the probabilities. Even though she well knows the fates of lost children. Even though she's a doctor and can separate facts from faith. Even though her life has changed completely, so much, since my disappearance. Even though. Despite all the rational talk and the twists and turns, Mother has refused to move out of the apartment where we lived together before my disappearance. My room is exactly as it was, the gallery of family pictures on my bookshelf, my pictures here and there on tables, a fresh pink carnation in front of my school picture, the one that was said to be soulful. It was that picture, my most recent, that appeared in all the newspapers after Linda had been found, and on television crime shows and web pages. It was that one that was on the cover of the book Mother wrote, an expression of hope, of course.

A few readers thought that they had seen me somewhere. One person who approached Mother anonymously was absolutely certain he had seen our pictures on some internet porn sites. But when Penalty Box and a police unit specializing in internet sex crimes investigated the issue, no shocking photos were found, only a couple of cute bikini pictures from the kids' galleries.

Mother was perplexed about the pictures, but only for a nanosecond since she had feared the worst; and what that was, she didn't even dare to consider. So she was relieved when nothing was found, even though Penalty Box told her nothing was certain, that there could have been something, and that those kinds of sites come and go. What was here a moment ago is already far away, over there. That's the strategy in these cases: the police will do all they can, and after that they'll just hope that higher powers exist, he said to my mother.

Luckily Mother never saw the pornographic pictures taken of Linda and me; she had enough to deal with the few facts and inferences the police were able to cobble together. Anyway, Mother would never have identified me from the pictures at the Wet Pet Club. Or those many others. Those pictures were not meant for mothers.

During the first years, Mother asked over and over again: Why? Why did her daughter disappear just like that, without a trace? Why had her daughter vanished into thin air? And if her daughter went somewhere of her own free will, why in the world did she leave? And why was it that this happened to her, Sara Martin? First, the love of her life dies of cancer, and then her daughter disappears? But no, my daughter IS alive, she MUST be alive! That's what Mother decided.

Later Mother tried to contact me through the media. I found several magazine interviews where she said I could and should return whenever, from wherever, and in whatever shape I was in. If I was just alive and returned, regardless of whatever experiences or twists of fate I'd endured, Mother wouldn't blame me for anything. Mother wouldn't ask me to explain. Mother wouldn't pressure, scare, or threaten. Mother would never ask me why.

Those questions she'd save for the Man Upstairs.

2.

On the Baptist's scholarly articles and the dust jackets and back covers of the books he wrote, there always was the same picture, a picture from his youth, in which the Baptist—Bruno Max Huber—glances over his left shoulder, eyes squinting, thick eyebrows, stubbly beard, a dimple near his lips, and a diamond in the earlobe facing the camera.

What would Mother think about the picture? What if I could have secretly sent one of the Baptist's books to Mother, slipping a note between the pages: Hi Mom, I'm living with the author of this book far away from home. He's quite an interesting guy, now that I've gotten to know him better. Maybe not a dream son-in-law, but rich and handsome—at least he was when he was younger.

I've had time to toy with all kinds of ideas.

Sometimes I've wondered: What if I had met him somewhere as that barely-thirty-year-old man in the picture? Maybe during a language course in Brighton, a summer vacation in Malta, or traveling in Miami with Linda—if she and I would've ever made it that far from home?

What if Mother had met him somewhere? Run into Bruno Max Huber at some conference abroad? Would Mother have liked him? Sometimes I've imagined their meeting. I try to picture them in the same room, my mother and Bruno Max Huber. What would they talk about? Somehow I think they would have a lot to talk about. The Baptist is a person you simply have to listen to.

From my previous life, I remember only two photographs. One is the school picture I especially hated for its tilt-your-head-delicately pretense. The other is an early birthday picture, which Mother still has on her nightstand, the one she wrote about in her first book, which she published less than three years after my disappearance.

The name of the book is *Monday*, and in it Mother describes in detail the day when she realized that I had gone missing. That was Mother's last week at work. That Friday afternoon, she closed her private gynecology office and took extended leave of absence. For a long time, Mother could not return to her office, and the receptionist kept organizing the office papers; she called patients with cancellations, and fielded the reactions of astonished and angry clients. Paula Pauliina—her name, indeed, was Paula Pauliina—had also been our house cleaner once a week throughout my childhood, and also frequently the babysitter when Father and Mother weren't home. Paula Pauliina lived with her old mother, sewed and knitted, did genealogy, took correspondence courses, and who knows what else? She did something new every year, mostly learned from the local community education classes. The new edition of *Every Woman's Household Hints* contained numerous tips sent in by Paula Pauliina. Mother often said that if Paula Pauliina didn't exist, she would need to be invented.

There's one memory I've been thinking a lot about lately. It's a moment like this:

"I'm bad, I'm bad," sings little Jasmin. She is sitting in Father's lap and relishing the attention. Father has a beard, and it tickles the back of her neck. Jasmin giggles and swings the fluffy, tinkling bunny she's just found inside a gift package. Jasmin has blonde, curly hair, and she giggles charmingly all around. She shakes the bunny. It jingles. The bunny sways and swings. Paula Pauliina glows. She had made the stuffed bunny, and had hidden a jingle bell inside the bunny's stomach. That way you always know where the little child is.

Mother and Father are smiling. Everyone is there when Jasmin turns five: Family, friends, neighbors, acquaintances. Her kindergarten friends have also been invited. Michael Jackson and the Spice Girls are playing on the jukebox. The boys are fascinated with that fat, shining, red jukebox in the corner of the room—Jasmin's birthday present from Mother and Father. One of the boys is already trying to climb it. Someone's sister pulls the boy by his pant leg. Get down! The boys are wearing T-shirts and baggy pants, lots to grab from. The girls wear spangled tops and lace blouses, miniskirts, and satin dresses. You can see their ribcages shining through.

"I'm bad," sings Jasmin in Father's lap. She waves at the photographer. She giggles and giggles. She has picked five raspberries off her birthday cake and stuck them on her fingertips. Probably not appropriate, but who's going to scold her on her birthday! Jasmin snaps the raspberries from her fingertips and the photographer snaps photos. Jasmin starts from her thumb, then the pinkie, and the ring finger. She makes a V-sign with two fingers, a raspberry victory sign. The guests are applauding. The bunny floats and eventually flies off. Oops-a-daisy. It jingles. Paula Pauliina quickly picks up the bunny and hands it back to Jasmin. The cake has five candles. The raspberries are sweet. Outside, the sun is shining. A perfect composition. A perfect light. A perfect day to turn five. Jasmin is called the birthday girl, and for the first time she feels all way down in her stomach how good it feels. Birthdays, to be the birthday girl. The center of attention. Admired. To be important. "I'm bad," sings the girl, full of her own charm, on her fifth birthday. Then she blows out the candles, all at once. Applause. Five years later she will be given a live rabbit as a present. Ten years later she will have gone missing. She's allowed only to take her chinchilla rabbit, the one that resembles her childhood pet.

3.

You have great skin, all sonnets and ice cream, and you're clearly totally Satan's property, said the Baptist to me when we met for the first time at the Wet Pet Club.

He said he had been observing me for a long time by then, although I hadn't noticed him among all those heavy-breathing older men who, like him, had been sitting or standing in semidarkness. Well, the Baptist always did wear that wide-brimmed hat, but so, too, did some of the others.

Oh, said I. I'd taken a happy pill, and was ready for some crazy fun, the end result of which would be the rustle of bills filling the inside of my new light-brown Mulberry handbag.

Show me everything that Satan has taught you, he whispered and leaned back in his booth, his arms and legs stretched out. Then I'll give you a grade, on a flaming-to-hellish scale, he said slowly, as if testing my knowledge of English, and smiled with his dark eyes. He was a big man, almost six foot six, with long hair, a broad mouth, and those captivating eyes with the dark brows. And the hat. He liked broad-brimmed hats and caps pulled low to shadow his face.

He visited me many times after that—I didn't even count how many times—first in the back room of the Pet Shop and later countless times at the Wet Pet Club. First he demanded that I giggle; he kept tickling me as I sat in his lap, then he wanted me to masturbate him, then he yelled at me, and then he paid double for me. Eventually he reserved me only for himself. I was his girl. And my purse kept filling with more and more bills, and I finally upgraded it to the newest style, even though Linda could never understand what fascinated me about that particular designer bag. She herself swore by the name of Vuitton, favored by all those zero-sized models; those bags didn't have any silly pictures of trees or running greyhounds.

Was Linda sometimes jealous that the Baptist chose me? I never thought about it back then. Even though Lido pulled a fast one and offered me to others when the Baptist was not around. And even though the brown-skinned Staring-Randi tried to protect me, like some idiot. Eventually, the Baptist found out about all of this, of course.

He always sat in the same corner—in the shadow, next to the glowing plastic pole. He talked to me at length about Satan and the flames of hell, about how I was actually only glazed with sin, but not thoroughly absorbed within it—in other words, I was potentially savable. He asked that I dance for him, first on the pole and then I sat on his lap. And of course he took pictures of me, lots of pictures. He paid Lido separately for permission to take pictures of me at the club.

He said his name was Jim Thompson. All the girls were circling around him and talking about him a lot. He had been a regular at the WPC already for some time; it was said that he was some kind of businessman who traveled around the world in these certain networks, and that he had always liked young girls—he never visited adult women.

Some girls told me as a fact that it was he, Jim Thompson, who was behind all this, that he was the big boss, even above Lido, and he managed the whole business from some other country as the mysterious Mr. Dakota. Some of the girls had occasionally heard talk about a Mr. Dakota, and we immediately decided that someone with a name like that must be the actual big boss. We were sure we were part of some larger network; we felt excited and important. We couldn't imagine that little Lido, with his silver-tipped boots, would alone be the one behind all this.

4.

December 17, 200...

...Art historian, scholar of religion and sexual ethics, Bruno Max Huber was in demand as a lecturer at universities and conferences around the world.

Bruno Max Huber was an inspiring teacher and a tireless cheerleader for his students. He was regarded as a genuine renaissance man whose expertise stretched from visual arts to baroque music, from chastity belts and orchids to medieval masquerade games.

Just like the undersigned, many remember Bruno Max Huber's tall and slender shape, always carrying Herodotus in his briefcase, always at the opening nights of new museums, art exhibitions, and charity galas. Bruno Max Huber traveled often, and liked it. He always accepted offers that intrigued him, and was, indeed, a dinner speaker in demand both at universities and high-powered businesses. He was also known for his open-mindedness and his unprejudiced disposition. He regularly donated to numerous AIDS research centers around the world. In addition, in recent years, he directed his energies and resources toward fighting human trafficking, a cause close to his heart.

Part of the eccentricity of Bruno Max Huber was the fact that he had never revealed the year and place of his birth. According to most accounts, he was born in A., in the early 1940s. During his university days, he changed his name, and after he emigrated, he never returned to his native land.

Bruno Max Huber liked to keep his private life to himself. He occasionally withdrew to work in the complete solitude of his castle-like home situated in the city of H.

Bruno Max Huber's expertise in the area of erotic art was without peer. Until the last few years, he was considered to be the foremost expert and a key buyer at art auctions. The undersigned has no knowledge of the fate of Huber's art collection, estimated to be immeasurably valuable. Bruno Max Huber was not known to have any next of kin, and he was buried in a private ceremony.

Bruno Max Huber received many international awards and honors in his field. He received honorary doctorates from universities in several countries. His works have been translated into many languages. The scientific and the artistic communities will miss a great person.

ANDREAS S. *The author is Bruno Max Huber's longtime friend and colleague.*

5.

That year, spring came late. Five months after my disappearance, when the snow finally melted, Mother founded FALL, the Family Association for the Loved ones of the Lost. During the last week in May, she appeared on a TV talk show, and was flooded with calls from parents and relatives whose loved ones were also missing.

Despite some discouragement from the police, Mother decided to organize a celebration of life service for me, to which she invited a few members of the media. It was not a memorial, but an occasion for sorrow and hope. A forum to share feelings. The service was meant for all those whose loved ones were still missing. During the service, Mother read a story that she had written, "Girl on an Unknown Path," which was partially based on my diary entries. Pictures of me at various ages were shown on a screen.

The newspapers published a lot of stories about Linda and me. We became almost like celebrities, as though we had won *Idol* or some other TV game show. How proud we would have been to witness our own success! And, how much creativity Mother had been hiding! What a surprise! She, who had always said that she loathed tabloids and the covers of women's magazines, now didn't hesitate to have her face plastered all over them, "for the cause of the lost girls." In interviews, Mother often remarked that boys return home, but girls never do. Mother had started reading poetry and had found a pair of lines by a Hungarian religious poet named Pilinszky. Later Mother had the text written in black letters on white marble. She had a tombstone made for me, which she kept in the basement storage room in our building, inside that big red Samsonite suitcase of hers.

When Linda was found at the beginning of May, but I was not, the police Violent Crimes Unit ramped up its efforts. With Penalty Box in the lead. Mother decided to dedicate herself fully to support-group work. She redecorated her empty Ob/Gyn office and used it as the headquarters for the Family Association for the Loved ones of the Lost.

Mother asked Paula Pauliina to join her. Mother had hoped that her longtime employee would be able to continue to work for her, but Paula Pauliina categorically declined. She was really upset that even she had been interrogated, not just once, but three times, about my disappearance. It didn't help having my mother console her, assuring her that everyone close to the victim was questioned many times, to discover if they might have happened to remember anything new. Anything might be important. Paula Pauliina was upset, and for a long time she didn't want anything to do with Mother.

Linda's mother initially took part in FALL activities as an energetic and active member, fundraiser, and event hostess, but she ran out of energy. Her daughter was no longer just missing, she was dead, and no one knew the circumstances leading to her death. The former beauty queen was crushed by the reopening of the investigation, the incessant media interest in Linda's death as well as in her life. They dug up everything. Her first-born daughter's death, her divorces, the allegations of embezzlement against her first husband, drunk driving charges, shoplifting cases, boyfriends. The following spring, Linda's mother was found on the floor of her entrance foyer, having suffocated in her own vomit, with tranquilizers and alcohol in her bloodstream.

So it was my mother alone who became the poster child of grief. Sara Martin became the Listener to Those Left Behind. She appeared continuously in the media, and she started her own blog, Mother's Gloomblog, which became very popular. She surprised even herself by openly talking about her pain. She discussed her career and her failed first marriage, her own sexuality, her methods for raising children, her religious or irreligious inclinations. She confessed that after my disappearance she began writing letters to the editor on all kinds of topics. She confessed that she had been looking for further injustices in the world into which she could pour her grief. She revealed that she had written my name on two voting ballots, and had filtered her energy into excessive exercise and dieting. During the year after my disappearance, Mother lost more than twenty pounds.

When Penalty Box later received tips from his informants about me and some domestic child porn websites, Mother asked him what it might mean. Penalty Box told her that a girl who looked like me had been seen in pornographic films and magazines. A Dutch informant had identified me in a picture and drawn conclusions about my home country from the curtains, electrical outlets, and door knobs that appeared in the movie. Even though it was again highly unlikely that anything would come up, Penalty Box wanted to make the rounds among a few known enthusiasts. You just might hear something new.

It had been a couple of years since his previous rounds, and the game was changing rapidly. It was full of creative playmakers, Penalty Box explained, stroking his beard. Lots of small, quick players. By the time you get there, only the net is still quivering. And the ice is silent. Frost on the plexiglass. Mother was fond of

Penalty Box's analogies. If anyone were to find Jasmin, it would be Penalty Box, she thought.

Even though Mother had led herself to believe and accept that it was not totally out of the question that Linda's and my fates had something to do with the underworld, violence, and who knows what kinds of perversions, deep down Mother didn't believe in such a thing. So Mother wanted to join Penalty Box on his rounds, and even though Penalty Box initially didn't think it was a good idea, he allowed Mother to come. He prepared her with an analogy she will never forget. The men in this field—and they are mostly men, explained Penalty Box—are just like stamp-collectors; they are detail-oriented, fanatic guys dedicated to just that one thing. They are hamsters who like to hang out with other hamsters.

I've often tried to imagine my mother going from one adult toy store to another, photo studios masked as massage parlors, and live dance strip clubs where girls and boys were available for purchase for adult games.

In some of those places, stories circulated of me and Linda. Former Wet Pet Club clients still hung around, and our pictures were probably still passed around the inner circles, but of course nobody uttered a word to the police.

They never traced me through that path. It sure feels like we're waiting for the puck to drop, but we're not giving up, said Penalty Box, again and again. He had his intuitions after Linda was found and after the Pet Shop investigation. Young men with foreign backgrounds had been hanging around the shopping center around the time we disappeared. Some had been questioned, backgrounds investigated. Some had rap sheets for assault and battery, some had even done time for rape, as was the case too often. Penalty Box was after something there, but what? He had no proof.

Was it the water bears that can live in hot springs, at the top of the Himalayas, under endless ice, or at the bottom of the ocean? I recently learned about water bears in the Baptist's library. They can stop their metabolism and move into a state of cryptobiosis. They can survive for years in a dried-up state, then return, just like that, to the world of the living.

And the girls, the Pet Shop girls, those who remained and were quiet as mice, looked at pictures of my mother and read her stories in magazines and maybe even met her in some context. Irina, Beata, Niina, Sandra...any one of them could have given a tip, but none opened her mouth. They continued with their schools, short-term jobs, and lives, as if nothing had happened.

Later, my father offered reward money for any valuable tip, but with the exception of a few fortune hunters, nobody took the bait.

You are out there somewhere, living your lives of which I have no clue, but what I know for sure is that not a single one of you has forgotten me and Linda and the Pet Shop.

Mother received a massive response, hundreds and hundreds of stories of disappearances; and she sometimes felt people almost forgot about me in the middle of all that commotion. She then always returned to my last diary, the one that was left in the locked drawer of my desk. Eventually she knew it by heart. At times, she had the feeling that she had written it herself. Sometimes, during the darkest hours of the night, she was positive that I had never existed, that she had imagined me, a daughter with the name of Jasmin Victoria Martin, and so therefore she must immediately call Penalty Box and tell him the whole embarrassing truth.

After a few years, Mother went back to school. Who would have believed it? Mother applied to a cosmetology school and, in addition to cutting and curling, she started to study Indian scalp massage. Indisputably, it was a strange move on Mother's part. But I do understand her, pursuing something that had interested her since childhood. Yet, in a family of doctors, daughters could not become hairdressers.

Mother writes in her blog, Mother's Gloomblog, that it may have been hairdressing that saved her during the first years of my disappearance. Other people's hair. In her support group meetings, they brushed hair and massaged scalps. For a time, Mother even considered buying the salon that Anita had left behind.

How do I feel, writing about Mother? It's like eating a mix of salty licorice and gummy bears.

6.

During the first year, I was not allowed to watch TV alone, nor listen to the radio, even though all I had wanted was to listen to music, any music. The Baptist was strict. My healing should be as complete as possible. First, I was allowed to listen to classical music, either as played by the Baptist himself or on cassettes he gave to me. I occasionally asked for other types of music, and sometimes the Baptist brought me some, other times not. Every once in a while, he gave long, in-depth explanations as to why a particular singer or band was not suitable for my healing process. The boys in this or that band looked like whores, or their music contained too many references to sex or drugs or, most often, to both.

During the second or third year he allowed me to start reading books; that is, books that the Baptist brought me. One at a time. First, of course, the Bible. At the same time, he gave me a pencil and some paper, first a single sheet and then gradually more. Initially, I kicked up a fuss and ate the paper, broke the pencil, heaved, and then threw up. I had often watched how my classmate Merita, who suffered from bulimia, did it, and I was able to shoot a spray of vomit quicker than the Baptist could react. Shrugging his shoulders, the Baptist called Esther to my room and asked her to clean it up while I looked on, snorting.

As time passed, I started to keep a diary, although in the beginning I had to explain to the Baptist what I had written, sentence by sentence. I sometimes entertained myself by lying in my translations. But I knew that the Baptist was not really listening anyway, since he oftentimes declared he was not interested in my rancid and sinful former life. Sometimes, in between the floorboards, I hid pieces of paper on which I had written: the Baptist is a perv, the Baptist is a disturbed dickhead. I always ate those pieces of paper before Esther cleaned my room.

What a murderer lived in me. I killed him in dozens of ways, each more punishing than the next. I slashed him, stabbed him, skewered him with pieces of glass and with knives, smashed his head with a chair and a statue, shot him with a hunting rifle I had stolen from the gun cabinet, poisoned him with insecticides, pushed him from the balcony and down the staircase, doused him with gasoline and burned him like a torch, pressed a pillow into his face, drugged him and buried him alive, tied barbed wire around his neck from behind, punctured his eyes, chopped off his hands at his wrists, mutilated his genitals with acid, pushed an antique sword straight into his heart...

And now I'm looking at him with caring eyes, like my own child. I'm now your patient, he says to me and tries to smile. But don't bother trying to cure me, he whispers. Not even ground peacock bones can cure this one.

I could overdose him on any of the countless medicines I give him every day; I could stick a syringe into his withered arm so deep that the needle would come through on the other side. How easy it would be. But I know that he will be repaired soon. That's what he always says himself. *Repaired*. *Redeemed, cleansed*, at the same time as taken away. Eventually there will be mercy for all of us. He believes in it.

Sometimes I tried to ask Rebekah whether she had similar desires and fantasies with regard to the Baptist. She never quite understood what I meant. Yes, during these years I actually made a new friend, even though we didn't have the opportunity to know each other for long. Rebekah didn't know her real age; she was likely a few years younger than me, but she looked considerably older. When we met, she had already been practicing her profession for several years.

I lived in an underground, windowless room my first few weeks. Later, I suffered my punishments there after my escape attempts and other mischief. Rebekah brought me food and drink.

Sometimes I asked her to stay with me, and she, goodhearted as she was, pitied me. I wrapped myself around her, shook her arms, and cried. Her head came only to my shoulders, and she was so slim and slender that I occasionally thought her bones were being crushed when I squeezed her. Her black hair tickled my eyelids. She smelled foreign, mossy, and sweet.

For weeks, maybe months, Rebekah had drifted up and down the streets in the city of M. in the neighboring country. Her pimp had died in a gunfight, and so she had passed the nights on beaches, slept on beach loungers, and found food in hotel garbage cans. For the rest of her life, Rebekah dreamt about that time—she imagined herself to be in Barbados, Calcutta,

Rio. Her hands and feet were tied, and her skin was burned with cigarettes.

I couldn't bear to listen. I told her to go to hell.

I howled like a wolf. Why am I here? What the hell am I doing here? I pounded the wall with my fists until I cut my skin. I heard nothing but the humming of my own blood and the beating of my heart.

With my own blood I wrote on the wall: I WANT TO GO HOME.

Rebekah was puzzled: ending up with the Baptist had meant a dramatic improvement in her circumstances. She had always wanted first and foremost to belong to someone. That, if anything, had happened with the Baptist.

Whereas I've learned a foreign language, art history, gardening, restoring plaster statues, gilding, and remodeling, the Baptist taught Rebekah to read and write in her native language.

During the windowless times, we communicated mostly by facial expressions and hand gestures, and by the sailors' English that Rebekah spoke fast in her high-pitched voice. I begged, prayed, threatened, and cussed, even bribed Rebekah to let me go, help me escape. I was not like her, I didn't belong here, whatever damned place this was.

Rebekah showed me by her gestures that I had to quit crying. The Baptist would take good care of me, just as he had with her. They had a nice, large yard, a variety of animals, and a horse I could ride. Bianca, Bianca, Bianca, Rebekah repeated. I flipped her my middle finger, and she fell silent. Then she showed me the newest thing the Baptist had taught her: a headstand. Upside down, she stared at me with those large protruding eyes, and smiled broadly with her yellow, gapped teeth. I had to laugh. Then she picked up the untouched food tray from the floor and walked out.

I heard later that she was HIV-positive. Rebekah had fallen for some Nordic tourist boy, who had promised to take her with him. But the boy never showed up at the agreed-upon meeting place. He'd managed to pass the disease to Rebekah. She should have guessed it from his appearance. But because boys like him had never before noticed her, well, that was that. After telling me her simple story in broken English, Rebekah burst into tears. I hugged her. I was afraid of crushing her delicate bones. I remembered how Linda's muscular body had felt when we, in early fall, were jumping on her bed, dancing wildly, holding on to each other.

Then, I didn't have the strength to think about what was waiting for me outside or upstairs. I was tired, nightmares tormented me, and I was worried about Mother and Jason and Miss Frank. Esther, who came to clean the bathroom—if that's what you can call the recess and the drain in the wall—drew her hand across her throat every time she saw the rabbit.

Don't mind Esther, Rebekah comforted me. Esther is a deaf-mute, a former go-go dancer from the bars in the city of P., and she wouldn't hurt a fly. She'll surely take good care of your rabbit. And you too, when the Baptist is away.

I turned my back and stared hard into the wall of the windowless room.

A few days later Rebekah told me more about her former jobs. Girlie bars, pole caves, dusky basement corners, back alley dumpsters. That part of her life included high points with the tourist clubs, then lows, and the lows of lows, with her customer base eventually consisting of more pervs, drunks, drug addicts, all kinds of beach-garbage-hauling lunatics.

I met Rebekah a few more times. She cleaned the Baptist's rooms and carefully wiped dust from the paintings and antique ivory objects. She died a year later. The Baptist buried her in his garden, next to the wall. Esther cried quietly, and I recalled my first nights at the Baptist's place, Rebekah's thin, scarred arms, the smell of moss, the first head standing lesson.

Whatever little that's left of my soul... Can you say that? You won't question it.

Sometimes I felt such pain that I cried for days, and my eyelids eventually swelled shut. I asked the Baptist to kill me. If not right away, at least before long—when he had had enough of me, and I guessed that it would happen soon. I had nothing in my room that would've helped me do it myself, and the Baptist was careful so I would never have access to any such things. After my phases of crying and bitching, he once more had reason to wash me again and again, wash me clean of all my filthy thoughts and my dirty imagination. I sometimes wondered whether the sponge vendors in the alleys and at the market ever wondered why this man needed so many sponges. Every time, the natural sponge had to be clean, just lifted from the sea. Maybe the Baptist eventually realized it, since one day he decided to teach me how to dive for sponges. He himself could not do it; he was afraid of water, everywhere but on his palm.

At night, after the Baptist had left my room, I thought about the traces I had left in my home country. A secret hiding place in the brick wall of the bike shed in my apartment building's basement; writings on the school bathroom door; drawings on school desks; finger paintings from kindergarten; report cards; class pictures; artwork on the walls of my art classroom; dreams recorded in friendship books; my own gallery on the internet, pictures of horses and fieldtrips, those few pictures we took of ourselves at Linda's house...

I was surprised when the Baptist ordered Mother's book for me on the internet. He thought it was good that I read, and didn't constantly beg for a television or a computer for my room. He thought it was important that I maintain my native language, and he kept asking in his politely careless manner what Mother wrote about me in her book. Is she still waiting? Does she still believe that she will one day see me? Otherwise he always emphasized that he was not interested in my background or my history; he had zeroed me out, blown a big wind through me, made me into a new person.

The Baptist spoke several languages fluently and wrote his work papers in at least two languages, and I sometimes thought he would probably easily learn my language as well. He would learn it just like that, only to read Mother's book, and to find out what I wrote in my diary and what I surfed on the internet; that is, when he eventually allowed me that; at first, an hour a day.

During the first years—the Baptist rationed me new liberties for Christmas, and sometimes also at Easter. When I was finally allowed to use the computer, I could not, of course, participate in any chat groups, and I could not look at the pages and blogs from my country except in his presence. I never told him I was afraid that somehow I would hear about Mother's death, that Mother hadn't been able to carry such sorrow and uncertainty any longer. I was afraid that Mother would die far away from me, full of inconsolable grief. I guess I was also a bit sad for my little brother, Jason, who was already living with Father and his new wife, and continued warming pieces of pizza in the microwave and liked to kick a soccer ball against the wall.

Isolation was the consequence of the smallest offense when the Baptist so decided. He followed all my activities with the help of a camera that had been installed in my room, and he found pleasure in commenting, through a loudspeaker, on my movements.

Gradually, as a reward for good behavior, I was allowed to chat and surf more freely, but, of course, only on approved pages. If I tried to cheat, punishment followed. And I did try to cheat, initially every time, even though I knew well how the Baptist enjoyed punishment and the associated rituals of torment. I did learn to be obedient, little by little, the kind of Ruth he wanted me to be. I wanted a smoother life; I was tired of being afraid and always trying to anticipate what came next.

Around the same time, he allowed me to move around his house on my own accord, that three-story stone house surrounded by high walls. A house that, according to the Baptist, had originally been a nuns' hospital and later, among other things, a brothel for soldiers on leave in the countryside. The house was mammoth, with wide hallways, arched ceilings, water basins recessed in the walls, fountains. The Baptist told me he had used his entire fortune to renovate and decorate it. No wonder. He had more paintings on the walls, sculptures on pedestals, and books in bookcases than in my hometown's art museum and neighborhood library.

Of course, right away, I asked the Baptist an unbelievably stupid question: Had he himself really read all those books? He simultaneously howled and smirked. He hated stupidity as much as he hated harlotry. Stupidity is Satan's middle name. Stupidity is Satan's form of existence. Stupidity breeds from Satan. As Augustine already said, unclean sexuality impedes the use of reason.

Of course all those things Baptist wanted me to do with him, what he taught me to do with him, were not filthy sexuality, but were part of an ancient sacred act that cleansed the mind and soul.

I still remember that agitated beginning. Alright, he had read all the books and seen all the exhibitions and watched all the classic movies, et cetera. He was a cultured person from head to toe, and culture was

God's middle name, the highest form of existence, soul's zenith, et cetera.

Satan dwelled in me obstinately, at least during the first years. *Now I wish to introduce the following idea. Between the ages of nine and fourteen there are maidens who, to certain bewitched travelers twice or many times older than they, reveal their true nature, which is not human, but...*the Baptist quoted one of his soul mates.

Once I asked him how many girl prisoners he had had before me, and what would happen to me when he got tired of me? Then the Baptist became angry and locked me in the windowless room, as usual, without Miss Frank. We had agreed there would be no stupid questions! he remarked coldly, as he locked the door. Another time I asked if he had ever been married. Then I had to stay in my own room for a couple of days, without food and without Miss Frank. For my part, I threw a scarf on the spy-camera and stayed away from the bed. I didn't understand why he became so enraged. I slept on the closet floor and imagined that I was home, among my stuffed animals. I was always sure that the Baptist would never harm my rabbit. I didn't believe he would do it, even though later things happened as they did. Strangely, Miss Frank had managed to escape and was found in the yard, in the claws of a hawk. The hawk had just sunk its beak into Miss Frank's neck and the poor rabbit tried to leap here and there and shake loose of its grip. Miss Frank was so plump that the bird eventually dropped her at the edge of the wall, where I then buried her.

Sitting on the floor of the closet, I kept thinking about the stories I had heard about Jim Thompson from the Pet Shop girls. It evidently was only one of the many pseudonyms used by the Baptist. They were things that seemed so strange and challenging, even unbelievable, back then. Not anymore. He, this tall man, who wore a hat, had always had little girls around him. He liked the fact that young girls washed and massaged him, danced for him, masturbated him, had a certain kind of sex with him, and played certain kinds of erotic games with him. And allowed him to take pictures of them for the family album. That's the way the Baptist had lived. Who knows for how long? I didn't know how many girls he had had before me, but now I know that I am the first one he has taken with him from far away, and I also know that I am the last one.

Monday

by Sara Martin

Morning. I am digging for my cell phone. Handbag. Early morning. Office hours are starting.

And somebody is already sitting there, at a quarter before eight, because this damn good-hearted receptionist has once again let someone in too early.

I am digging for my cell phone inside my handbag, and—look: A dread-locked girl without her mother, hanging her head, is browsing through a women's magazine, likely an abortion. Or maybe the girl has condylomata? Getting her first prescription for contraceptives? I can't remember right away. I read the day's schedule beforehand, in the metro as always, but now can't seem to recall.

I pass the first client of the day and the week and smile in a friendly way, digging toward the bottom of my handbag for my phone, which, instead of some carefully considered melody, has just the default deskphone ring. Mikael's favorite ring, reminding him of cinema adaptations of Chandler, detectives' offices filled with cigarette smoke. Out of the corner of my eye, I glance toward the television at the back of the room—the receptionist's wish, veiled in altruism—and on the morning program they are interviewing the eyewitnesses of who-knows-what calamity; right now the screen is showing a shabby couple standing on a slushy street with a shopping cart before them. An industrial building has burned to the ground during the night; the work of extinguishing the fire will continue for several more hours; there is no information about victims. Because of the possibility of chemicals in the building, the area has been cordoned off, and the neighboring buildings have been closed for the day.

I stop for a second to watch. Some people have been given the day off, the week off, or need to change jobs, I think, and then I walk past my assistant; well, she has a name too.

"Good morning, Paula Pauliina." I let the Monday-morning greeting come out from the side of my mouth. She lifts her head, returns a perky greeting. After her break, caused by my week-long trip, she looks at me as if she really had missed me. She is knitting again, some strange-shaped garment; it's touching and at the same time somehow quaintly old-fashioned; perhaps it also relaxes the clients. I can't be fatally ill since that person over there is just knitting...

Paula Pauliina emits the familiar scent of her perfume, and the skin under her eyes is, if possible, darker than usual. I must ask if she is still taking those iron pills, and as I am opening the door, I remember that she has had some worries about her elderly mother who has again fallen in the hallway and hurt her hip. Or could there even be some male friends in the picture because she has been a bit absentminded recently? I am, however, not going to inquire about it under any circumstances, for Paula Pauliina is one of those people who will freely start confiding, and that could easily go on forever. Paula Pauliina is a sheep, so gentle, and she will eat from your hand. It should be enough for her to receive, for free, two basic examinations a year plus the hormone pills, along with a decent salary for housecleaning and the occasional trip to the grocery store. So, she should look elsewhere for her spiritual care.

Behind the door, my back against the inner door of the consulting room, I finally manage to get the angular phone into my hand—dear Mother—and I answer it.

"Yes?"

“We-e-ell, we-e-ll,” says Muma. “Well, you finally answered. I was getting ready to hang up. Why doesn‘t your answering machine turn on? I don’t know how many times I’ve already tried calling you.”

And so-o-o forth.

I couldn’t really talk with Mother right now. I tell her that I’m still totally just-returned-from-a-trip tired, the waiting room is Monday-full, and my papers are still scattered around; could Muma call back later? Or I could call, when I found a suitable break.

“Papers always need to be kept in order, whether or not you are tired,” remarks Muma, quick as a weasel. “My secretary always organized everything on Monday mornings. She actually came to work two hours earlier on Mondays. Mrs. August. You certainly remember Mrs. August. Too bad there aren’t people like her anymore. All I had to do was ask the first patient to come in. And a hot cup of tea waiting on a saucer, a napkin tucked through the cup handle, two lumps of sugar, and a shortbread biscuit. Always one shortbread biscuit.”

“Really, Mother, it’s a bad time right now. And yes, is everything okay? Jasmin has already left for school, and how has everything been? Hopefully well, since I haven’t heard anything.”

“We-e-ll,” says Muma and lets out a cough. “See, you didn’t have your phone turned on. I’ve tried to call a number of times. And even sent those text messages, but a message has always come back that they were not received. So.” Muma lets out another cough. “Everything else has gone really well, I’m feeling fine and your father is doing great, but I just wanted to let you know that we let Jasmiina go and stay with that girlfriend of hers for the whole week.”

Muma pauses.

I pause.

“Jasmiina is an extremely wise and sensible girl,” continues Muma. “But for a couple of days she has not answered her phone either, and I was wondering if she may have exceeded her minutes or..."

I am shaking my head as if trying to get water out of my ears, some atavistic remnant; it's as if I had not heard my mother's message properly. Then I go back to the beginning, unwind what I had heard. "What the hell does it mean that Jasmin has spent the whole week at her girlfriend's place? I have, you know, returned last night from a damn tiring conference trip, and Jasmin was supposed to be with you till this very morning, to be exact. Go directly to school from your place, and then to practice, and then come home in the evening. That was the agreement. That was the exact goddamn agreement. And quit calling my daughter Jasmiina. Her name is Jasmin."

"I knew you would get mad since we didn't ask you," says Muma, and sighs. "I wish you sometimes kept your phone on. When I used to go to conferences, you know, I always received the messages on little pieces of notepaper and someone would come and pull my sleeve when you were small, even if something really insignificant had happened. And I always would call home right away. Right away I would call home."

I am quiet. Mother's history is full of important people, grand historical events, and unquestionable decisions. My grandmother Mary, for instance, had posed in the same picture with Hitler in the year of the Berlin Olympics, a counselor of education and a fitness instructor; what can you say to that? Portraits of German shepherds were next to the pictures of humans on the bookshelves of my mother's childhood home.

"Jasmiina asked so nicely," continues Muma. Asked nicely. "And said that you would certainly let her. As I hear you let her drive the Vespa, too. Even though, let me say, I'm a bit surprised. Traffic nowadays is nothing but racecars; even I am sometimes afraid to drive, although I've never had an accident."

I am quiet, quiet, quiet. Muma goes on, goes on and goes on. A Duracell bunny.

"And that girlfriend is such a sweetie," adds Muma. "Like a picture of her mother, by the way. And since they had an exam week and everything. The girls wanted to study together. Your father and I thought that it was just a matter of course. And I'm sure that Fred wouldn't have had anything against it either."

Now the ex is dragged into it. With my free hand I press my diaphragm and breathe.

"Jasmin did not have an exam week; it's not for another two weeks."

And then the conversation breaks down. First, Mother starts to feel guilt and then rage. Daughter feels rage and then worry. I declare that I can no longer trust even my own parents, to which Muma remarks, what a great help Muma and Papsi have been to me in all the turns of my life. And besides, *touché*, why hadn't the girl's father taken her for the week, or were relations with Fred still so poisoned? And how is Jason, does the boy still like it better at his father's, and so on. And so on.

"I'll call back at some point," I finally snort, "clients are waiting."

"Please do, and, dear girl, try to keep that phone of yours on and remember to organize the papers. The patients have become so demanding, and, besides, everybody has friends who are lawyers," she adds before I hang up.

I stand with my back against the door in the dusky room and feel the need to kick some large object. Why didn't I ever take up kick-boxing? I could now beat a punching bag with black gloves the size of a balloon. Cuss. Yell my voice hoarse. Afterwards, laugh. Laugh at poisoned relationships with men, lawyers, shortbread biscuits.

I glance at the screen of my gray cell phone. The phone has, indeed, been turned off a lot, occasionally switched to silent mode, and, at times and in the morning rush, forgotten in the hotel room, as so often happens at conferences.

Mom-mmy, calls little Jasmin's voice from the kindergarten entrance hall. So when are you gonna pick me up? You sure you're gonna be on time?

I dial Jasmin's number and wait until a male voice tells me that I can't reach the number I have dialed. Why is the tone of his voice so scornful? One would think that piece of news could be delivered in a friendlier manner. I shove my cell phone back into my handbag and turn on all the lights in my room. The handbag and the briefcase onto the table, then three steps to the rack, the fresh white coat on, and then turn toward the work table. Where there is no teacup, no lumps of sugar, no biscuits. Even though I think Paula Pauliina would prepare all those things if I just hinted for them. But I'm fine as it is. All the routines of a normal morning, except that the floor is slanting. Big time.

I hold onto the side of the table and feel my temple. A bump is a bump.

At half past five in the morning, the hall table had fallen, crashed down. One of the three legs had given in and the entire top fell to the floor. I was awakened by the noise, the sound of shattering glass. When I had gotten up to see what had happened, I found everything that had been on the table piled in a huge mess, the crystal bowl shattered to pieces. My baptism bowl. After I picked up the things, among which there was a business card left by the overnight guest, Umberto—was his name really Umberto?—I had bumped my head on the wall and fallen to the floor. Luckily no one was around to see.

The overnight guest had already left—an early plane had been waiting. When I came to, I stood up, collected the things that had been on the table, took the broken glass to the trash can, looked at the pieces there, at the bottom of the plastic bag, among coffee grounds, cried a little—the minister had long ago dipped the tips of his fingers in that bowl and given me my name and place in the congregation—then I had clicked the coffeemaker on and automatically dropped two slices of wholegrain toast into the toaster, remembered that I was home alone, and had pulled the second slice out at the last moment. I had left that tad-too-dark piece of bread on the kitchen table as an orphan. Jasmin's slice.

Mom-mmy, cut me a piece of boat-bread please! asks little Jasmin with her nose flat against the side of the sink. Please Mommy please please.

Fred liked the end pieces, too.

Help. For the second time in fifteen minutes I am thinking about the ex. And that is exactly two times too many.

I lean against the reception table and look at the photograph on my table, dig out the phone from my bag, and dial Jasmin's number again.

Why is the girl not answering?

I ask aloud. Why don't you answer? Damn kid. What kind of a joke is this now?

The dialed number cannot be reached, says the male voice, and it sounds like the guy himself is tired of repeating the same thing over and over.

Daughter's cell phone, pink and shell-shaped, is somewhere, turned off, but where? Hopefully at school. In class. In the side pocket of her backpack. In the back pocket of her jeans. Maybe hanging from her neck?

I feel the need to mobilize. Should I make a list of all the things that need to be taken into consideration right away? Should I call the school? Hospitals? The police? Where else should I call? The third time I'm thinking about the ex, and it's still early in the morning: I should maybe tell the girl's father, but not yet. He would make me feel guilty, and I can't take it now. Besides, Fred would tell my concerns to Jason, even though I would insist he not.

Tell him what? That Jasmin has not been at the grandparents' place for a week and now is not answering her phone?

I shake my head.

Am I being stupid? A mother hen? Of course, everything is fine. But. If. Despite. Maybe. To be sure. All of a sudden it feels like all the doors and windows are wide open, and temperatures dropping as winter suddenly blows in. I remember the picture on TV a moment ago: a wide-eyed homeless couple is staring from behind their shopping cart. Flames are licking the red brick building. They are talking about millions in damages. What in the world were they pushing in that cart? Empty bottles, rubber boots found in the garbage, a broken umbrella?

Go to hell, all of you.

The school office number is busy all the time, and I can't remember her homeroom teacher's name. Should I remember it? Should your phone always be turned on? Even when you start playing around with a foreign colleague? Whose back has thick hair? Whose name is Umberto?

I feel like laughing.

Should I really be seriously worried now? Really? Should I go to her school? Should I cancel my appointments for the day? Invite a colleague to help? Excuse me, but my child has all of a sudden disappeared somewhere and won't answer her phone, could you come and help out?

Ha-haa. A teenage girl won't answer her phone and Mommy gets nervous. The girl feels a bit of air under her wings for the first time in her life, and Mommy doesn't understand. Father and daughter like end-pieces, they cut incisions on the side, make boat-bread, yum, have a good trip, favorable winds.

The thoughts are flying. No, the girl has certainly not gone to her father, nor has she stayed at home for a week with her girlfriend; it was way too clean there, everything in place, a week of silence to welcome Mother and Mother's occasional overnight guest. A mother can sense such a thing, of course.

What about the summer cottage? What if the girls have gone to the summer cottage? Invited some friends, had some country fun?

Then I remember that we don't have a cottage any more, it was sold soon after our divorce. I glance at my watch, and for a few moments ponder what other sensible things I could do, and how embarrassing it will be to start asking around. I browse through the phonebook on my desk, leave a message on Linda Rossi's mother's answering machine, and ask her to call back as soon as possible.

If Mikael lived, this would not have happened, either. The thought always comes so quickly; it always slides in from some crevasse of my mind, without warning. All the things that would have happened, and would not have happened, if Mikael had lived. The ifs of sleepless early morning moments.

I'm looking at the knuckles of my right hand on which the overnight guest had pressed his teeth when getting out of bed. An alpha-male. Hairs that tickled my cheek. There were hairs even between his toes. Umberto, I snort. The teeth marks had faded. And most likely, the generally sympathetic alpha-urologist wouldn't show up anymore either, ever. I am not going to feel guilty. Yet, somewhere far away Mother's voice keeps asking why I didn't call from the conference, and why the phone was turned off still for all of Sunday night.

I, Sara Martin, specialist in gynecology, competent in my profession, and careful in my human relations, sigh deeply and glance at my watch again. Monday morning.

I place the narrow reading glasses on my nose and begin to familiarize myself with the paperwork of the girl who has arrived too early and is sitting in the waiting room.

The girl is seventeen years old and she hopes to be given contraceptive pills. I place the normal arsenal on the table, a couple of booklet guides, condoms, intrauterine devices, and various progesterone pills—rattling pill cases that look like a doll's ruler. Doll's ruler is what Jasmin always called them, this disappeared daughter, or whom I imagine to have disappeared.

I'm looking at the selection in front of me. My favorite brand for someone that young is, come to think of it, Yasmin. Only mild side effects, usually. Luckily the girl's mother has not come with her. Sometimes it's difficult to keep them away from the office.

I take off my glasses and rub the bridge of my nose. I wonder if the dreadlocked girl has had her first intercourse. Will she turn red when I ask about partners, a steady boyfriend? There are so many different kinds, shy ones and bold ones, shoplifters and pot smokers. You never know what you'll find under that skirt, the Bearded Professor used to say; and the young female students protested, Goddammit, you can't say that. Well, what then, the Bearded Prof continued as if amused, rubbing the corners of his jaw, you never know what you'll find inside the jeans, or what? For a moment I remember the prof with the gray hair, whom everybody addressed formally, and, contrary to what one might think, the formality made many things easier.

A moment before I invite the girl in, I write a text message, "Call Mom as soon as you can." I look at the message on the screen of my cell phone and delete "as soon as you can."

The Year of the Peacock

✳

The Year of the Peacock differs from the Year of the Cobra, from carnivals, kites, fireworks, and water music. During the Year of the Peacock, people don't hang wreaths on their necks or wear flowers in their hair. In the processions, people don't carry paper tigers or dragons; there are no silk lanterns swinging on tree branches, and no one has released paper flowers to float on the waves.

The Year of the Peacock is a year of manhood. Big bonfires burn high, swords flash in duels, and march music fills the air. The Year of the Peacock is a time of growth and bravery, a desire for conquest. During the Year of the Peacock you are expected to surpass your limitations, disengage yourself from all pettiness and pedantry, pretexts, and pretended modesty.

Now we are living the Year of the Peacock, you over there and me over here. Now or never. You have to make space for new things. Dare to test the boundaries. Begin a journey.

✳

Lido has wrestled since he was a little boy; Lido has done business with Zhirinovsky; Lido has arm-wrestled with Putin; Lido has had a thing with Natasha Poly. Lido has crazy ideas and wild impulses; Lido is unbelievably fair; and Lido certainly knows how to dress in style.

Uncle Chanu has also met Lido. He seems to be one of those modern gentlemen, says Uncle Chanu about Lido. Do you want Uncle Chanu to write a letter of recommendation for you? Maybe that will calm Mother down. After all, Chanu is Mother's cousin. Dear Mother, naturally, is worried and talks about the twelve bicycling spirits that are spouting their prophecies and threats; but *ciao* to you, dear Mother, your cousin Chanu left to explore the world a long time ago, and he lives here in this city, and lo and behold, he's in a position to offer his young relative, Karim, his first job in the laundry business he, Chanu, owns. Everything's cool and safe, dear Mother. The laundry steam brings memories of spring at home before the rains, dear Mother. You have to try out your wings sometime. Let the spirits say what they will.

And now, what you need to listen to all the way to the end, little brother, is the story about Lido's background. In the first and second years, Lido lived in a blackened concrete suburb, in a dilapidated two-room apartment, and had never held a cell phone or typed on a computer keyboard until one morning when he abruptly decided to say fuck all this and leave that fuckin' collapsed country, because finally there was a chance to do so. Surrounding the concrete factory was a whole city of unemployed toothless old men, Lido's father among them, boys collecting firewood from the smoke-burned woods, and mother and sisters on the street corner, selling roasted chestnuts and bouquets of withered lilies-of-the-valley.

One morning he got tired of looking at all that crap and decided to take charge of his own life. And he left. Since then, everything has happened very fast for him. Well, he has had some trouble at times with various authorities, but who wouldn't? Including Uncle Chanu.

Okay, okay. To the point. Get away from that place. What the hell will school and grammar and arithmetic do for you if you're gonna stay in the same shitty place for the rest of your life? Unless you want to start protecting gum trees and mountain butterflies. Hey, the opportunities are up here, in the north. You can't argue with that, my esteemed, genius little brother. Neither can those bicycling spirits.

*

The little brother who stayed attached to Mother's apron strings, is he as handsome? Lido asks Ringo, whose former name is Karim. And of course Lido's real name isn't Lido either. It wouldn't even cross anyone's mind, especially Karim's (now Ringo's), to try to pry a real name from Lido.

Ringo shows Lido a wallet-size photo, snapped at the railway station in C., which he has brought with him for this particular purpose. Standing straight like a pole, Lido stares at the picture, stares through the progressively tinted glasses at the tip of his nose. Is *that* a boy? Does he own a set of balls? Fucking hell. Maybe I should start a boy-business, says Lido, waving his arms and moving the picture from one hand to the other. Fuck, what a fucktoy. Invite him here right away. And ask others too, Tobi, Nawal, all those friends. The paperwork's gonna be a piece of cake, no problem. Why the fuck are you all so beautiful in that part of the world?

Lido's face is pockmarked, his eyes are small, lips are thick, and his hair is thin. His ears don't match. But it doesn't matter, Lido has other qualities. Money, arrogance, women; in other words, looks aren't everything, thinks Ringo, and puts Little Brother's photo back in his wallet. Next to Mother Lalla's picture, and Father's picture, and Anil's picture. You can't help feeling a bit homesick every now and then, far away from home. Ringo notices that he misses his native language as well and hopes, for that reason too, that Randi will come soon. Uncle Chanu is a man of few words, and the people in this country have made him even more quiet, when he was only trying to serve and please the customers and appear sophisticated at the same time.

*

Ringo received maybe ten paychecks from Uncle Chanu before he met Lido. Or, actually it was Lido who met Ringo, then still Karim Suraweera, safely employed in his mother's cousin's laundry. Lido was a regular customer at Chanu's laundry, and was of the opinion that *pakis* did a better job washing laundry than *chinks* or *coons*, and that's why Lido always had his suits cleaned and pressed to a T at Chanu's. That's why Uncle gave Lido special deals, and difficult stains were removed at no extra charge. What else could he have done? Chanu handed over the clear, thin clothes bags on their metal hangers to Lido, bowed and said, "Be so kind." Karim laughed. "You don't say that anymore! You don't bow like that anymore! You don't have to be so formal anymore!"

Uncle Chanu leaned against the old cash register, which he wouldn't give up even though nobody used such things anymore. He marked down the number of treated stains, and roughly their type, on a piece of paper. Sometimes he felt like asking Lido the origins of all those stains, as well as the stains on the various women's garments, but he didn't because, naturally, it wasn't any of his business. He washed and ironed and steamed and dry-cleaned everything, from white silk shirts and jeans with rhinestones to the teeny-tiny skirts and bikini tops. One summer, Uncle Chanu had customers who belonged to a traveling circus, and their laundry looked no different.

Lido always liked to stay at the laundry counter and talk. He watched female customers and paged through the English football magazines that Chanu's children from London had sent. And then once, while hanging around, he casually asked about Chanu's young male relative's future plans. Karim Suraweera's future plans? Nobody had ever asked what Karim planned to do or what Karim would like. Even at home everyone kept asking only what the smart little brother would do after school. Certainly the little brother would go on to study something fine, being smart and all, law or medicine or politics. No one, however, saw the little brother as a soldier.

Lido, however, did ask Karim. And when he heard that Karim did not pray several times a day in any direction, nor had he gotten into trouble with law enforcement, he said that Karim would be suitable to work for him. Like now, right away? Then he asked what was wrong with Karim's hands. Karim got embarrassed, turned red down to his collar, and stuck his hands where they almost always were anyway: in his pockets. Sharp-sighted Lido had noticed Karim's palms right away. Ringo's last job in his home country had been in a paint shop where they manufactured various timepieces that glowed in the dark. And you couldn't get rid of the phosphorus with any thinners or turpentines. Many of the workers walked around with gloves on their hands, even years after having quit the job. In the evenings, after his day at the paint shop, Ringo also used to drive a taxi, but the customers got scared every time he took off his gloves to collect their fare.

Soon after that, the big brother sends the little brother some money and a plane ticket. Fantastic opportunities are waiting here in the north. Nobody would believe how easy everything is. Randi, also, can get a job with Lido, see the real world, earn some money, be a man.

Lalla Suraweera's cousin Chanu is a good guy but belongs to the days gone by. He was even afraid of the little old ladies in the block who thought there were all kinds of weird things at Chanu's laundry: a water bowl with flower petals sitting on the counter and a teapot with strange-smelling tea for customers while they were waiting. One of the old women had once complained to the city's sanitary inspector about the hygiene in the laundry; and after the inspector's visit, Chanu came to believe that the whole block was laughing at him and that customers were eyeing him suspiciously.

Certainly Chanu could have had other business opportunities beyond the small and sweaty laundry; that's what Lido said, too. He could work as some kind of an intermediary or use the laundry as a front. Smuggling animals, for instance, was real easy, and people paid in spades for all kinds of endangered insects, reptiles, and small monkeys. Lido knew a lot of mud-faced brothers who worked pretty successfully in that field. But Chanu had lost his nerve and gotten antsy simply because of bacteria-fearing old hags. Chanu pretended not to understand Lido's hints. Chanu could not do something like that.

Think, little brother, what it would look like if ants romped around inside skinny little Chanu's pants. Chanu has always been so fussy about his clothes, dressing up embarrassingly neat even on workdays: a burgundy tie, carefully polished shoes, and nicely pressed gray pants. A hat on his head when he ventures out. Sweet-smelling hairspray for his thick hair.

My friend Lido is totally different. Lido doesn't need to fear anyone's fist nor anyone's laughter. Lido is on top of things. Lido has a network, connections. In London. In Calcutta. In Stockholm. In Havana. In Buenos Aires. Lido actually says sometimes that he is like a full-service department store.

Ringo ponders whether to tell little brother about Lido's actual inventory: hormone products, girls, collections, money laundering, entertainment for anyone's taste. Everyone watches for Lido; many fear for their lives around the pockmarked ponytail man.

Ringo couldn't list everything Lido actually bought and sold and negotiated, nor could anyone else, but the Suraweera genes are not impatient. On the contrary, they wait very patiently. Something new will be on its way, of course, in the Year of the Peacock.

*

One morning, Randi Suraweera carries the green fabric bag that Mother has sewn for him over his shoulder and wears a strange expression that nobody has seen before. Father's camouflage jacket is functioning as a bag. Something had been sown into its seams, but Randi didn't yet know what it was. Father left, too, although for the mountain—but only for the spring, and only because of the butterflies. He was looking for Map butterflies, rarities, which according to Mother resembled shredded paper after they had been placed in the display case.

Small birds are bustling about in the bushes, and the house is being scrubbed, water splashing across the floor. A wind blows from the direction of the forest, and Mother Dearest wipes her forehead with her elbow and squints, supposedly because of the sunshine, supposedly because of the smoke coming from the clearing of bushes on the riverbank. But we know that it's because Randi has decided to follow his big brother Karim's bold example; Karim, who in his new manhood in the Year of the Peacock is now called Ringo. Mother is scrubbing the house because she doesn't want to watch Randi pack. Big sister Anil is helping him. She brings a sweater from the closet, and a scarf and thicker socks, asking if these are northern outfits.

Mother has been pleading to all the spirits bicycling on the earth for her younger son not to leave. She senses trouble. The bicycling spirits know it. Altogether there are twelve of them, and Mother knows them all.

The Smeller of Shadows is most worried about Randi. That's the spirit that stirs the greatest restlessness in mothers, and so too in Lalitha Suraweera.

But this time Mother Lalla's stories of the spirit world will not keep the little brother down. Bye-bye to the spirits. The boat is waiting. A distant land is waiting; a land of opportunities.

"So far away," says Mother, "everything is different. Everything, absolutely everything." Mother's cousin Chanu has told her so. "You need sweaters made of coarse material and knitted gloves, scarves, fur-lined hats, high boots; it's cold up here, and also so different. Your skin will crack, your fingernails will break, your tongue can freeze against your mouth if you yawn in cold weather."

"Fortunately, it's a different *somewhere*," replies Randi, pulling the zipper closed on a small red traveling bag. "In a different kind of a place there are new opportunities," Randi mumbles. "And Chanu has gotten along fine there, so why wouldn't we? Why wouldn't I?"

The eternal little brother finally dares. The little brother seizes an opportunity. Grabs his fate by the beard and pulls. The little brother grows up to be a man. Not a little boy anymore but a real man. Up there in the north nobody would say, Hop hop, Randi. Or, do this, do that, Randi. You must never do that, Randi. Or, Remember your responsibilities and your duties, Randi. You are the first one in your family to do this and that, Randi. Randi here, Randi there.

From this time forward, the little brother will choose for himself. The little brother wants to experiment with life after school. Nobody will laugh at him anymore.

Diary

1.

Autumn starts from here, wrote a girl named Jasmin Martin in her diary on the last night of her summer vacation, in a diary of recycled paper between textured covers, with a picture of a bunny rabbit in the middle. A cute, small bunny was on the cover of the diary, which was bought from a store opposed to animal testing. This is respectful of nature. Friendly. Sensible. Simple. Hopeful. A fresh breeze.

Autumn starts from here. Every autumn is a new beginning. New makeup tips, new fashion catalogues, new looks. You can even lose a little weight in the thighs. You can find a new hairstyle. Pluck your eyebrows or leave them bushy. You can have a crush on a new boy. Or at least find a new girlfriend, especially if the last one is a little bit passé. Jasmin's former girlfriend Merita had almost died. Simple. Hopeless. She stopped eating. A beautiful girl who thought she was a fat pig, and so in half a year changed into someone resembling a prisoner at a concentration camp.

The diary was a gift from Merita, the vegetarian, the animal activist, the energy-saver, the one who worries about globalization. Could Jasmin have done something more? Jasmin has already thought this through: No, she could not have helped any more in any way. That was Merita's fate, just as the fate of Mother's and Father's marriage was divorce, and that of Diana was a short life. Diana died of something strange; she became debilitated, stopped eating, and withered away. Diana was a gift from Mother and Father when Jasmin turned ten.

The girl named Jasmin Martin drew hearts in the margins of her diary and examined her face in the table mirror—the profile, from bottom up, from top to bottom, directly from the front. Thin lips, thin hair, thin eyebrows, thin eyelashes. How in the world can one person accumulate so much thinness? Yes, except the cheeks. Jasmin sucked her cheeks in and turned her face in front of the mirror. Model material? Well, the girls in the model competitions on television were not so much more beautiful, more slender, or more statuesque. Except the American girls, but that was a different story.

Besides, when school starts, you choose new favorite words. *Neat*, *awesome*, *simple* were already so last year. You should pick up a new favorite color and stop biting your nails, but still be certain to practice cartwheels and splits and to exercise your abdominal and thigh muscles every night. More strength, more tone, but not a huge mass of muscle. And if you only could find a mascara that doesn't smudge all the way down your cheeks. Really. And Jasmin can't tolerate weekly piano lessons anymore, despite what Mother might say. There were also tense negotiations regarding riding. Jasmin would have quit her riding lessons back in the spring, but Mother had strongly resisted the idea. Jasmin was puzzled and angry. The lessons were expensive, and Mother had to take her to the stables twice a week. You see, Father did not participate in it out of principle. So, quitting it should be a relief for Mother. She would have had more time to stay at work, however late, listening to the endless troubles women had, or writing answers for the doctor's column in the women's magazine.

Jasmin wrote a couple more lines, closed the diary, and hid it in her closet under the stuffed animals. That's the place where Jasmin every now and then put her oldest stuffed animals, flung them there by their tails or long ears—but in a moment, after seeing their shaggy shapes in the dimness of the closet, she, teary-eyed, then dug them out from there. There had been a dinosaur period and a panda period, a period of fabric birds, a period of green teddy bears, a time for fleece snakes, knitted ladybugs, and piglets made of foamy plastic. The stuffed history of Jasmin's childhood.

Excuse me, friends. I was thoughtless. You still belong to my life, you who are clotted with saliva, smelling of drool, dim-eyed. I will never forsake you.

And then there were tamagotchis and their many relatives. Jasmin had placed all her Japanese digital pets in a row at the bottom of a sock box. The yellow ones and the green ones, the red and the golden little oval pets, of whose nursing Mother eventually grew tired, since they had to be fed and medicated all the time, and little Jasmin's patience never reached the levels such care-giving required. And when the tiny charge died, the display had a small creature who'd sprouted wings on its back floating in a shower of stars with text: *Goodbye I loved you*. Jasmin cried inconsolably and wanted right away to rekindle the pet back into life with the touch of a pen.

Jasmin was looking at her room. Something needed to be done. The posters had been changed at the end of summer. Gwen Stefani, Shakira, and Christina Aguilera were put up; the only old one was the giant Norah Jones, which Mikael had brought from a trip. Mikael always brought posters; Mother brought notebooks. Sometimes when he had been young, Mikael had dreamed about being a photographer, and Mother had written poems. Then they both had ended up as doctors. Simple. Great. Transparent. The dreams of youth smoldered in the gifts they brought back, but Mother and Mikael never noticed it themselves.

How do you like it? Mikael had asked when the black-eyed Norah Jones was put up on the wall. Really nice.

What else could you say? Mikael liked the whispering voice of Ravi Shankar's daughter, but it wasn't really Jasmin's thing. Yeah, yeah, Norah played the piano beautifully, but even that wasn't Jasmin's thing.

So what was Jasmin's thing? Strawberry ice cream, girls' parties at someone's house when the parents were at the movies, toffee candy, lace-trimmed bras. And, well, just a little bit: Tony from upstairs, the boy that all the parents liked, a boy just like that. Polite, cute, clean, helped with computer problems, even though he never tired of lecturing about modern life's excessive dependence on technology. He brought misdelivered mail and walked grandmothers across the icy yard, a crystal clear future for him as a doctor in a developing country or a lawyer for the underprivileged. He had the world's weirdest little sister, Téa, a spectacled girl who was easily scared and liked to scribble on graph paper.

For a moment, Jasmin thought about Tony's pale face, his straggly curls, his front teeth that were a little bit crooked, his pure white T-shirts and baggy jeans; maybe even Tony was not really Jasmin's thing. Even though he did like Kurt Cobain. Even though he thought Bono was an awesome rocker. Even though he was good at soccer and knew how to bowl.

Maybe Norah should finally be replaced with, say, Jennifer Lopez. But then on the other hand, no. And so, Ravi Shankar's child stayed on the wall.

It had been a year and two months since Mikael had died. It still made her cry, when she started to think about it. Mikael's picture was in the drawer of the nightstand, face down; so she wouldn't look at it all the time anymore. A blond man with a thin face, a dimple in his chin; people kept telling Jasmin how much she resembled her father. To which Jasmin laughed—that's really great, you mean how much I look like my stepfather? Many people didn't know that Mikael was not Jasmin's real father. Right away, he had become somehow closer than Jasmin's own father had ever been. For that—also for that—Jasmin felt guilty, for not being able to relax with Fred the way she had with Mikael. Unnecessary, said the little voice right in her ear. That's how it always reasoned, that little voice, but Jasmin still felt bad for thinking about Fred that way.

Before Mikael died he had looked just like a baby—bald, with a round face, and yet still thin. The tubes were aerial roots or vines attached to him. Mikael was like a third-world child from a social studies textbook.

Autumn starts from here.

A girl named Jasmin Martin threw herself on the bed, flat on her back. In her mind she planned *the agenda for a wonderful day*. In the morning, healthy cereal and plain yogurt, honey on top of it; then to school, where the lessons would just fly by—poof—while chatting with friends; then a quick-quick trip home and, with the strength derived from the very healthy snack that Mother had made, to the gym to work out, vigorous exercise in preparation for the fall competitions; then with the bubbly cheerleading friends to a neighborhood coffeehouse for a large latte, even though Mother didn't approve, since the caffeine made it difficult to fall asleep; then home and dinner into the microwave, unless Mother had already come home; then the homework plus instant messaging and webcamming on the computer and watching music videos until Mother, in a stern, yet still smiling voice, would come to wish her good night.

Mother always went to bed by eleven at the latest, after she'd watched a TV show—*CSI, 24 Hours, West Wing, ER*. Sometimes they both watched *Living Single*, had an evening snack, and almost always laughed at different parts of the show. Mother thought the series was quite daring, and Jasmin replied with a yawn.

Don’t you think so? Mother asked, wondering. And then: Good night, Jassu.

Moth-err. Mother still called her Jassu, even though there had been a lot of discussion about that.

Besides, Jasmin would start using her middle name as soon as she herself could decide. Victoria Martin. Vic-tor-ia. Victoria sounds somehow tantalizing and sexy. *Special. Fatal.* Jasmin seemed ordinary, completely too ordinary. Average. Normal. A dull prototype.

Autumn starts from here. Autumn. Starts. From. Here. The future Victoria Martin yawned. She and Mother lived together now, just the two of them; and in a way it was fun, even though Mother was occasionally quite sad, but you couldn’t say it aloud because it might have sounded odd. Of course Jasmin missed her little brother every now and then, but to be really truthful, only every now and then. And they did have lunch with Jason during the weekends, sometimes went to the movies and shopping, the three of them.

Jasmin pondered. Sometimes it seemed that Mother had no more expectations. Mother did not become excited about anything. Mother did not oppose anything. Mother just allowed things to happen. After Mikael’s death, Mother took sick leave for a long time and planned her own funeral—the decorations, flower arrangements, guest list, music, and so on—but fortunately, she eventually moved past that phase. And now Mother laughed at it all.

Mother’s sister Seidi says that Mother should start to date, but Jasmin doesn't know what to think about that either. What if Mother brought home candidates? But where would she even find them? At work, at least, she doesn’t see any men, laughed Jasmin. Paula Pauliina was no guy-magnet either. Sometimes Mother and Jasmin entertained themselves by imagining what kind of man would fall for Paula Pauliina.

Well, there's the internet, Mother had laughed. Aren't there dating sites just for people like her? You can place all kinds of touched-up photographs there. There, everything is possible.

Once an old guy had tried to come to Mother's office to be examined. He was no transsexual, but had somehow mistakenly thought that Mother would look at his equipment, just as she would look at a woman's. He insisted on an internal examination, an ultrasound, the full repertoire. Mother explained the issue, refused, and still the man tried to climb up on the examination table. Mother struggled with him while he was opening his zipper and pulling down his pants. Finally, Paula Pauliina had come to help with a baseball bat; she always kept it under her table. She had played Finnish baseball, *pesäpallo*, in her youth, and always mentioned it. The bat was useful when clients turned difficult. Once a drug addict had become restless, thinking that the large-leafed plant on the window sill was hemp, and had wanted to eat it on the spot.

Then, even then, Mother had remarked that if Paula Pauliina did not exist, she would need to be invented.

Often before going to bed, as she was doing now, Jasmin browsed the internet to see if her friends had anything to say, to comment on some heated discussion, to check out the new pictures added to her friends' galleries, to watch a music video, before going to the bathroom to examine her face in the mirror. She reached for another mirror to help evaluate her profile. Lifted up her hair and checked out her jaw, her neck. Quite nice. Quite okay. But.

What was that but? It always felt that it wasn't just as it should be. A delicate neck, looked bony, bird-like. And the chin was somehow puny. The cheeks did not have such angular bones as the girls on the cover of *Cosmo* always had.

But sweetie, Mother would always say in her slightly irritated tone. You are a normally-developed girl, very pretty and sweet and lovely.

Pretty. Sweet. Lovely.

You are not lacking anything.

Piano lessons, riding, GPA. Piano lessons, riding, GPA. Jasmin covered her ears with her hands and read her mother's lips.

Jasmin leafed through the magazines and threw them on the floor, spreading all over the place, faces on the covers. In the morning, all the cute little faces would say *Good morning, guys! How are you, guys!* and Jasmin would push them a bit further away. Disperse, you teenage beauties! I'm tired of you with your turbo lips and your super-white-toothed smiles, your sex tips and your most embarrassing experiences!

But not really. Jasmin held a couple of the magazines in her hand and looked at those brown and blue and green eyes, the long curling eyelashes, the perfect skin, and rounded breasts.

Pretty, sweet, lovely—but, first and foremost, sexy!

How can they be so beautiful and skinny and tempting? So original? So perfect? As if they were of a different race.

Jasmin had already been going to the Girls' House for a couple of years. All kinds of girls were hanging around there from all kinds of countries, but they were not like that. They had zits and blackheads and split ends and lard on their hips and yellow teeth zigzagged in their mouths.

At the Girls' House, in small groups, they discussed menstruation and the problems of immigrants; they learned to fry eggs and boil potatoes and bake coffee bread, and, at times, they sewed different seams with a sewing machine. Sometimes they told ghost stories or real stories that were almost more horrible than the headless dead people who haunted houses during the nights; some girls told how they had nearly been forced to marry their cousins when they were only nine.

The walls had been painted in rainbow colors, and the couches were deep and soft. You didn't have to do anything if you didn't want to; you could just sit with headphones on. And absolutely no guys ever found their way there. No thank you to guy stuff. Guys were odd, especially the tractor types. They just came and rolled and never asked if anything was right or wrong, a good thing or a bad thing. That's what tractor types were like. Did that expression also come from Paula Pauliina? Quite a few expressions did. Listening to her talk in Mother's waiting room, while waiting for Mother's workday to end, was actually fun. The plastic knitting needles snapped against each other; sometimes she hummed or asked about school achievements; sometimes she played solitaire on the computer and talked to herself at the same time. She said that Jasmin had to study hard; she said she would have become goodness-knows-what kind of a government official if her family had had money while she was growing up. But they didn't.

And do not come into my dreams, Jasmin said. But come they did. Ashleys, Jessicas, Parises, Rihannas, they came and had their wild parties in Jasmin's head. Their makeup was super-precise, their clothes were sexy, and they kept walking again and again over Jasmin, who just lay in her bed. How could they step so brilliantly in their stiletto heels? How could they sip their drinks without smudging their lipstick? How did they hold those long cigarettes at the tips of their thin fingers without dropping ashes on the floor or without burning holes in their fancy clothes? And how did they know what to say to boys? And what to do in any situation?

They were busy. There was so much to do, makeup and fitting appointments, performances, and so they did not hear when Jasmin asked for advice from them, and so eventually she asked them to leave.

You invited us, said Paris Hilton in a gentle voice with puckered lips. May I introduce myself? I'm Paris. Johnny Depp's partner is Paradis. Try not to get us mixed up. Many millions and cup sizes separate us.

I'm awfully sorry, but my autumn starts from here, and I need to rest and gather strength for all the possible new things, Jasmin told them.

What new things? Natalie Portman laughed. What new things, tell us? What is your favorite drink? Care for a smoke? Do you already have a boyfriend? Have you already gotten it on, if you know what I mean? Jimbajamba, horizontal mamba? Ha ha ha. Lindsey Lohan is the worst. Do you dare to party without panties? Do you already belong to the commando gang? How many have you already had? What kind of feedback have you gotten regarding your machinery?

Jasmin was trying and trying in vain, but they kept inviting more people to the party.

My room is too small for all of you, Jasmin began, but her voice was lost in the buzz of voices. I don't even have anything to serve you. Still, she tried.

Listen, we have enough of everything, absolutely everything, Keira Knightley said, smiling. And looking at the dark-haired girl, Jasmin could do nothing but agree. How could even her elbow be so perfect, and what is that little place again, the dent of the clavicle, just like a marble sculpture?

Get up, Jasmin, it's already seven o'clock! School morning!

Good morning, Jasmin Martin. A fine good morning! You are Jasmin. Five feet six-and-a-half inches tall.

Ninety-nine pounds. A teenager. School, riding, cheerleading, piano playing. What's new? New cosmetics, new clothes, new favorite words, maybe a new friend? What's REALLY new?

When Mikael was still alive, Jasmin had wished that Mother and Mikael were not so busy, would not travel so much. Jasmin didn't really like to stay with Father and Hannah. Hannah seemed so young that Jasmin didn't want to listen to her, and the baby seemed to be the center of the universe for them.

It was actually nice to stay at Muma and Papsi's place, but you had to engage in long conversations with them on strange topics, or listen to them reminisce about their time as physicians, how medicine had developed and patients had become more cumbersome, and all that sort of stuff. Mother and Father's wonderful wedding a long time ago, sniffle. The sadness of divorce, sniffle. Little Jason who misses his mother and sister, sniffle-sniffle. And Muma and Papsi always took a nap, together, after five-o'clock tea. And they took daily walks, together. And always watched black-and-white movies on videos, together. And at some point you always had to look at Papsi's stamp collection, the most recent finds and the special cancellation marks.

Actually it was fun, staying at Muma's and Papsi's, just like starting school, but you really just couldn't admit it. Or, you could talk about it with someone like Tony. Tony also had cool "granderstanders"—yeah, that was Tony's humor. Granderstanders: grandparents who could understand—Tony was cool, no denying it. Mother liked him too. And Father. And Mikael had liked him. He had teased Jasmin about Tony, and that had been irritating. And embarrassing, really.

It's already ten after seven! Mother's sleepy eyes in the doorway. Hurry up!

Jasmin rubbed her eyes and looked at the clock. Mother kept putting it back on her nightstand, even though Jasmin kept moving it to the shelf.

The whole gang fortunately had finally left the party scene. In the aftermath, the room always seemed somehow darker, and it seemed as though they had left a fragrance hanging in the room—a sweet, full, Jenniferlopez-like smell.

Jasmin stretched out. There were familiar smells coming from the kitchen, the morning television, their theme music, the hosts' laughter.

2.

Jasmin was looking out the window into the schoolyard where the first-graders were flocking around their teacher. Jasmin wouldn't have been able to say what she was expecting, but the feeling of anticipation was quivering somewhere in her stomach area. Or lower. Jasmin had not really been with anyone yet. After a couple of beers and a cider, she had been sliding very close to it with a few boys, and even Tony had already fondled Jasmin's clitoris and inserted his finger into her, and Jasmin had caressed Tony's stiffened organ, but then his little sister had knocked on the door and so on. Plop.

Toward the end of spring, Mother and Jasmin had been wondering together if it would make sense for Jasmin to switch schools in the fall. There were plenty of good choices, and to please Mother, Jasmin had actually visited one school that focused on science, but her enthusiasm ended there. Jasmin had already made it clear that she did not want to become a physician.

Jasmin snorted at the first-graders who were walking behind their teacher, and stretched out to check a text message that had made her phone blink and vibrate. It was from Viola, asking about meeting her after school.

Even though already last spring Jasmin had decided to quit riding lessons, she still had taken a few individual lessons at her cousin's stable at the beginning of summer vacation. Viola couldn't understand how Jasmin could quit riding and say good-bye to all the wonderful horses just like that, and Jasmin didn't care to explain—or, actually, she really couldn't. The same thing with piano lessons. And Girl Scouts. And Cousin Viola didn't understand cheerleading. She regarded it as some sort of bimbo sport. That's just fine. Or was it rather Viola's mother who thought that cheerleading was not a real hobby? In any case, Viola could now ride by herself. Jasmin was no longer interested in the smell of the stables; it wasn't exciting anymore.

The first day of school, wrote Jasmin in her diary that evening. This will not qualify for the Chronicle of Wonders. The class is what it is; some snarling idiot asked if Jasmin was still a virgin. Yawn. The teachers were mostly the same: some pleasant people and some not so pleasant.

People were asking about Merita, and Jasmin told them what she knew. That Merita had spent the whole summer in the hospital and had gained just enough weight so that she was no longer in immediate danger of dying. But she was too tired to start school yet. And so on and so forth.

Jasmin had not gone to see Merita since June. Mother had tried to persuade her to go; it would be really important for a friend. Jasmin told her she would go but ended up never going. She herself didn't really know why. She just didn't want to see Merita anymore, to see Merita as she was. It may have reminded her too much of Mikael's final weeks. The head deep in the pillows, hollow cheeks. No thank you.

Even the cheerleading team was almost the same, the Funky Sweet Angel Team. A couple of girls had dropped out, and a new one had joined, a small, slender, and beautiful one, Vanessa. She would probably get the role of the climber if she was good enough. The Funky Sweet Angel Team was supposed to compete abroad before Christmas. The older girls had already been to who knows where, but Mother did not allow Jasmin to go. Despite the fact that Jasmin had progressed hugely during the year, and she might even have been considered for climber of the group, in spite of having grown so tall.

Jasmin dug out *Sugar* magazine from under her pillow and browsed it. In this special issue they were introducing American teams. Glittery tops, short satin skirts, pure white shining slippers. Rhinestones, spangles, pearls, lamé. Hip hip hop! We are the top!

Jasmin had explained it to Mother. Who knows for how many times. Look. The climber is the top-most girl, the one who performs stunts above the lifters and the bases. The jumps in the air were difficult and felt wonderful in your head and in the pit of your stomach. Everybody wanted to be a climber, including Jasmin, and this fall there might be an opportunity for that; that is, if the cute, tiny little Vanessa did not butt in.

That's great, real nice, Mother had said, peeking absentmindedly over her book. It's nice you've found your own sport and have a goal.

Real nice! But is this my thing? Jasmin felt like screaming. Real nice! What is my sport and my goal? How do I know?

Monday

by Sara Martin

In the middle of seeing the second client of the day—a young woman, convinced about the abnormality of her labia major—Linda's mother, Anita Rossi, calls. She speaks fast, in a high-pitched voice. She has not seen her daughter in a week; she's been under the impression all this time that the girls were at my house, that Linda had specifically told her that Jasmin had said they could stay at our place for the whole week.

"Wow. Is that so?" I say slowly, and step to open the trash can, drop the gloves into the trash can, then glance at the woman who is lying on her back, and, with a clear nod of my head, tell her she can get up now.

"And now," says Anita Rossi vehemently, "Linda is not answering her phone. It's not like her at all. We have an agreement that she must always let me know if she's staying out late or if there's a change in plans. I kept wondering a little because there haven't even been any text messages, but I just assumed they were having such a good time at your place."

Why didn't you call and make sure that everything was fine and that it was okay with me, I ask in my mind, but then I remember that most likely I would not have answered the phone anyway.

"So, there's been a misunderstanding, or they've misled us," I say, a little tensely. I glance at the woman who is getting up from the examination table and, lowering my voice, add that "Jasmin was supposed to stay the entire week at her grandparents', but I've just learned that she has not been there either. Neither has she been at home. So evidently the girls have been somewhere together. But where? And where are they now?"

"Do you have a summer place?" I ask. "Another place in the country? A summer villa?"

"No," Anita answers, and I hear a little laugh. "Not even a cottage."

I feel uncertain. Why am I the only one asking the questions?

"What about grandparents? Relatives?" I continue, nevertheless.

"All of them live, or are staying, abroad," says Anita.

"Does Jasmin carry a lot of cash with her?" Anita asks.

"I don't know," I say, and think I should check Jasmin's bank account. "What about Linda?" I ask, thinking that Anita probably knows nothing about money problems. After Mikael's death I had often thought I should take another job in order to afford everything I needed.

"I just thought about that," Anita answered. "Maybe they've gone somewhere. You know, traveling. Gotten some stupid idea. Who knows? Maybe they've gone away with some friends."

We're quiet for a while. Disbelief takes over, and then it starts to break down. Neither of us wants to say it first. Does your daughter often have stupid ideas? Is your daughter an idiot? Should we really be seriously worried? Then I ask Anita when she had last seen her daughter.

"Let me see," says Anita, and inhales her cigarette. "A week ago Sunday. They both came over here. I thought they were on their way to your house. They were packing some clothes and cosmetics with them. They were fussing. And they had that chinchilla rabbit with them."

"Chinchilla rabbit?" I say, and I can't help thinking that Anita Rossi had been crowned Miss Europe sometime near the end of the seventies. A handsome throne, a crown, and a mink robe. Did beauty queens, the fake royalty, still use things like that then?

"I thought it was your rabbit," continues Anita. "Because Jasmin always has it with her."

Pause-pause-pause.

"And you?" Anita asks. "When did you last see Jasmin?"

When did I? I was busily packing my suitcase a week ago on Sunday, and I was looking for a leather belt that Mikael had brought me from Paris, when I noticed that Jasmin had it. She was wearing jeans, and the belt was hanging low on her hips. I was in a hurry, the plane was leaving at half past three, and I was already late. I made a remark about the belt, and Jasmin, of course, snapped back. Muma and Papsi never nag me about small things, she reminded me.

I glance at the woman who stands nervously next to the dressing screen. I apologize to her about the interruption and tell Anita that I know absolutely nothing about a rabbit, and then I ask her to call the school immediately—I will at some point call the Pet Shop and the Girls' House, if need be.

I don't think we should call the police quite yet, I think aloud, hoping that Anita would have something intelligent to add. The woman next to the screen stiffens even more. "Oh, how horrible," says Anita Rossi. And it's only then that I allow myself to hear the salon noises in the background, women talking to one another, hairdryers roaring, clinking, the laughter, the delighted exclamations.

I swallow the suspicious question about Linda that I had had on the tip of my tongue, finish the phone call, and think about what to say to the woman whose labia are within the limits of normal, somewhat large and slightly asymmetric, but totally normal, quite okay, provided they don't chafe when she walks and moves or during intercourse.

After explaining the issue, I see the somewhat sulky client out and keep repeating to myself: This is happening to me now, this is true, this kind of thing may happen to anyone. Again, I call Jasmin's cell phone and, while listening to the same automated answer, I glance at the next patient's chart. A woman around thirty, a police officer, childless, healthy, a routine examination. Fortunately.

When I peek through the door and call the woman's name, I feel that the voice comes from somewhere far away, a foreign voice.

I push my finger into the woman's vagina and feel around the opening of the uterus. My probing may be harsh, raw, hardened by routine, but so be it. Today it's like that. I look out through the window. The wind is blowing. The tree branches are whisking around, naked. The woman on the examination table is a police officer, exceptionally tense. She keeps gasping for air and stares intently at the ceiling. She would like to become pregnant in the near future, but she is afraid of giving birth and would like to make sure well in advance that she will not have to give birth vaginally. I'd like to ask what kind of police officer could be so afraid of bearing a child.

I think about pain, about different thresholds of pain; I ask her about the regularity of her periods and how long they last and when she had her last pap smear. The last what? The woman cramps so badly now that I have to stop the internal examination. Cervical cell exam, I continue. A wave of exhaustion flows over me, and I ask the police officer to get dressed. She wears street clothes. What if I asked her what I should do? In exchange for telling me what I should do, I'll write you a diagnosis about your narrow hips; I'll let you escape with a C-section if only you tell me where Jasmin might be, and how she can be found as quickly as possible.

Only a few hours after Sara Martin had given birth, the doctor came to tell the young mother that something was wrong with the newborn baby. Fred was standing there at the foot of the bed, looking at his wife with hunched shoulders, his face long and pale. I don't believe you, the young mother had said, quietly, without raising her voice. You cannot make me believe. I refuse.

And then what happened: the blushing young doctor had looked at his papers again—and lo, he had come to the wrong room, to the wrong woman, the problem had been with a baby boy. And the mother who had just given birth watched how the doctor walked out of the room, and soon heard a piercing shriek from the next room. It was like a nightmare that came back every now and then to the baby girl's mother. As if she had gotten hold of fate, pressed her hand on the evil eye, blown out the angry flame. The mother refused to accept the bad luck. She transferred it to another person. Sometimes she thought that fate would pay it back some time. The shrieking woman would return one day; she would come to the office with her deformed baby boy and demand to see Jasmin. Shall we trade?

Sometimes in the mornings I wake up to Mikael standing at the foot of my bed, watching me with sad eyes, his shoulders slightly hunched. I had also tried to fight for Mikael—I won't believe, I won't accept—but it didn't work. Mikael should have fought harder for himself. Been more forceful, I think. Mikael was skillful, capable, thoughtful, smooth, suitable, everything but forceful. It was Mikael's tenderness and intensity that caught your attention right away.

After asking the grateful police officer the routine questions about nutrition and lifestyle, I shake her hand and close the doors behind her. Double doors, which women prefer. Not a word can be heard in the waiting room. Total privacy in the office, and before and after in the waiting room, where they read the women's magazines, with glamorous celebrities, women living multilayered and colorful lives, who open up and spill everything. In a way, I like the contradiction, even though I don't understand it.

For some, life means looking for something from everyone, everywhere. In some people, you feel it immediately, at the door, even before shaking their hand. It's the toughness in their eyes, the tenseness of their breath, the cock of their hips.

A picture of Mikael's withered penis flashes across my eyes. A heartbreaking sight. The neck of a bird that has flown into the window. Mikael let me watch. Touch. Till the very end. Even that had a first time and a last time. Sometimes, when Mikael was sleeping his pain-medicated sleep, I held it in my mouth. I've never told anyone about it, how much comfort it brought me to hold that limp and withered penis in my mouth during our last nights together.

Before the next patient I dictate notes about the police officer who fears giving birth, and, atypically, add into the otherwise routine report that it's life that the woman is afraid of, rather than giving birth; and then I call my parents' landline.

Papsi answers the phone as slowly as always. I have no time to start my worried, accusatory torrent of words when Father already starts recounting the events of the morning.

"Muma just went for a walk with her girlfriend, and after that she'll go to play bridge, don't you remember? Bridge every Monday. Muma won't be back until afternoon. I'm reading the newspaper and watching television," he continues. "I'll glue a couple of new stamps in the album; soon it will be time for the stamp expo again." Papsi's voice is calm and cheerful, jovial. A hearty laugh and large warm hands, a pediatrician's hands. Sometimes I even felt jealous for all those children Father likely patted and pampered in his daily work. I wanted to sit in my father's lap forever. Can I build my cottage here? I sometimes asked.

"There's a huge warehouse fire in the eastern part of the city," Papsi tells me. "I think I can smell the smoke all the way here. An extensive fire, some big storage building. Hopefully it's nothing toxic. The fire chief they interviewed looked like my younger brother when he was young. They still don't know what caused the fire. Probably those immigrants again, some of those mafia men?"

I'm quiet.

"Hello?" says Papsi. "Hello?"

All of a sudden, I want to go home, home to the peaceful wood house in the peaceful neighborhood where Mother and Father live, two doctors who have been together for almost fifty years. I want to throw myself onto the dark-green sofa and eat chocolate candy from that stemmed serving bowl Mother always takes out well before Christmas.

"You had such a beautiful wedding," says Papsi. "A really beautiful wedding." He means my wedding to Fred in the old manor house by the sea. It was a beautiful wedding, and expensive.

"And you shouldn't worry about Jasmiina," Papsi says in his soft voice. "She told us she was going to that good friend of hers. They would study together for exams, surf on the computer, eat chips, drink Coca-Cola, and, of course, talk about boys."

"I guess so," I say quietly and sigh. Go ahead and mention paper dolls, glossy pictures, and lollipops. But where is Jasmin now?

After the phone call, I text Anita. Has Linda run away before?

A heavy feeling in the pit of the stomach, aching lower back, painful intercourse, spotting.

Tapping my temple, I record the symptoms of the client who sits in front of me, hoping that the examination will not reveal anything abnormal. A thirty-eight-year-old secretary. Even if the lump were to be harmless, a temporary cyst, finding out is always stressful. A referral for further tests is a serious next step to hear, and across the desk I can sense the anxiety that creeps into the woman. I don't believe you. It's not true. My thoughts return to the hours after having given birth, to my newborn daughter with whom there COULD NOT be anything wrong.

Moth-err, waves Jasmin at the school gate when the bell rings. I'm going in now, Mother! And there she disappears, among the others who are rushing inside. Bye, Mother!

At ten thirty, Paula Pauliina informs me that a very persistent woman on the phone insists that she speak with me, even though she is not a patient of mine. I initially hear Paula Pauliina say "perverse woman," and it takes me a moment to figure it out.

Put her through, I say to my perky receptionist. I write Paula Pauliina's name and the name of an iron supplement on a prescription and lift the receiver. Anita apologizes for calling my office directly and continues in a breathless voice, saying that Linda has never been gone without letting her know, and that the girls have not been in school for the whole past week, and they don't seem to be there right now either. Their friends have not missed school, and are there now. She has also learned that our daughters have had other absences during the fall, and lately quite a few. The principal himself made that observation. The principal? What good is such an observation?

And no one contacted the girls' homes, I mutter aloud, goosebumps on my arms. Simultaneously I remember that I haven't been at home and I haven't checked my email; something I usually would've done immediately after getting home, but my thoughts had been focused on the overnight guest.

"We should probably do something," says Anita. "If nobody else has heard anything, we need to report this."

"We do," I reply.

"To the police," says Anita. "Still today."

"Yes, of course."

A strong wave of nausea swells inside me. I look at the woman behind the curtain who is getting undressed, and I ask Anita if it would be okay for her to come and see me around five.

"At your office, you mean?" she asks.

"First here, yes," I answer absentmindedly and think about the last patient of the day, an elderly woman who has a tumor in her ovary. I wonder if I would like to see the mother of my daughter's friend, a former beauty queen, on my examination table. Sometimes, in the heat of an argument, Jasmin would remark that Linda's mother and I were like night and day.

But in one sense we are completely identical: for one week, neither of us has missed her daughter.

After the phone call, I review the file on the next patient. I look at the clock, and select a cell phone number. I hold the phone next to my ear, until the male voice again tells me that I am calling in vain.

I open my mouth and hold up a pocket mirror to look at my tongue. The nausea continues. Does my tongue look strange? Should I gargle with Betadine? I have to work all day today. I have to make it through the day. Women are waiting. More and more women are waiting. And is there really a smell of smoke in the air? At least my eyes feel sensitive, runny. From the pocket of my white coat, I pull out a handkerchief and wipe my eyes.

I examine the woman's breasts, and on the left side my finger finds something barely noticeable yet sharp, not quite the size of a pinhead. I try to remember the woman's year of birth and the date of her last mammogram, and then I ask her to feel her left breast herself. I guide her fingers, stop on the spot, press lightly. The woman's face becomes pale and tight, her eyes fill with tears.

"What is it?" she asks. "What can it be? I have a young daughter, a very young daughter!"

I calm her. "It could be a totally innocent concentration of calcium in a gland, post-partum, temporary, but it should be checked out."

The woman gets up quickly from the examination table and goes in front of the mirror, looks at her breasts. She slaps her left breast. Tears are running along her cheeks.

"I'm not going to disappear," the woman says, looks at me from the mirror, and sniffs. "Like my mother. She died from this," the woman says, "when I was ten."

I write her a referral for an ultrasound. I suggest that she go as soon as possible. "Of course!" the woman says when she leaves, with an almost angry look on her face, wiping her cheeks.

After the woman has left, Paula Pauliina sticks her head in the door, lets me know about a last-minute cancellation, pauses theatrically, darn cancellations, and reminds me of the phone office hour.

"Can you smell smoke?" I ask.

"Oh yeah," Paula Pauliina shrugs her shoulders. "Maybe a bit. It's that big fire over there."

My receptionist stands in the doorway and sniffs the air around her. Is it she herself who always buys that perfume? She wears a brownish-green blouse and a matching long skirt. The wool vest she must have knitted herself, cable knit, large, with buttons a bit clown-like. As Christmas presents, I've received scarves and socks from her; I can probably expect something like that this year too. One Christmas Eve, Paula Pauliina had gone to play bingo. She left the place only after they started to close. And she had been the first one in line to wait for it to open again on Boxing Day morning. She was not at all embarrassed to tell me things like that. She plays bingo and the lottery, does crossword puzzles, visits the amusement park gambling hall during the summer, which is a bit odd, but maybe we all have our odd sides. Muma has her bridge, and Papsi has his stamp albums and men's sauna club twice a month.

"Alright," I say and let out a deep sigh. Hunger growls in my stomach. Deep down in the pit of my stomach, after a long while, there's that certain feeling. My vagina has been pulsing rhythmically around a man's penis. I've shaken in waves after a long time. Then I think about a rabbit. What rabbit did the girls have with them? I glance at the clock and ask how many people there are waiting on the lines.

"Nine," answers Paula Pauliina from behind her desk. Her computer is on, and when I try to see what pages she has open, she steps in front of the monitor and seems to blush. For a long time, she's taken all kinds of computer courses at the continuing education center. My first net-dependent receptionist. For a Christmas present, I'm going to buy her Estée Lauder. Or is she more the White Linen or Private Collection type?

"I'll take those phone calls in a moment, but I need to make one phone call first," I say, and hand the iron prescription to Paula Pauliina. I call the Pet Shop, where the girls have been working each afternoon since the beginning of October as part-time assistants. The answering machine tells me that the Pet Shop is closed today, Monday, because of an illness. I wonder how the animals get taken care of when the shop is closed, but the first person who wants to renew her prescription interrupts my thoughts.

Thirty minutes into my phone office time, there is still one more phone call, from Anita Rossi.

"Oh, I've been so busy," Anita says. She has called both of her ex-husbands, her mother and some of the girls' classmates, but absolutely no one has seen the girls anywhere in a week. In the same breath, Anita tells me that she has spoken with her therapist and her priest and her personal trainer. And really, Linda has never taken off on her own; and even though sometimes she's been a nerve-wracking ditz—but aren't they all at that age—Linda has always been a sweet and extremely considerate child. Once, for instance, when Anita had been sleeping an exceptionally-deep Sunday morning sleep, Linda had tried to attach on her mother's finger a sculptured nail that she had found on the hallway floor, using a glue that said it fixes everything—wood, glass, porcelain, leather—but Linda had attached it the wrong way and wanted to know if Mother would be mad. Linda always wanted to please Mother.

Ditz. I taste the expression used by Anita. A ditz of a girl. Is Jasmin a ditz? I can't tell. Rather, I would say that Jasmin is serious. Disciplined and conscientious. Almost a control freak. She even cleans her room without a special reminder. Has always cleaned her plate, even though sometimes so quickly her stomach has started to ache.

I think slowly, Should I go home right away? To Jasmin's room? Inspect the place? Lift up her mattress? Search through her closets and drawers? The computer? Search for what? Rabbit droppings? A foreign smell? Chatroom links?

For some reason I tell Anita about a morning three years ago. It was a completely ordinary Monday morning. The coffeemaker was hissing. Mikael and I had divided the morning paper into its first and last sections; we alternated the sections we read first every day. While carefully cracking the shell of his breakfast egg, Mikael lifted his eyes and said that he might not see the next summer. How so? I asked, smiling. I had fallen in love with Mikael's sense of humor from the moment we first met. But now I was wrong. Mikael took my hand and told me about the worsening headaches and the problems with his eyesight, for which he had gone to get some tests. It was a tumor, and in an especially difficult location. Mikael used a few Latin words and phrases, which I allowed to sink peacefully into my professional register. Then I handed him a plate for the egg shells and glanced at the clock. I asked something else. Physician talk. Death before summer. Why should one hurry now? We finished eating breakfast in silence, Mikael sipping his coffee and me my tea, and when he stood up from the table, Mikael said, I love you all so much. I don't want you and Jasmin to have to suffer for me. Let's talk more in the evening. The front door slammed closed.

What are we going to do now? Jasmin asked from behind her partly-open door, her hair tousled, her eyes not yet teary, but almost.

"What are we going to do now?" asks Anita Rossi. I wake up, and remember the earlier discussion I had had with Jasmin, the last conversation about some wide leather belt that Mikael had brought me as a souvenir, which she had borrowed without permission. After a squabble that didn't go anywhere, I had said, You should at least drink your chocolate milk.

To be a gynecologist requires a certain attitude, a certain approach. Perhaps each gynecologist has her or his own rituals. In the beginning, I always thought about anal intercourse with Fred. No longer so. I push my middle finger into the woman's anus and feel her uterus from both sides by stroking her stomach on the outside. The uterus is a bit out of position, which fits well with the symptoms that brought the woman to see me. One of the ovaries is clearly smaller than the other. Among all the clients I've seen today, this woman is the first whose pubic hair is completely natural. The thought startles me. I can't imagine myself on the table at a beauty parlor, having myself reshaped. Is it some old-fashioned bashfulness? Laziness or lack of style, or merely a lack of time?

Who would even be looking at your hairs like that? says Muma's voice.

Oh, who knows who? I reply.

Moth-err, I'm taking a shower! Go away! shouts Jasmin from behind the shower curtain. Go away! Disappear! Get lost!

The woman gives a yelp. She has four children, and she is not planning to have any more. She asks for sterilization or a hysterectomy or whatever other means might be available. I draw her a picture of her ovaries and her uterus, and at the same time I think how in the mornings I used to leave a note on the kitchen table, and on that note I drew my own picture, a round face, round eyes. Sweetie, it's a busy morning, busy week, I'll be late today, there's food on the stove. All kinds of goodies in the refrigerator. Kisses, Mother.

I'm starting to shake. The pen nearly flies out of my fingers. I look at the picture I just drew: It looks more like a girl with braids than a woman's ovaries. Has it already been more than a week since I last heard the pink Moomin alarm clock ring in the room next to mine? Wake up, it's a fun day ahead, wake up now! Jasmin still wanted to use the same alarm clock that she received for her sixth birthday. The girl even wanted to renew her subscription to the *Mickey Mouse Club* magazine for

Christmas. *Mickey Mouse* and *Cosmopolitan*, both. Okay then, I had finally agreed. At the time, Fred had opposed even the *Mickey Mouse Club* magazine—such American garbage. I didn't even mention *Cosmopolitan*.

The pink Moomin maiden's bottom was chipped, and covered with a small Band-Aid. One time Jasmin had flung her singing alarm clock to the other corner of her room, the Band-Aid a reminder. Jasmin put it there herself, a mini Band-Aid. No more harsh handling, laughed Jasmin, and kissed the alarm clock.

I'm thinking about the toast I had thrown in the trash this morning. Jasmin's toast, soft, warm.

It's like diving into black water. That's how the author of *The Little Prince* described the descent into the Sahara in the middle of the night.

This woman, who has lost her child, rinses her face with cold water and looks at herself in the mirror of the small dressing room. Where is your daughter? she asks her reflection in the mirror.

You have lost your child. You lost your child in the night of the Sahara.

After wiping her face with a tissue, this mother calls the cell phone again. The number cannot be reached. A dive into black water. A well. A sewer. Fuck you, says this mother to the unknown man who can only keep saying again and again that the number cannot be reached. Poor man.

I call again. Another time. And again. Repeatedly. I keep pushing the numbers. Fuck. Poor mother. Poor Jasmin. Did you get tired of my cooking? Did I tell you the wrong bedtime stories? Was I too stingy? Did I not take you shopping often enough? Didn't you see your father often enough? Where in the world are you hiding, sweetie, call me as soon as you can, I say tenderly, as if an answering machine would click on at the other end of the phone line.

Then I call home, to the landline, and wait with tears in my eyes. The white phone is ringing there on the kitchen table, under the little bulletin board. Maybe the girl has gone home and is taking a shower, as she often does, and can't hear. What if she has returned from her adventure, is now a bit ashamed, has to invent a good explanation and practice apologizing? Soon she's going to miss her mother. And father. Both fathers.

For a long time after Mikael's death I used to carry his cell phone with me. It held his friends and colleagues—his phone network, the background picture he had chosen: Jasmin's and my face cheek to cheek, and "Imagine" for his ring tone. Once he and I were in Berlin together when somebody blew up a bomb, they may have been Kurds or something, I can't remember what they were protesting. Are there any doctors here? someone kept shrieking. Dear God, is there a doctor here? A thick smell of smoke, then too. Coughing, with burning eyes, Mikael and I led people out of the subway corridor, toward the light.

Before I invite the next client in, I call Saku at the university. Saku sounds surprised and somehow humbly delighted, and I almost regret having called. My brother does research on shame, and after initial doubts, he has achieved status as some kind of an expert in analyzing national characteristics. I explain my concern to my brother and realize only now for the first time that I have never asked Saku to look after Jasmin during my trip. On the other hand it was a given that I had never asked Seidi; Seidi lived out in the country, and our relationship was not like that. But would Saku, who lived in the apartment building almost next door, have agreed?

I'm quiet for a long time, then I start to cry.

Saku asks simple questions, comforts, and encourages me. "When the puppy gets hungry, she'll come home.

But she's not that kind of girl. The girl is in the middle of a transition and is acting out all kinds of things. It's actually good to do something radical. It's a healthy sign."

"Radical?" I sniff.

"I entered puberty at the age of thirty-six, and it wasn't really a good thing," said Saku.

I recall how Saku sat through his whole summer vacation in his dark apartment and didn't want to see anyone. Muma and Papsi were worried. They called me, too, several times a day. Heartbroken? Papsi inquired, and I didn't deny that it might be so.

"Would you like to talk?" Saku suggests. "How about lunch at the Thai place close to you? What's the name of it again?"

"Szechuan," I answer.

Always ready. Saku is a good person. Saku has had nothing but his work. Recently he'd had a close male friend even though I could never bring myself to ask about him. Was he in the travel business? They took so many trips abroad together, always to warm countries, most recently to Cambodia.

And the fact that one can't admit her brother has a male friend, and that this is the reason her daughter can't go and stay with this brother—is this so? Is that it?

I wonder if Saku has, at last, a prospect for a wife. A fiancée. Muma and Papsi keep asking, and I don't know how to answer. I imagine myself explaining to Muma how a man can cause heartache to another man. Muma ponders this thoroughly. Yes, yeees. That's right. I suppose that's how it is then.

"I'm sorry," I say to my brother.

"Don't worry," Saku says.

"Trouble does not look like this," I continue.

"It's better to walk ten miles safely than to take a dangerous shortcut."

“I’d be sad if I could,” said a woman in the rapids. And so forth. For a moment I’m that big sister with braids and Saku is that little brother with freckles, baseball cap reversed. And again I would like to say, Let’s not take Seidi with us, okay? Let’s not tell Seidi, okay?

When the next client suddenly whimpers on the examination table, and I see bloody sores, I ask if the woman has had intercourse during the past twenty-four hours. And had the woman herself wanted to have intercourse? Had there been some kind of game? Was the partner someone she knew? And so on. When the client’s tears start to trickle on her cheeks, I stop the examination right away, pull off the gloves, stomp on the trash-can lever so that the metal clanks, and drop the gloves in the bin. The woman gets up to a sitting position with difficulty, and I take her by her hand. Maybe a bit too firmly.

“I’ve never come to see you before,” she sobs. “I sometimes read your column in the magazine, and once I even wrote you about something. Of course under a fake name. And you actually answered my question, and now I came because I couldn’t even think about seeing anyone else.” She leans more heavily against my shoulder.

I let the woman talk. I ask for more details, trying to remember where I had placed the contact information for the crisis center, the brochure, the steps to be taken. It’s all the same. I grasp the woman by her shoulders and tell her that she should go right away to see the police and after that to the Women’s Crisis Center, where she could talk to somebody about all of this.

“Police?” the woman cries out.

I’ll meet you there soon, I keep thinking. I don’t want to go there either.

Crying, the woman gets dressed, takes the piece of paper on which I've written the phone numbers and addresses, and the medical report. I suggest that she take a taxi. I ask her if she has a friend where she could spend the night. When the woman closes the door after her, I open the window and light a long, thin cigarette, the ones I sometimes buy on impulse at the airport. A few years back my gynecologist's column was in a women's magazine, and I almost drowned in the mail. After Mikael's death I took a break, but now I've started again. It's good work for evenings and weekends.

"We're out of the brochures," hollers Paula Pauliina from the door. "Not one left. Gotta order some more."

Paula Pauliina stares at my cigarette for a moment, shrugs her shoulders almost imperceptibly, and then closes the outer door. I can hear her spraying deodorizer. "Get a life," I say half-aloud and take a really deep drag.

I look at the hunched woman, my last client, who is crossing the street and walking directly across the slushy park, into the dimness of the trees. I think about the space between my own legs; last night it was only the second man since Mikael's death to touch me there.

Mother

1.

Mother published my diary entries from the early autumn as part of her own book. When the Baptist learned about it, his anger flared. How could my mother profit from her own daughter's intimate diary? At the time, I was still depressed and so insecure that I didn't quite dare to laugh at the Baptist's opinions. I just listened to him quietly. He talked about it continuously, and reminded me that he had at last rescued me from everything bad, he was the one who had cleansed my body and my soul, separated me from my formerly inconsequential and self-destructive life. Now I was Ruth, and I belonged to the Baptist.

Mother writes in her book that after my disappearance she read my diary day and night. She eventually showed it to Penalty Box and the young female psychiatrist whom she had met at the police station, but they found absolutely no new clues to my disappearance in it. Besides, the diary entries suddenly end at the beginning of October. There's very little about Linda in there, and only a brief mention of the Pet Shop. *Today was the first afternoon we were at work.*

At that time, Penalty Box spoke with my mother on an almost weekly basis. He asked how Mother was doing, and sometimes inquired about Jason as well. He reminded Mother that my case was being investigated as a possible homicide, especially since Linda's body had been found. And that, despite all, your own life must continue. You shouldn't become mired in this.

Even so, every day Mother wished there would be a small sign of life from me. That somebody somewhere—even on the other side of the world—would have seen me. That from somewhere a teeny tiny piece of proof that I was alive would appear. Or even proof that I was dead. A sign of death. Mother had gotten used to that thought too. That I had met the same fate as my friend, but that I was hidden, deeper, elsewhere, tucked in the earth.

In a big arc, my cell phone flew over the boat's railing into the sea. I watched it, and, over the noise of the boat's engine, heard the Baptist say that it was something that belonged to Jasmin; Ruth did not need it anymore. Since then I haven't had a cell phone of my own. To be clear, I haven't had anything of my own, except for Miss Frank. Everything I have I've received from the Baptist.

Like a cartoonist or a child, I still sometimes imagine my little pink cell phone slowly sinking to the bottom of the sea. While drifting downward, it rings and blinks its light, and fish come to marvel at its presence. And then an ugly, scaly sea monster falls in love with it, in true romantic fashion.

The Baptist soon lost interest in my country's events: The search for me, the police, my mother's prolific mourning, if any of that had ever really stirred him. He assured me that I would quickly forget my background and my old surroundings, and that nobody would search for me at his place. No connection could ever be made. Nothing. And, little by little, I'd learn to appreciate my new life, the archeology, the artwork, the books, the landscape, the ancient garden plants. Even him.

True, the police would never connect my disappearance and Linda's death to the Pet Shop, nor the Pet Shop to the fire at the warehouse. More than one motorcycle gang had meeting places close to the warehouse, and, toward the end of autumn, the police had suspected a possible retaliation strike. In addition, there were earlier small fires in the neighborhood, set by homeless people and kids playing with matches near the fishing marina. And young partygoers at raves, which the police and the fire inspectors sometimes raided. Illegal bars and clubs had never been found in the area, nor had anyone ever looked for them.

Among our classmates, all kinds of rumors circulated after our disappearance: First, a pervert school inspector had kidnapped us; we had won the lottery and were traveling around the world; we had committed a double suicide and fell through the ice into the sea outside the city; fearing disclosure of our lesbian relationship, we'd decided to run away to escape our parents' condemnation; we had met some suspicious immigrants at the Pet Shop, became infatuated with them, and left the country with them. The police regarded those rumors as typical teenage urban legends and didn't take them seriously.

The girls who had been working with us at the Pet Shop never said a word about us, and nobody ever ratted on Randi. He was probably already back home when the authorities started calculating the damages caused by the massive fire.

2.

I often thought about Randi. Randi with slender fingers, Randi who smelled of cinnamon. I didn't know that a man could be so sweet, so beautiful. I didn't know that anyone's feelings could be hurt so much as when I asked him about the smell of cinnamon.

Randi Suraweera, who was lured by his big brother Ringo to the city of O., *to the country of oversized people*, as Ringo once put it after a few too many beers. Randi's hands, so small around the rims of his beer mug. I never saw him get drunk. He was our "protector"—for me and the other girls, the next one up the ladder from the driver—which means quite low in the strange hierarchy of Lido's business empire.

There is always someone who lures someone else. Ringo painted such fancy pictures of my country's standard of living and work opportunities that Randi couldn't help but leave his mother and family behind and head far north to try his luck. That's how it went, I think. Poor Randi. I remember well what their apartment was like: two small musty rooms in a house of concrete blocks, next to a coal power plant in an industrial district, windows blackened by soot.

Randi wasn't like Lido's other men. He always carried a small canvas shoulder bag with a book or two in it and a bundle of letters tied with a rubber band. Hanif Kureishi, Nadeem Aslam—who are they? Linda asked Randi about the books peeking out of the bag. At the time, Randi was sitting in his typical pose, a book in his hand, on a recliner with his feet on the table, not seeing or hearing anything else. His big brother often laughed at him, roughed up his thick, dark hair, poked at him, and kicked him gently. When Randi wasn't reading, he was writing letters, using light-yellow lined paper. It looked funny; we hadn't seen anyone write a letter in years.

Randi folded the letters twice, inserted them into envelopes, and sealed them—ready to go. Then he stuck the letters in his canvas bag. Sometimes in the back room, I looked in the bag, and sniffed the small things inside—all with a faint aroma of cinnamon—and spelled the names on the envelopes: Lalitha Suraweera, Anil Suraweera.

He could not resist the suspense, the temptation, the difference. He, too, was misled, deceived many times over, changing into a person he himself had a hard time recognizing in the end. A couple of years ago, I still thought I would contact him. I would tell him that it was Linda who was responsible for the letters disappearing from the canvas bag; Linda was the one who took them. We looked at the small drawings he had made in the margins of the letters and laughed with the other girls about the curly words, since we couldn't understand anything.

And I would tell him that neither he, nor any of those drooling old men, ever understood anything about us. We were not the Scandinavian girls that he or his big brother imagined us to be. They didn't really even exist, except in their imaginations.

At the same time, I would tell Randi that it's because of him that I'm here; it's because of him that I ended up where I did. Or should I say that it was because of his brother Ringo? If his brother had not lured him to my country, deceiving him with his big promises, would Linda and I ever have stayed at the Pet Shop?

One day I gave the letters we had taken from Randi's bag to the Baptist. How they had ended up in my bag, I couldn't recall. As I guessed, the Baptist was able to read the writing. The Baptist read the letters to me, translating them as he read. He kept smiling and raising his eyebrows, and occasionally stopped to stare at me, in the way I had learned to fear. He asked me if I had had sexual intercourse with the boy who had written the letters, and he didn't believe me when I denied it and swore that I hadn't. Sometimes these moments had a very ugly ending. The Baptist tied me up, and when I screamed at him and blamed him for the fire and Linda's death, he pushed soap into my mouth until I vomited. Eventually he opened my leather belt and penetrated me without saying a word, painfully, as it always was in moments like that. With trembling hands, he finally buckled my belt, put the little key in his pocket, and cried. Sitting on the floor he cried, with his chin against his chest and his back against the wall. I belonged to him and to nobody else.

Before leaving, he said he would draw a bath for me. Did I want lavender or orange oil in the water?

3.

One of the envelopes had been addressed to Vanilla Bebe. If I remember right, Randi stuck the letter in my hand after a gang-bang party in his putrid apartment. I didn't want any letters then, especially from him.

In the envelope there was only a drawing of me next to the rabbit cage, a shockingly detailed pencil drawing. Who knows when he had drawn it.

So, I am Vanilla Bebe. Or I was, during the days of the Wet Pet Club. Linda was Pink Cream. These were names Lido had given us, ancient pornographic codes, as the Baptist puts it. Banana Split. One needs two minds, a night mind and a day mind. I know it now. The girl who threw her cell phone into the sea was Vanilla Bebe, formerly named Jasmin, but the girl who watched the evening sky darken over the sea was Ruth.

Every now and then, Ruth wrote letters, letters for the Baptist to read that were not meant to be sent anywhere, of course. Actually, they had been written only to cheer him up. Sometimes after returning from trips, the Baptist was gloomy, quiet, and irritable, and I tried to entertain him with stuff I had written, veiled in the form of a letter. Sometimes he was patient enough to listen as I read; he sat deep in an armchair and pressed his fingertips together, clearly lost in his own thoughts; and I continued reading even though I knew he had something else on his mind, maybe meetings with the group of men, the brotherhood, to which he once had said he belonged.

At some point I started to fear that the Baptist would bring a new girl with him from his trips, since he told me that I was already an old woman, and soon he would not want to touch me anymore. But he didn't bring anyone, and I stopped thinking about it.

The Year of the Peacock

*

And so it happened that despite all the bicycling spirits, and especially in defiance of the Smeller of Shadows, this son of Lalla Suraweera named Randi is sitting on the deck of a merchant vessel and looking out over the sea for as long as he can, since in a moment he must retreat into the corridors of the ship, where for the rest of the trip he will only be able to stare at the sea through a fogged window. Spices in one direction, electronics in the other.

Randi holds a small red travel bag in his lap as well as the canvas shoulder bag with notebooks and pencils and cedar-scented paper inside. In the red zippered bag he has clothes, a dusty sweater that his sister found somewhere near the bottom of a closet—the one that, according to Mother, a relative from Ireland had sent and that nobody ever wore—socks, underwear, a couple of photos in plastic sleeves, a few books, tobacco, and a ringing bowl. Yes, as the final thing, before turning away, Mother Lalla had handed him a ringing bowl. Randi, this son of hers, knew that it was important to Mother, an inherited piece from decades ago. It, too, had something to do with the spirits, the spirits' drinking bowl or whatever, originally the ancestors' fingerbowl. This is how it was supposed to go: When you put water in the metal bowl and rubbed around its rim, it made a ringing sound. One sound when you used a piece of wood, a different one when you used an iron nail. Some people played the bowls for a living. Eyes closed, heads tilted, swaying and groaning while rubbing the rim of the bowl. Mother and Father's old relatives. People from times gone by. A noisy washbowl, Karim used to joke, when Randi, as an enthusiastic little boy, imitated them and rubbed the rims of the bowl with a piece of bark. Randi thought the sound was nice, especially when you rubbed the bowl with your fingertips. The sound went to the marrow of his spine and tickled at the root of his neck, the same feeling as when he had watched the girls in silk shirts frolicking in the pouring rain.

*

FROM ANIL'S LETTER TO RANDI

Mother is down in the dumps for yet another week, but she may have finally gotten used to the fact that men leave. Big cities are calling. Our father, on the other hand, never talked about leaving. The wide world did not interest him, no far-away green forests or desert oases, no money, and no fortune. I wish that we could remember more about Father, and not just those stories told by others. I've finally organized Father's butterfly collection, and even though Mother first resisted the idea of hanging them on the walls, I did it anyway. They're not the same as the head of a deer or a wild boar; they won't scare anyone to death when he turns on the lights in the hall. I especially like the butterfly that Father labeled Sleepy Orange.

It's nice that you have started writing letters. It's comforting to our Mother. Right now she's cooking food, and believe it or not, she still sets the table for both of you boys, at your own places.

So, working at a pet shop? That's what Mother says to me all the time, with a furrowed brow, her black eyebrows looking like one dark tulip in the middle of her forehead. She's worried, as always when there's a change of plans. You know, she starts to pick at her knuckles... Oh, oh, oh. I thought you were going to work at Cousin's laundry? People always need clean clothes and they need food; but over there do they also need live animals that people buy in a store, just like bread? And what is that pet shop like? What kind of animals can even live up there? Mother is confused. I tell her that it's not like you guys are living on some ice sheets, or in igloos. Send Mother a photo so she will believe me.

And then there's that other thing, which, of course, I won't mention to Mother. I hope in that pet shop of yours you won't get mixed up with any trapping or smuggling of wild animals. There are plenty of rings for that. Our friends and relatives have fortunately never had anything to do with them, but I've read about them in the papers, and Mother's cousin Chanu has told us horror stories. True, our animals wouldn't even survive there, I'm absolutely sure about that. I'm a little bit embarrassed about Mother: she believes everything she's told, never suspicious about anything. Since you left, she just cleans the house, scours, and wipes from dawn till dusk. And chats with those spirits of hers. Oh, I wish they had more days off.

Up there in the north, I suppose even the women are different—tall, blonde, and beautiful—and they won't be as easily led on as we are here, right? Do you even dare tell me?

Take good care of yourself, okay? Karim promised he would teach you the ways of the world, too, but I'm not quite sure what those ways really are, and I can't say anything else here, except to come back home as a man that Mother could be proud of.

*

FROM RANDI'S LETTER TO ANIL SURAWEERA

Thanks, Sis, for asking. Everything's gone really well. First, I've taken it easy, trying to get used to the climate. Karim has shown me the city and introduced me to different places here.

The pet shop manager, Lido, seems to be a cool guy. At first I didn't quite know how to talk to him; he reminds me of one of the actors in *The Red Avenger*. Remember that show we used to watch all the time a couple of years ago?

Lido is a man of the world. You can see it right away. He's figured out that rich young people in the big cities in this corner of the world want lots of special things during their leisure time, and they're ready to pay for them. What are we going to do about it? Lido asks, and then answers: Fuck (sorry, this is Lido's talk), we'll get those rich kids the special things they want. Anything they ask for, we'll get for them. Easy as fucking pie, that's what Lido says. That's how Lido talks.

My job description isn't quite clear to me yet, but one thing I can already tell you is that at least my fingertips won't turn brown like they do when peeling cinnamon.

So Mother is worried about the pet shop? Tell Mother that it's a place where you can buy different kinds of pets, birds and fishes, house crickets, snails, prairie mice, frogs, and even a desert iguana, which is already old. I myself wouldn't take it home to die, but some people think it's really exotic and ask about it every day. As part of the shop, there's also a photo studio, where people can get keepsake photos with their pets. That's what people here like. They send cards with animal designs to each other for Christmas and birthdays, that's what I've heard. These people really care about animals. Some young people talk about animal rights and set foxes free from the fox farms where they're bred for fur coats. I hear that Lido has a wolf coat, and I wonder if they raise wolves here on farms. I'm too embarrassed to ask, especially Lido. Oh, and in addition to the pet shop, Lido also owns some nightclub or games arcade. He's always in a hurry and sometimes smokes two cigarettes at the same time.

I'm going to study hard, learn everything I need to learn. I know that Mother wanted me to apply to a university or work for some big company, but this is my solution. This is the first step for me, and who knows what kind of ladder it will turn out to be! Do I sound just like Karim? I may be overly enthusiastic. It sure is cold in here though, and I'm freezing almost all the time; tomorrow Karim and I will go to look for warmer overcoats. We can't afford fur coats, and I wouldn't really like to go anywhere wearing something like that, since Uncle Chanu told me that a person wearing a fur coat may get covered with spray paint or rotten eggs. Otherwise we've had a friendly welcome, and our language skills are okay for our circles.

Besides, Uncle Chanu has promised to help us with everything, should there be any problems. But I don't think we'll have much to do with him. Since Karim left, Chanu is taking care of the laundry with his wife, Lipak, and I think he's already dreaming about retirement. Maybe they'll return home someday, or travel to London, where one of their kids has that flourishing spice shop chain.

Oh, Karim and I are living in a really nice furnished apartment near downtown. For work we've got new cell phones that can display our country's weather info and sports news. We also got a brand new computer and two TV sets, one for each of us. Shelves full of movies. I just watched *Notting Hill*, and I watched it closely—who knows if I could've seen our relatives in street views? I didn't! On TV there are programs all night, and even though I don't understand everything, it looks interesting and at least different.

*

Is this what they mean by culture shock? wonders Randi one evening. He's standing on the balcony, trying to identify familiar constellations. In the evening, everything is easier. Walking in the streets, going to the store, moving up and down the stairs. During the day, Randi is scared to look around, let alone talk. He has already met Lido. They went to the Pet Shop to get acquainted with the place. Randi was stiff and quiet, indeed couldn't seem to get a word out of his mouth. It was embarrassing, but what could you do? Lido kept talking instead. Satisfied, he kept glancing at Randi. You are the guardians and protectors of my precious little treasures. With time, I'll find plenty of different sorts of jobs for you. No dirty work, no dangerous work, only clean work, easy work, interesting work, big boys' games. Very different from the work at your old uncle's laundry, many more possibilities, much more money.

I'm a fucking global entrepreneur, Lido explained to Randi. Your uncle Chanu is a good guy, but without a doubt he's just running a small business now. He should be brave and start something new, Lido said. He should fucking move forward. Develop an enterprise strategy, update the business. Girls, girls, girls. Lido whistled, looking at a small red harmonica he carried everywhere, even though he never played it.

Lido was quite a sight. Tattoos circled his arms and neck. Gold rings in his ears, a thick gold chain around his neck, and a matching one on his wrist. Gold shining from his mouth when he laughed. And rings as large as bottle tops, a big black stone on both of his index fingers. Lido looked at Randi sharply, lifted his right arm as if to make some kind of tribal greeting and said, Oh, fuck. He then patted Randi on both of his shoulders and cheeks, complimented his appearance, and said there would be a demand for Randi in all sorts of markets, and that the girls would certainly like him. And boys. And men. And animals. Everybody, everybody. Lido let out a satisfied laugh. Randi will end up providing plenty of joy to Lido. Randi listened to him, shifting from one foot to the other, without any expression. It looked cool, even though Randi was nervous as shit. Just like a king's servant. Lido was ecstatic.

Linda

1.

Linda stepped through the doorway to the classroom, stumbled on the doorsill, and almost fell, not because she was clumsy, but because from the very beginning she wanted everyone's attention. Welcome to our class, Linda Rossi.

It's here that everything really begins. There is always someone who attracts someone else. Someone always gives in gladly to the temptation. Thanks to Linda, I've grown to be a woman because of all that has happened. In Mother's world, the question would be, Why? But Linda had the better question to offer: Why not?

There was an empty desk next to mine, and that's where Linda sat down. Satsuma body balm, melon lip-gloss, peach deodorant, and that super-strong hairspray, recommended by movie stars, that doesn't make your hair brittle. A scent of coconut floated from her hands, and even her sigh had a fragrance to it, that of strawberry bubble gum. Everyone watched in silence when the honey-blonde creature, made of all things sweet and soft, sat down in the place where my best friend Merita had sat in the spring until she stopped eating and was taken to the hospital to be fed intravenously. Hey guys, said Linda, turning around in her seat. I smiled quickly in the direction of this vision that had seated herself next to me, nodded, and then turned to look out the window.

How can anyone be such a human-sized sugar cookie? The first thing I wanted to do was to take a bite of Linda. Bite a piece of that translucent freckled arm, soft skin that breathed and emitted some special radiance into the environment. What would it have tasted like? At least it would have melted in my mouth.

I just got back from Miami on Sunday, Linda said. Still totally jet-lagged. Like, help, is it a.m. or p.m. now? Would you hang out with me during recess, Linda whispered to me when the bell rang. So what's your name? Martin, oh. I don't know, like, anybody around here. Do they have a candy machine in this school? What kind of cell phone do you have? What do you use to shave? Do you have a webcam?

Nothing like that had ever happened to me before with anyone; by that evening we were sitting in Linda's pale yellow room, on a big bed, our legs crossed, looking at Linda's pictures from Miami on a computer screen. Long-legged, tanned people at the shore on South Beach. Linda's mother was one of those people. On South Beach, everything is pastel colors—changing booths, kiosks, houses, Linda explained enthusiastically. There are no better-looking guys anywhere! And how they treated women!

I was looking at pictures of beautiful people and looking also at Linda's beautiful pale yellow room, the walls covered with huge posters of beautiful people—Marilyn, Madonna, Anna Nicole Smith, Pamela Anderson. I was looking at the unbelievably beautiful scenes of Miami and listening to the flawlessly beautiful Linda, who was apologizing for her American accent—which I barely noticed, except maybe at times, just a tad.

For the first time in my life I was overwhelmed by beauty. I felt dizzy. I felt like singing some song of praise, maybe a hymn. That's how strongly I was struck.

You listening? asked Linda, with tiny wrinkles at the base of her nose. The sweetest resentment I had ever seen.

Yeah, I'm listening!

Linda's aunt lived in Florida, and Linda visited her every year. At Aunt Angela's everything was always absolutely wonderful, and Linda wanted to stay there forever, or at least for a year as an exchange student, but Mom wouldn't let her. Yet. A battle of attrition had been going on, though. As I watched Linda and listened to her, I knew she would win every possible battle.

This one's from the alligator farm, look at that Indian boy, isn't he awesome? Linda said, explaining the pictures. A boy with well-developed muscles was holding a half-meter-long baby alligator in his lap. I was looking at the small animal; Linda was looking at the boy's bulging biceps, which, undeniably, were gorgeous. They reminded me of the picture in *The Little Prince* of a snake that had swallowed an elephant.

I had never been to America, even though that's where, of course, I had always wanted to go. Mother had been there a few times for conferences, and Mikael, too, for the same thing. But there was no use even talking about it with Fred. Fred always said that they would never let him enter the U.S. with his political background, going back to his student years.

So tell me about your family? asked Linda with her head tilted.

I had to think. It's complicated. And I answered: My old father and my little brother, Dad's new wife, and their baby, live on the other side of town. My new father, Mikael, is dead, but when he was still alive he took care of what's between people's ears, and my mother, with whom I live, takes care of what's between women's legs.

It sounded outrageously good. Absolutely fabulous. How did that come out of my mouth?

Linda obviously liked it. She laughed. She kept stretching her long tanned legs on the bed. Wow, said Linda. Wow, wow.

I talked more than I had planned. I told her that one set of my grandparents were medical doctors. I didn't mention anything about Fred's mother and father. I had met them so rarely that I could not have said anything more than that they live in the north and are some sort of believers in a funny way.

That means you are really cool! shrieked Linda. You can teach me math and chemistry, but I bet you that I know more about anatomy than you do!

The joke was kind of old and lame, but what did Linda Rossi do to illustrate her joke? She dug out her breasts—they were not only tanned but also well formed—and told me that everyone calls her Pamela Anderson's twin, that she loves Destiny's Child, that she can give really good French kisses, that she had been practicing them since she was six using giant-size bubble gum and sometimes even with poster putty since that required more tongue power, that she has slept with about fifteen boys, that her zodiac sign is Scorpio, that she had just broken up with Bob, who was too old, that she no longer ate red meat, and that she no longer believed in God.

The first thing we did was to save each other's number in our cell phones. We discussed our favorite music, movies, TV series, and actors. We tried out different cosmetic products. We blow-dried and sprayed each other's hair. We watched ourselves together and individually in all ten mirrors; never have I seen so many different kinds of mirrors at anyone's home—full-size mirrors, makeup mirrors, door mirrors, enlarging mirrors, pocket mirrors. Sometimes I counted them for fun, but I always got mixed up.

We talked about everything from the very beginning. It was easy to talk to Linda. She asked straightforward, simple questions, and her replies to my questions were comprehensive—she had a lot to say even if you didn't ask her any questions. She told me that she would undoubtedly like to live with her aunt and the aunt's boyfriend in their brand new house on South Miami Beach, just as soon as school was over. Or, if she could somehow acquire a nice pile of money, she would move there right away. Her aunt would certainly take her. All the best stores are on Collins Avenue: Urban Outfitters, Express Only, Paul Frank.

And Linda *loved* the internet. She couldn't live without the internet. She could sit in front of the computer as long as she wanted—no stupid three hours per day rules—and she surfed, insatiably, on all kinds of pages, maintained Skype-connections all over the world, sent her pictures to different galleries and took part in dozens of chat groups, and regularly read celebrity blogs. According to Linda, she had learned everything she knew about sex on the internet; that is, everything useful. Linda had also dated a couple of boys she had met online, but they had always been much uglier than in their picture, almost thirty years old, and once, even, a boy had turned out to be a girl. But that was okay. Linda liked surprises and excitement.

What's your motto? Linda asked, then waited, her head tilted.

Linda's was: No problem. Life is cool.

2.

C'mon Jasmin, Linda said. She sat cross-legged on her bed and patted the pillow beside her. Let's tell each other about our families' prescription-drug addictions, the co-dependencies, the problems with alcohol, the affairs, and the neuroses. She had just read an interview with Drew Barrymore, and she totally identified with the young actress.

I had never told anyone anything like that about Mother, or about Father or Mikael, or especially about

Mother's grief after Mikael's death. For a long time her grief was so great that I wasn't sure she would survive.

Linda's mother had been to rehab twice, she had panic attacks, and occasionally breathed into a paper bag. The latest boyfriend had left her mother for some twenty-year-old. *Fuck you*, says Linda, frowning her forehead. Mom was really in love with that guy. And the guy got mixed up with some Belorussian babe, who took money for her services. Now Mom was planning a hysterectomy and another facelift. Aunt Angela had already had three facelifts, and she had been diagnosed as bipolar, and her son had Angelman Syndrome. Linda's biological father was a businessman, and he never wore anything other than silk underwear.

And so on.

Linda said that there are no skeletons in her family's closets. On the other hand, it would be hard to fit any skeletons into those closets since Mom has so many millions of clothes! Linda's mom wanted everything to be open, o-p-e-n, everything must be spoken of with the proper names. Mom had given Linda her first lessons in sex education when she was six, before anyone could give her wrong information.

Linda sighed. She wished her mom had also taught her boyfriends. Some of them came into Linda's room after her mom had fallen asleep, to tell her some pitiful versions of the *Little Red Riding Hood*.

Linda had a big flat-screen TV in her room, facing the bed. She liked to watch game shows and talent contests, and in the evenings she dialed the phone numbers on the screen to vote for her favorites. Linda had once been in the audience for a popular talk show, seated in the front row, and she had even been allowed to send greetings: Hi there, Daddy, wherever you are, make a lot of money, and give me plenty too, okay.

Linda had four holes in one earlobe and five in the other. Plenty of rings, many of them genuine; a dozen chains on her neck. And Linda also had a navel ring, two pink stones. I touched it, and I had never touched another girl's belly button in that way. I knew I wanted a belly button like that and a navel ring like that, and a brown soft tummy too, and I knew at the same time that Mother would never let me have a navel ring, nor anything else in the category of Linda's Personal Wonders.

No problem. I realized that I was telling Linda about Diana. How, when I turned ten, I had received a small fluffy ball of puff with a twitching nose, how wonderful its warm fur felt and how it cooed when I petted it, then how it just all of a sudden became sick from some strange illness, went limp, stopped eating, and withered away.

Linda sighed heavily. It seemed that her eyes were tearing up. Linda had never had a pet because Mom never liked animals. Except dead ones, on her, yes, Linda grinned. Especially the red fox because Mom's hair, or actually Mom's favorite hair dye, Foxy Lady, was exactly that color. And, Linda's mom had been completely freaked out by Jimi Hendrix; she had seen Jimi live at a gig somewhere on the Isle of Wight, and Mom still adored his style of clothes—the ruffled shirts, the satin pants, the scarves, and the Indian jewelry. She even had a Jimi-only scrapbook. Linda's mom liked to remind people that inside she would always be a die-hard hippie.

Let's get you another bunny, Linda said, with tears in her eyes. By the way, are you hooked up with anyone right now?

For a moment I wondered if Linda meant a pet, but I realized what she meant and thought really seriously, for a second, of telling her about Tony, about our cautious caresses and kisses, our movie nights, popcorn and apple juice—yes, Tony never drank American soft drinks, like he never went to fast food joints either. In one way, we had been together since spring, after we had danced the slow dances at the disco at school. And what about my cousin Viola, rider of horses, Girl Scout, who, on top of everything else, belonged to some sort of TLW movement, True Love Waits. You couldn't really open up about something like that to Linda.

Do you know what Rose Butt means? Oh you don't? When a totally *hypergorgeous* guy has fucked you, you have to get a rose tattoo on your butt, Linda laughed.

Who says so?

Well, Linda Rossi.

What if there are lots of men?

Then you have to continue up your back, honey. Then you will be a Rose Back. Rose Shoulder Blades. Rose Neck.

Linda only likes the good-looking ones. *Beautiful people*. Linda's biological father, the silk-underwear-only man, was a *really handsome* man, and all the women ran after him. The bio-father was not only well formed in every way but also *absolutely wonderful*. Linda could go to her father any time, at least when he was in the country. The only un-cool thing was that Father's *girlfriend* was jealous.

Sometimes I miss my daddy horrendously, smiled Linda. Too bad that Mikael died, she said.

Yes, it is.

I thought about Mikael. Sometimes it had felt strange to like Mikael almost more than my own father. Mikael was straightforward and athletic, played tennis and liked the sun. Mikael might have let Jasmin go to Miami with Linda, or at least would have let us finish asking. Fred would have shrieked the moment he heard the word Miami.

Linda took me by the hand to the hall and showed me her mom's handbag. It was a *real* Grace Kelly bag, Linda remarked. Everything Mom has is real. Mom can't stand anything fake. Once, in Morocco, Mom almost bought a fake Rolex, but luckily she came to her senses. Linda dumped everything in the bag on the hall table, and together we investigated its contents. Cosmetics, business cards, coins, crumpled bills. A picture of Linda's bio-father Ron, and it was indeed true, the man looked just like a movie star. A little bit like Don Johnson from *Miami Vice*, you know. Even that. I was completely sold. How can anyone have a father who looked like that? Linda took a couple of bills and, in an experienced manner, ironed them against her arm. They were large bills. I watched how Linda inserted the money between her breasts and then put the handbag back in its place.

Mom always gets a massage after going to the gym, Linda explained, and sometimes she doesn't come home for the night. The masseur is a handsome Viking, white hair and icy-blue eyes. Mom's emergency treatment. You can stay over if you want to. I know where Mom keeps the adult movies and she has magazines too, even though they're kind of tame.

I didn't tell Mother that during the days I went to my new friend's house, and that I had skipped hours of practices, hours and hours. At Linda's suggestion, I called the coach and complained that I had such a painful period that all I could do was lie in a dark room. Linda often used those kinds of excuses. Linda *actually* had really nasty periods; they lasted for several days and upset her stomach. For the pain, Linda took pills that were in fact meant for birth control. When I asked her what her mom thought about it, she laughed and wanted to know why her mother would have anything to do with it? Her father had always taken care of her doctor and dentist bills, paid for her medications, and he never asked questions. For a long time, Linda had been bilking her father for money for the dentist, even though she didn't have one. The luck of a child of divorce.

I knew something about it as well. Mainly the fact that after the divorce Father completely dropped out of my life. Judging from his presents last Christmas, he thinks I still do puzzles and read books about horses and stables. At Christmas dinner, when I explained to Father for the umpteenth time what cheerleading is all about and told him about our Funky Sweet Angel team, he thought the conversation was about some fairytale play at the school Christmas show. And once, when I was again explaining to him all the particulars of cheerleading, he looked at me as if he were hearing about all of this for the first time.

I didn't tell Linda that soon I would have my first test as a climber. That, in fact, I *absolutely* should be practicing hard. I had a feeling that Linda would not appreciate something like that. How could I explain it in a cool way, that at practice we jump with both feet together and scream with shiny pom-poms in our hands, and someone gets lifted to the top and then is tossed around for a while up there. Splits and somersaults and cartwheels. It sounded like something kindergartners do.

Wow. Shall we watch *Lesbian Hippies*? Linda asked, as if it were the most natural thing in the world, to start watching a porno movie at two in the afternoon while our fellow students were still in home economics class, practicing how to thicken mushroom gravy.

Monday
by Sara Martin

Children, more children. Don't they understand that children not only appear out of nothing, but that they can also disappear into nothing? The stork brings, the hawk takes away.

After the gypsy woman, pregnant with her sixth child, has left, I let out a deep sigh, drop my work sandals on the floor, and put my legs up on the desk. And, at the same time, the next one is already on her way in. Or not quite. It's Paula Pauliina, who has something to say. She peeks in from the door and talks in a low conspiratorial voice: THAT ONE just canceled her appointment for today; THAT ONE is still on the phone, she's asking for a new appointment, shall I tell HER that she'll still be charged the full amount since she canceled at the last minute?

"Things come up, just give her a new appointment," I answer meekly. Paula Pauliina looks at me for a moment, as if not believing her ears, then nods and closes the door.

THAT ONE is Mikael's former squeeze, a remnant of his youth. She comes to my office often, who knows what for? A healthy, middle-aged woman. She started it right after Mikael and I married. Mysterious reasons that I don't want to think about.

The gypsy woman left a lingering smell. She had had two difficult miscarriages before her most recent pregnancy. The husband was always gone, sitting in jail, blaming his wife for losing the babies. The woman told me the story with her arms folded, laughing. That's how it is with everyone. With the women of our tribe. Nobody can't do nothin' about her fate, ya know. Big gold earrings, with a heart dangling inside. Rings on all her fingers. When I reminded her about the importance of personal hygiene, the woman started to hum.

The most troublesome patients often come around two p.m. First, they collect themselves at home or work, have a sturdy lunch, and then come to the office with a full and rumbling stomach. Now too, the pale young woman, a batik scarf tied in a tight bundle on the top of her head, starts it from the doorway: "I'm not going to give birth in any institution. I'll do it at home, in candlelight, on a jute carpet."

I listen calmly as she describes her diet, her yoga positions, the blessing of the placenta, and other requirements of her lifestyle. I ask what this future mother is going to do if there are complications with the birth. Complications? The young woman is surprised. She rolls a ring at the base of her nose. I sigh deeply and ask the pale woman to lie down on the examination table. I ask her the last time she had had her blood count checked.

If Jasmin does not come home, I can never be a grandmother!

I yelp, and the young woman looks at me, surprised.

Don't have children, I feel like saying. Damn it, do not have children. One bright day they'll disappear, and you won't be able to deal with it, not with a head like yours.

Fortunately, on Mondays there are also plenty of routine checkups, women wanting to change their birth control prescriptions, or delicately ask about estrogen supplements, or about the possibility of trying to have another child.

Often, and actually from the very beginning, I had thought about focusing on research only, but especially after Mikael's death, I realized how much I would miss human contact. So, contrary to my plans, I stretched my Monday and Friday office hours till seven in the evening. At times, I didn't even take the one-hour lunch break I had promised myself, but just ate the yogurt or sandwich that Paula Pauliina had brought, standing on my feet, and I would see as many patients as would come. And did they come. Beautiful women with tight vaginas. Ugly women with smelly ones. Stretched labia and scarred perinea. Abnormalities, accidents, injuries, sickness, pain.

No day has been the same as another.

This day has not been identical to any. I call Anita's cell phone, but the number is busy. I try again, but the number is still busy.

Now they've been found, I think. Anita is on the phone, scolding them, telling them to come directly home, right away. This time you got lucky, just a little shock. Don't even think about trying this again.

The number is still busy. Paula Pauliina knocks on the door lightly, peeks in, and taps her watch. I nod. I know I'm behind schedule. Why does she have to hassle me now? I leave a message on Anita's answering machine, think about it for a while, and then say to myself that when they come back, let's give them a homecoming party. That sounds odd. I hang up and look at Jasmin's school picture. Let's go shopping when you come back, let's shop for five hours in a row, let's check out all the Zaras and JCs and H&Ms. I'll buy five Kenneth Cole bags, Manolo Blahnik shoes, a Chanel top, and Dior makeup. Underwear from Victoria's Secret. Everything.

People tell me that I dress young, and maybe so, but not always, I think. I've never wanted to hear anyone say, You look just like sisters. No, actually, I've always wanted to look like my daughter's mother.

Moth-err, I don't want any birthday parties with cake anymore, okay? Declared Jasmin, slamming the door behind her. And through the mail slot: Remember, Mom, I don't want any huggy-kissy family parties!

“Okay,” I say aloud. I pull myself up, dial the number of my daughter’s father, and leave a brief message: Important information about Jasmin. Would you please call?

It always hurts when I think about Jason. I last saw the boy at a café on Father’s Day. They were having such fun there, on the other side of town. Where there is soccer and fun stuff. The new wife works at the airport. When I asked earlier—straight out—if Fred’s new wife was maybe a flight attendant, it turned out that Hannah was a salesperson in a tax-free shop. Even my guess about her age could not have been more off. At least she’s over twenty. And what did she offer as a fragrance sample? Boss?

Jason had an opinion about that too. Really nice. Now everyone has someone.

What Little Is Left of My Soul

1.

Origamis were confusing. For a long time, I got them mixed up with orgasms, and I used to wonder when Mother told Mikael on the phone that she had created many beautiful orgasms during her lunch break. How various things can cause misunderstandings. Before ikebana, origamis were Mother's favorite hobby. You could find the little folded white birds everywhere in our home. You could infer Mother's moods from them. Sometimes she folded them carelessly so that the birds resembled crumpled paper napkins rather than origami birds; sometimes she folded a flock of a dozen birds using bright red copy paper. We attached strings to them and hung them in the windows.

I've often wondered how many origamis Mother made from prescription slips or other pieces of paper lying around on her desk that Monday when I disappeared. I'm sure that she made them, although she doesn't mention it in the book.

She had skillful hands, and she was able to conjure up a teeny-tiny bird from a piece of paper no bigger than the size of a postage stamp. Mother had marvelous hands. Had I been allowed to have just a part of Mother to visit me, I would have wished for her hands. I've had hundreds of dreams about them.

Especially during the first year, I would wake up in the middle of the night and think I was at home, in my own room, in my own bed. I bounced up, stretched, and called Mother. I wondered why the alarm clock had not rung, and why Mother didn't show up at the door, woohooing me. For a moment I'd think it was some kind of holiday, and Mother had already gone to work and was letting me sleep in.

Slowly, I'd remember everything.

Linda's shrieks; gargling in the Pet Shop bathroom; Lido's laughter; the lighted dancing pole; sweaty, rough palms on my body; the clinking of glasses; the cigarette smoke; the fire; the Baptist, who is carrying me in his arms; a rabbit that jumped back and forth...

Metal bars on the windows, thick like fingers.

A door, locked from the outside.

The pale, scarred Esther carrying the breakfast tray, smiling with her big, brownish teeth.

During the ensuing years, before I'd fall asleep, I'd play the time machine game: In the morning when I woke up, I'd be in such and such a day of my former life. I'd wake up to such and such a morning, and the day would continue as it had when I really lived it. It was really difficult to remember certain days in strict detail, at least complete days, but there were those too. Some childhood birthdays, the first day of the first trip abroad at the hotel and the pool, the day when Jason was born, the day when Mother and Father told us they were getting a divorce, the day of Mikael's death, the day when Merita was taken to the hospital, the day when Linda came to our class.

Every now and then in the morning, when he was cleaning me up, the Baptist would ask me what kind of dreams I had been having. Every time I'd answer him that I didn't have any dreams in his house. Everyone has dreams, he would say, always as tersely, dipping the sponge in a bowl of water that he had sprinkled with coconut shavings. I dreamt of you for a long time before we met, he'd say.

But you'll never enter my dreams, I swore quietly to myself. But that oath, like so many of my other oaths, didn't last long.

2.

After the divorce, Fred met Hannah before he had had time to put a nameplate on the door of his new apartment. The young new wife always said she didn't want to get involved with anything regarding the divorce, especially issues of child care. She was never really interested in getting to know Father's children, but she declared from the very beginning that she wanted children of her own. Sometimes I feel sorry for Jason, who had to live with Hannah and Father, but Jason always claimed that it really was fun. They ate out a lot and often went to the airport together.

At that time, Father was still at the Ministry of Foreign Affairs and was working on something to do with development aid. He was also an expert for UNICEF and the Red Cross, until he and a friend with similar political views started an alternative advertising agency. Actually, progressive—that was the word Father always used in all contexts. Socially-conscious advertising. Global views. Mother thought that Father was stuck in the good old days, which meant that he had never given up his leftist thinking to enter the modern world. Mother called herself a liberal. To which Father always snorted, "bourgeois is as bourgeois does."

Their fights before the divorce were more amusing than scary. Father thought that taking riding lessons was bourgeois, and that was what they bickered about, especially when the stable bill came due. Mother's private practice was also a luxury, and Father thought that Mother should be working at a public hospital or something like that, where women who had no financial resources could get health care.

I would never have believed that those two would end up getting back together.

3.

The woman brought a pink orchid growing in a glass jar and mushroom pastries she had baked herself. She was dressed tastefully; and even though she was almost my mother's age, Mother thought she looked at least ten years younger. She was warm, empathetic, and didn't avoid long, silent moments. She had a small leather-covered notebook in which she wrote. A photographer also appeared, a small weasely-looking man, who didn't talk much. Later, Mother noticed that he had stolen a couple of photos that she had placed on top of the bookshelf.

Does Mother plan to mark the anniversary of the disappearance, and what might those plans be?

Does the biological father of the missing daughter blame his ex-wife for the disappearance?

Is there a particular reason why the daughter called her biological father "Fred" and not "Father"?

How have the missing girl's grandparents dealt with this ordeal?

Does Mother have phantom sightings? Does she stop people in the streets, department stores, bars, restaurants?

Does Mother visit restaurants more often than before?

What about smoking? Has she thought about starting it up again?

Does Mother stay in touch with her former colleagues and friends?

Does Mother take mood-altering drugs or sleeping pills? Has she had suicidal thoughts?

How long is Mother planning to continue leading the Family Association for the Loved ones of the Lost? Is the organization profitable?

Did Mother know Anita Rossi well? What kind of picture was Mother left with of Anita Rossi as a mother and human being?

Mother had mentioned somewhere that she'd read some Buddhist books and gone to hug Mother Amma—why hasn't the Lutheran Church satisfied Mother's spiritual longing?

In cases like this should the church provide crisis counseling? Has Mother seen the movie *Hardcore*—and if she has, might her daughter be found in a place similar to where Catherine was found in the movie?

And so on and so forth.

Mother listened to her patiently—where do people like this come from?

But every bad thing always brings something good too, according to Mother's motto from later times. During the interview, Mother conceived the idea for her book: *Monday*.

4.

During the weeks after our disappearance, emotions took control of everything at school.

Candles were lit on our desks till the beginning of the Christmas break. Let's hope that Jasmin and Linda will be found, said the teachers with heavy looks, during the first days; then the candles were lit, and after a short silence, class began. In the teachers' lounge, a small lantern burned on a long table, and every morning, people asked if there had been any news. When the class pictures that had been taken at the beginning of the fall semester arrived, our pictures were marked with circles. The teacher's lounge had a picture of the two of us on its bulletin board until the end of the school year.

All kinds of rumors circulated in the teachers' lounge. Somebody said that in the spring and early fall, Tony and I often used to walk home from school together, or we'd stop at a nearby café. At school they questioned Tony about me; it was suspected that he knew something about our disappearance. Four times the police talked to him, and it was from him that Penalty Box received the best character descriptions of both me and Linda.

It was at the beginning of the week of our disappearance that I saw Tony for the last time. He and his little sister were coming to the Pet Shop to buy some plants for their aquarium; I was just leaving the shop. I was wearing heavy Joe Blasco makeup that Linda had stolen and intended for backroom use, and I was in a hurry to get home and into the shower before Mother arrived. Tony didn't recognize me at first. I tried to sneak through the door without saying hi, but Tony's little sister caught my arm. A small pair of tongs.

Téa was truly a strange six-year-old. Exactly three years later she blurted out in the middle of the family dinner that she might know where a certain Jasmin Victoria Martin was.

Well, where?

Over there, far away, where Katrina also visited.

Which Katrina?

And Wilma too.

She's talking about hurricanes.

Is Jasmin in Florida?

How would I know? answered Téa and kept eating.

Her family was used to things like this. Téa played complicated computer games and drew cathedrals and historical staircases on graph paper from her memory. She took care of an imaginary dog, Ilona, and talked with an entire cast of imaginary friends before going to bed. She didn't like loud voices or touching, and she agreed to wash only once a week.

You smell odd, Téa said to me at the Pet Shop door. She jumped up in the air with both feet together, as she used to do when she got excited. Hahaa, I know *what* you smell like…that is, what your *face* smells like!

Well? I asked, startled, glancing at Tony, who kept looking at me, then his strange little sister, and then me again. He could not decide which one was crazier.

Sunday mornings, answered Téa in a serious tone, with her head tilted.

These were the things Tony said on the third floor of the police station, in room number eight. He tried to be accurate and transparent, and he tried to choose his words wisely, but time after time he got nervous and upset about the situation, and ended up crying uncontrollably on Penalty Box's shoulder. Take your time thinking, go ahead and take your time, Penalty Box coached Tony. Take your time. All details, even the small ones, can be important. Absolutely everything is important. They also chatted between the interviews about sports, about ice hockey world championships, about soccer, and occasionally Penalty Box asked Tony about love, girls, dating, and jealousy, waiting and watching for every gesture and shift in tone of voice, because no possibility was out of the question. Penalty Box was a versatile player; he could handle the younger generation—everyone knew that.

But he would have wanted to get more out of Tony. Not that he would have seriously suspected this sensitive boyfriend, but the boy may have known something that he himself could not articulate. That happened often with young people, even more so with children.

And what might that Sunday morning have meant?

Tony thought and thought.

Penalty Box pondered it over and over.

It took years before the answer arrived.

5.

The last movie I saw in a theater was *21 Grams*.

Tony was so excited to see the movie; Sean Penn was his favorite actor. After the movie, we went to Tony's, snuck into his room, surfed the net, laughed at various photo galleries, smoked a cigarette in front of the open window, lit up incense that Tony's father had brought from a business trip to Thailand, kissed and kissed. My tongue was already numb, and my mucous membranes were hurting. Already for a few days there had been a tender spot on the roof of my mouth. Many Pet Shop girls had had mononucleosis or some yeast infection in their mouths, and I was afraid I had caught something like that.

Tony asked me if I recognized the scent. I was startled.

Jasmine incense, said Tony. He cleared his throat in his fist and asked me if I had somebody else. When I paused, he asked me who.

Then there was a knock on the door. Téa pulled the door open and peeked inside.

I am an explorer, said Téa with a grin and closed the door.

Rather a cuckoo clock, I sighed.

That's the reason why only one babysitter ever agreed to come to our house, and only one cleaning lady, smirked Tony. All the others run away and won't return, no matter how much they get paid.

Hemingway, Blixen, Duras, Ondaatje. El Greco, Picasso, Gauguin, Munch. Tony's lists had other names: displaced people, women and men in *The Communal Book of Moonlight*—that's what Tony called them. He imagined a similar life for himself, as a restless alien, on the road, far away from home. I thought it strange that Tony knew all the movies and read so much, and that he also read poems and stories written by women. When did he have time for this? What did he leave undone?

I would've wanted to tell him something of my own, to be wild and cool, to experience something intensely, to be unique and different, fatal, to dream about fame, but I couldn't. At times I was annoyed by my stupidity. Then again I told myself to blow it off, it didn't matter. I wouldn't become a professor of literature or a doctor of philosophy, no way! And probably not even an oceanographer, though Tony once became really excited—totally overexcited, as typical of him—when I told him about my little-girl dreams. Yeah! Exciting!

Every year I check out the list of students accepted to theater schools in my country, and I was not surprised when a couple of years ago I saw Tony's name among them. On the theater school's website, I later read a description of how some teachers had been moved to tears when Tony Kantor presented a piece he wrote himself, titled "The Scent of Jasmine."

The Year of the Peacock

✳

The Pet Shop was big, well lit, and well cared for, despite the fact that it was located on the lowest level of the shopping center, with its main entrance right next to the parking garage. The windows facing the street were high up by the ceiling, so even on sunny days, they only let in a little bit of sunshine. At times, you really didn't know what the weather was like, and it was difficult to guess the time of day based on the faint light from outside.

As his first order of business, Randi washed the narrow windows and door glass, which made the view a little clearer. Granted that you could only see into the gray parking garage from the front door, but still.

Randi liked the birds the most. Especially the big black-and-blue parrot named Conrad. Its previous owners had returned it to the Pet Shop because of difficulties in taking care of it; and even though it was viewed with curiosity and was talked to, no one wanted to buy it. It was big and couldn't fly; it just flapped about like a broken umbrella, letting out low sounds from its throat. *So what?* it asked everyone who cared to stand in front of it long enough—at other times it glared at people through the bars of its cage. It agreed to eat only one kind of seed, or rather the seed mixture that Randi offered from his hand.

Years later, when he was thinking back about everything that happened in the north, with a couple of deep scars in his palms, Randi wiped other things out of his mind and regretted that he had not taken Conrad for himself. Nobody else really cared about Conrad. Randi didn't want to even venture a guess about what happened to the bird. In his mind, he developed different survival scenarios for it. 1) Conrad escaped and flew into the forest next to the shopping center, where it was found by a birder who'd been wandering the woods with binoculars around his neck and who'd taken it home. 2) Conrad swooped into the parking garage next to the shopping center and settled in the back of a jeep, hiding there until it was found hours later when the family had arrived at their country house and the children made the decision for their father and mother to keep it, since it was clearly a present from Santa Claus, wasn't it! 3) Vanilla Bebe took it herself and continues to take good care of it.

The last version was probably the least likely, thought Randi with a quiet smile, looking at the small nicks in the life line of his right palm, left there by the bird's beak.

*

Despite having been the valedictorian in his class and the genius of the Suraweera family, Randi has luckily not started to think about the reasons for everything he had seen and heard in the Pet Shop. Lido has led him to understand that that type of thinking will not pay since there are no answers. Neither can a tobacco vendor stop to think, let alone moralize, his customers' various yearnings.

Hence, Randi doesn't even try to understand how, in the middle of a day, a man can pay to watch naked girls engaged in intercourse in various positions with many men at the same time and, simultaneously, drink beer and eat a sausage dipped in mustard. And eventually join the fun himself.

So Randi doesn't try to understand, and he doesn't talk to anyone about what he sees. And Ringo will certainly stand up for him, even though the big brother was initially a bit apprehensive when he saw Randi's reactions to the Pet Shop side businesses.

In this city, there are dozens of nightclubs and bars and massage parlors where they show special live performances, but the Wet Pet Club has its own unique spirit, as Lido says, fingering his harmonica. There are programs every night, from six p.m. till two a.m., and during the weekends the place is open till six in the morning. And how fucking delicately it's all handled, through the Pet Shop. Recruiting the girls, customer service, movie-making, movie presentations, distribution of the material. Even online moments available almost 'round the clock.

The Wet Pet Club is a private club, where you need a membership, recommendations, and a code to enter. This, of course, is required by the nature of the program—and the age of the girls. And the Wet Pet Club is not located downtown like many of the better known strip clubs, such as SexLux and Yerevan; it's in a suburb for a reason. It's the quality, not the quantity, of the customers that's most important, emphasizes Lido. We don't want any mass tourism here. We don't want to attract attention. We attract desire.

Looking from the outside, you'd never guess what the building hides inside! The large red-brick industrial building has served as a warehouse for many businesses. Most recently there was some kind of vegetable wholesale business, storage for spare car tires, and storage for a cleaning supply company. FRESH WHOLESALE still shines in big red neon letters on the building wall, and that gives the place its carnally corny nickname, which the girls and even some customers liked to use.

The bottom floor of the former vegetable wholesale business is a storage area for animal foods and supplies, and the smaller warehouse area serves as the cleaning supply storage. No one standing on the bottom floor could guess that upstairs there's a girl club with private rooms.

Nearby, there are other similar warehouses and industrial buildings. On weekends, some have hosted youth raves, and in others motorcycle gangs have established their club houses. The place was a good find for Lido. A Royal Flush.

Across from Fresh Wholesale, on the other side of the street, is an imported car business. Rows of variously-colored cars lining the yard look just like fish with shiny scales. Farther away, toward the shore, is a fishing marina and smaller wholesale warehouses.

✳

Information about Lido's most recent nude-party place travels quickly among certain circles of men, and it has become a "must" place for *those interested* and *those dedicated*. We don't really have customers or regulars; we have *those interested* and *those dedicated*, as Lido puts it precisely.

Undeniably, Ringo sometimes feels that he needs more sleep. Nightshifts are hard. But he doesn't complain. Especially not to Randi. Ringo has already earned so much that he's embarrassed to mention it in his letters. Or do you want to know, he asks his childhood friend, Toby. When are you coming here?

✳

FROM KARIM'S LETTER TO NAWAL

My friend Nawal, when little brother came to work for Lido, Lido had dozens of girls working for him simultaneously in his Pet Shop business. This kind of activity seems to attract people. The girls tell one another about it, and soon there may be more applicants than space for them. The money attracts them—and brand name clothes, VIP cards, and all sorts of backstage passes. I could never have imagined that this business would be so easy.

In the Wet Pet Club proper, about ten girls work every night. On weekends, often more. Beautiful young girls—all teenagers, guaranteed. All the girls come first to the Pet Shop and the studio; there have been no problems at any point. As Lido says, customer satisfaction is top priority. There is something for everyone, and plenty of choice.

Randi sends his greetings. He really likes it here, and we're living here like cats in cream. He's already noticed that the girls here like dark boys, and sometimes they're so eager that poor little brother doesn't know how to act.

Luckily, I know, and I take the girls out, sometimes many in the same night. Often I bring them to my apartment, and if things go as they should, everything gets recorded by the camera installed in my room. Really easy. When Randi wondered about these systems of mine—you know how Randi is, always wondering about things—I laughed and said that why shouldn't you be able to do business on the side too. You know I've always been interested in filmmaking. Dark boys and young girls sell well here. Everyone has started their own business this way, from small seeds—Lido too. When are you coming?

*

FROM RANDI'S LETTER TO LALITHA SURAWEERA

I hope you got the pictures I sent you in the mail. The views are from our balcony. When the sea freezes over, I'll send you pictures from the same place so you can see how different it looks. The apartment is spacious and comfortable and warm, and everything is going extremely well. We've been healthy and lived simply. During the day, I take care of the business of the pet shop, and little by little I'll get to do some more demanding chores. You can be proud of your sons. Father would be too.

*

FROM KARIM'S LETTER TO NAWAL

Please think again about coming here, my friend. You can study to be an accountant later—those books won't go anywhere. Here everything is going super smoothly. You still have time to be part of it all. Excitement, new experiences, money.

I don't have time to write long. Randi is mostly working in the Pet Shop; I take care of the club business. I'm actually now the *club manager*, as Lido said the other day. Lots of new girls are coming into the ring. All of them are young and eager. Now I also film the girls at the Wet Pet Club—mostly the contacts between the girls and customers. Lido asked me to *record the most interesting situations*, and that's what I've been doing. I act like some kind of movie director there. For once there is a good use for my phosphor-stained hands; everyone can see when I direct. Those pictures and films sell well. You'll find some demo pictures on the net at the following address. To log in, you need a username and password.

The Baptist

After he fully comprehended the true nature of the theory he had created, Darwin vomited for weeks, said the Baptist. In recent years, the Baptist had become more and more interested in Darwin and his life. Darwin's theory matched the current social reality too well. There was a demand for Darwin. His brand sold immediately.

Himmler had stomach pains, and he too kept throwing up, the Baptist reminded me. Felix Kersten tried to massage Himmler's stomach; the same man also treated Hitler's colic.

But Brother Herodotus ranked higher than everyone else in the Baptist's conception of men. The Baptist always had Herodotus's *The Histories* with him—a loved and hated little brown leather-covered volume.

What do you think? On his trips, did Herodotus often visit the temple prostitutes? For instance, in Babylon, the local women had to go to the temple once a year and engage in sexual acts with a complete stranger. This was considered an act of hospitality, and a symbolic fee had been determined for it. And what about this: Did Herodotus have perversions? Did he lust after choir boys or maybe after infants? Dogs, sheep, geese? Or maybe the old, the elderly, those whose bones would break during intercourse?

Hmm? The Baptist waited for my answer. At first, I thought that was part of his strange torments, a trial, the first act of some new play where my role would be something I hadn't experienced yet. I had learned to be careful, open to all possibilities. From which direction is the wind blowing this time? I had learned to anticipate every moment, to be prepared for anything.

Hmm? The Baptist really expected an answer. Expected, as if I were some colleague, a university professor; maybe that was also part of his sheer madness—it spread like air into the whole room, flowed everywhere, on top of us, and created a new home for me. A home where I, at times, felt quite comfortable.

First, I need to know who the hell Herodotus was, I said quietly. The previous night, the Baptist had been talking about Kierkegaard's problems with digestion, his fits of vomiting. The poor man had once visited a brothel, and, according to the Baptist, this solitary visit had an effect on his whole life till he died. On his philosophy and so on. After all, everything depends on such small things, the Baptist reminded me. Gripes, aching molars, deformed testicles, the ailments of history's great men.

Sometimes the Baptist showed me pictures and drawings, which were intended as illustrations for his new work. I had already become accustomed to seeing all kinds of pictures, but one picture stopped me.

They are girls from the Ouled Nail tribe, the Baptist said. They are claimed to have been lustful little whores even before age ten. That is why, in the olden days, they were brought in shiploads to Europe's exotic clubs. The Lady of the Camellias and Mata Hari were sweet aunts compared to these wriggling, painted porcelain pussies.

Baptist closed his eyes and squeezed the small alabaster sculpture he always carried with him. It was a naked girl, whose hands were raised above her head. Whether she was stretching or dancing or worshipping the moon—that was the subject among experts of complex theories and arguments, in whose development the Baptist had also taken part. This little piece of sculpture was one of the most valuable in the Baptist's collection.

Where were we again? asked the Baptist after a moment.

The girls of the Ouled Nail tribe.

At times, the Baptist would fall asleep, then suddenly wake, sit up in bed and look at me intently, as if seeing me for the first time. Have I mentioned to you a coastal hospital in Tyrrhenia? he might ask. Have I told you about the moment when I saw your picture for the first time in that internet gallery? Did you know that you had masturbated for me online many times before we even met? Sometimes the Baptist would ask me if I thought he was intelligent. I said he was, as far as I was concerned. I almost added that I might be lacking a certain kind of judgment, since for various reasons I had not attended school recently, but I didn't care. The Baptist had taught me everything that was necessary. That's what he always said. Also the right kind of judgment.

No Freud here, and no Jung—they would spoil everything, the Baptist whispered. Tell them that I'm not available. Instead, Erroll, Vladimir, and Evelyn may come. A brotherhood is a brotherhood, and a brotherhood has the rules of a brotherhood. Once upon a time, there was *A Game of Glass Beads,* its players...

The Baptist raised himself up. His face was wet with sweat. His bony cheeks were sticking out. Every day, there was more and more hair on his pillow, and I tried not to think about Mikael or Merita.

I lifted you up from the slushy street, I saved you from the gates of hell when the flames were already licking you.

Yeah, right, and left Linda there, and eventually burned down the whole building, I mumbled so quietly that he didn't hear. He had never talked about the horrible fire that we left behind us. He carelessly overlooked this fact, and he certainly never confessed to me that he had started it. I insisted and insisted, but he only got angry. He, who feared fire as much as water—he had never even lighted a campfire.

Over the years, the Baptist visited my home country a few times and returned with magazines and books, movies, and some of the foods I had spoken of.

The tastes in my mouth intoxicated me. The Baptist watched me as I ate, watched my expressions, the small noises I made. He found it interesting. He wanted to watch me eat via the camera in my room. Most likely it gave him some sort of gratification and he masturbated while I ate.

After his first trip, he told me that the Pet Shop was still in business, and that he had stood approximately in the place where the burned-down club had been located.

The illness, or rather the heavy medication, left the Baptist confused and delirious, at times for days. Some mornings he woke up with a clear mind and filled the large, cool room with little bits and pieces of his stories, which meandered and interrupted, moved in time and place. It was interesting to listen to them; the Baptist almost always combined the people and the events somehow differently than before. Maybe he had always been talking like that in order to cover his tracks. Sometimes he tenderly called someone Dominique. At times he talked about himself, how he'd become a believer, as a young man, about his calling to salvation. He called himself the dogcatcher of souls, someone who had saved dozens of children from the slavery of the sex industry and then baptized them into the purity of a new life. He talked about *Sexualia* and a worldwide brotherhood, selected men, some of whom studied quite exotic and far-fetched ideas. One translated ancient Egyptian texts into Greek and Sanskrit, one investigated the pronunciation of Latin in the universities of Southern Italy at the end of the twelfth century, another studied the cracks in Pompeian jars, yet another knew everything about the light of Holland, and another one had sacrificed his life to researching the formation of dunes.

Recently, he apologized to me.

What in the world are you apologizing to me for at this point?

The Baptist sighed deeply, closed his eyes, and shook his head slowly on his pillow. I knew what was to follow: Isaiah, Jeremiah, Song of Solomon. But he could no longer raise his voice. His favorite verses he recited in whispers.

It's very recently that the Baptist has returned to my beginning, the situation when he met me for the first time. He was in my country as a guest of one of the universities, and he stayed for another week and then a third because he could not leave. The reason for that was me. That's what the Baptist told me. He had seen me on the internet and in the Pet Shop and later at the club, and he kept coming back.

Monday

by Sara Martin

The girls have been raped, and they're lying in some sand pit at the outskirts of the city! At the moment this horror arrives, all my instruments are inside the woman. My hands start to shake.

There's no reason to euphemize. The girls have been strangled, and they've been beaten; they're sprawled, almost dead, in the trunk of a smelly car. They've been tied up with rope. Their faces are swollen. Several of their teeth are broken off. Their hair hangs down in tangled clumps. There's blood everywhere. Their limbs are in grotesque positions. The space between their legs is a gaping wound. Their eyes are gone.

Somehow I manage to finish the examination. I apologize to the middle-aged kindergarten teacher in case she feels that the examination has been cold and painful. I don't remember why she has had her uterus removed. For her prescription, I write: Jasmin Martin 100 mg, to be attached on clean, dry, hairless, and healthy area of skin on the lower back or buttock. I tear up the prescription and write another one. The customer keeps sweating, can't sleep, has put on weight; and soon I will be like her.

After the door closes, I take Mikael's cell phone, find my own name in it, and dial. The cell rings. After waiting for a while, I pick it up. I hear my own voice in both phones. "You don't exist anymore," I say aloud. "This is what deep sorrow is like," I whisper. I turn Mikael's phone off and drop it in the garbage bin. Thud. Smell of smoke, a piece of nearly-burned toast, and a night guest blowing smoke rings before he left. Where do they go, the smoke rings I blow? said the man in the bedroom doorway. It feels as if I'm still asleep, and it's only a moment from now that the three-legged table will collapse. A purple curtain glides in front of my eyes. There's blood everywhere. Limbs helter-skelter, broken pieces of a child.

I pour cold water on my face. Calm down, woman, for heaven's sake; the girls are just skipping school. They felt like spreading their wings a little and will be back in the evening, of course, right? RIGHT? I interrogate my own thoughts. I recall how it felt to skip a day of school; the feeling of freedom and space, walking in the city with your best friend during the lunch hour rush, imagining everyone else in a math class or sweating during a grammar test.

Mother never suspected anything. There was also the smoking phase, and the occasional drinking. At one point, one boyfriend changed fairly rapidly into another one. Things were taken from Father's medicine cabinet and his doctor's bag. Was there anything else? I don't think so. That's all. How light. The entire storehouse of sins!

I lean on the side of the examination table and think about what might be going on with Ella. We were known as Sordino and Soprano. In school, I was famous for my high-pitched cackle, for my giggling attacks. We were inseparable throughout our high school years and even after that, though Ella went to study to be a carpenter. She had always wanted to build boats. It still sounds so funny that I have to smile when I think about it. We wrote our dreams in each other's friendship books. First Ella wanted to become a carpenter, and then a boat builder. Ella did enter the program for carpentry in vocational school, and later continued somewhere along the coast as an apprentice boat builder, and never returned. She married a sea captain, who was quite a bit older, and they had three sons.

What did I write in Ella's book? I think for a moment. I have to confess that I don't remember. A researcher, something vague, neutral. Of course I didn't dare to mention anything about my dream of becoming a hairdresser. Even Ella would have laughed at that. Or would she have?

Everything feels distant, on a December Monday, sleet and the smell of smoke, and if this is a dream, I wanted to wake up now and return to that moment when I had gone to see what that thump I'd heard from the direction of the hall in the early morning really was. That's when I hit my head, banged it really hard. And hence a dream like this.

Or even farther back? How far back should I in fact travel? Till the time with Ella? High school choices? Ella went in the direction she chose, but what did I do?

Some colleagues would not willingly treat women dressed in head scarves, or at least in burkas, those black cloaks, but I've never seen any special reason for not seeing them. The mutilated clitorises were an abhorrence, and the first few times I admit I cried and once I even threw up; that was when a woman visited my office from whose small vaginal hole clear green puss had been trickling.

I've given birth control pills to Catholic girls, and haven't felt any guilt, except, of course, an eternal insufficiency because I had always believed in enlightenment. Everything would turn out fine if we only had more information. And there was information. So what?

The woman with the head scarf is eleven-weeks pregnant. She has come to my office in secret, of course. She's afraid, glancing at the window through the eye-slot of her scarf, wanting to know the details of pregnancy and giving birth. She suspects that her brothers have followed her and are waiting in the nearby park.

I invite the woman to sit down, and I hold her thin blackish-brown fingers that are like horse chestnut branches. I tell her that she should rest a lot during the early weeks of pregnancy and that giving birth is, in all cases, difficult. That the tear would be large, and recovery would last longer than normal.

"Normal?" the woman repeats, surprised.

"In our culture," I say almost with irritation. And I remember my daughter as a smiling baby, golden, curly topknot hair, chubby arms, the spongy bottoms of her feet. Fred's lips making the baby's stomach buzz so that she let out a high-pitched giggle. Takes after her mother. Sordino and Soprano. Today there's a real meeting within my head. Who invited them all? Jasmin. Hey girl, why would you go and do something like that? And what kind of a friend is that Linda really?

I pause and would say, if I could, that in our culture girls are not sexually mutilated, but I keep that inside me and ask the woman to undress for the examination. I hope she understands that I need her to undress completely from the waist down. And I hope I do not have to see anything that would make my very heart shudder. Not today.

After the woman is gone, I call Fred and leave another message on his answering machine. Then I call Jasmin again. When a woman's voice answers, I startle and ask where Jasmin is.

The woman tells me that there is no Jasmin at that number, that the person speaking is Lilga from Window Blinds Service, how can I help? You can't, I reply, cut off the call, and then call again. I wait until the wretched male voice tells me that the number cannot be reached.

A text message comes from Saku: “Have you heard anything?”

I reply: “Nothing.”

And, finally, from Fred: “This week in Rome. Hopefully no trouble. Keep me posted.”

In Rome, almost aloud I cry out. How can anyone be in Rome, at this time, on this Monday, in this sleety rain? What does Fred have to do in Rome, except be there on vacation with his Tax-Free Chick. So, where is Jason then?

For a moment I have a sense of dizziness, a very strong sense of dizziness. The room is upside down, and I‘m standing on my head, my feet toward the ceiling. With trembling hands, I write a message to Fred. I ask where Jason is, and I try to focus my eyes on the medicine ad on the wall. At the corners of my eyes there are still flickering zig-zags; what’s really missing here is a migraine attack.

When I call Anita’s number again, or still, it’s busy. The beeping noise again awakens new hope in me: What if Anita has just now gotten hold of the girls, and right now is talking with Linda, questioning, interrogating, scolding her; and in a moment she’ll order the fugitives back home immediately.

There are simultaneous messages from Seidi and Fred. My sister asks how I’m doing, and Fred informs me that our son is at home with Hannah.

I send a message to Jason right away. I ask him how he’s doing. I put my cell phone on the desk and think: Soon this nightmare will be over. Soon I’ll call everyone. Soon I’ll tell them that this is the best Monday of my life. That everything is well.

In my eyes, I see, for a long time, the previous patient’s mutilated vulva. Labia slashed with a piece of glass or a razor blade. A twenty-seven-year-old woman born in Somalia, I begin in my dictation, eleven weeks pregnant.

Then I just can't continue about how I couldn't do the internal examination without hurting the woman, how the woman bit her fist, how there was blood. I stop talking and just hum into the dictaphone. Some Cuban melody. I remember how Mikael and I were supposed to go to Cuba together; it was our shared dream. We even found time to take a few samba lessons. If I make it through this, I'll go to Havana.

I text an answer to Seidi: "All is well. No problem whatsoever." I wanted to add: Just stick to your own business, Sis.

I wonder if I should call Saku and ask why he had gone and told my sister about Jasmin. Otherwise Seidi would not be asking how I'm doing. Or am I unnecessarily suspicious? It could be that Seidi is genuinely interested. But on this particular Monday?

I decide to send a message to Saku as well. "Why did you have to fucking tell?" Then, just as I always do, I delete the word *fucking*. But there it stays, in my mind, and Saku knows it too.

This incident is my property, I think, before I look at the chart of the next patient. Let Seidi take care of her horses, let her live a healthy country life with her flannelshirt-clad, bearded husband, as she has done until now. Let Fred be in Rome. Let Saku eat the sushi fixed by his male friend, the chef. Let Muma and Papsi watch their TV series, let them sleep their beauty sleep, let them munch on bonbons.

Puberty is no safe haven, I say half aloud, hunched over the papers. Out of season, curfew, amputation.

Suddenly I miss my son terribly, little Jason, who is still innocent about all the temptations of the world, or is he? Little Jason would never leave his mother, would not run away. I press my arms against my stomach and imagine my son there, tousled hair, saying in a raspy voice, Mother don't squeeze me, I'm suffocating here. I check for a reply from Jason, and yes, there is one: "Just fine, how come?"

For a moment I'm almost relieved. The boy's living in a reality where this thing does not yet exist. He's outside this magic circle. I, too, would like to return there! I get some strength. I feel I'm a modern person, a modern mother, a modern woman, a modern specialist in gynecology. Little things won't startle me. But maybe some things will? I look at my daughter's school picture. I imagine the same picture on the side of a milk carton, a cereal box, a light pole. Jasmin has disappeared, have you seen her? Have you seen my daughter?

Linda

1.

Mother thought it was great that I had found a new friend, especially because of the sad thing that had happened to nice, sweet Merita. Next weekend you can go and stay overnight, and bring her to our house soon, says Mother. Yeah, yeah.

Mother thought that our home, located in a stern-looking Art Deco building, made a huge impression on all my friends: high ceilings, bay windows, ceramic stoves, parquet floors shining like mirrors, design furniture, and lots of books and paintings with sea motifs, which Mikael used to collect. Okay. But Linda's home in a small, new apartment building was modern and light, retro furniture and textiles on the walls, purchases from flea markets in Paris, large framed posters with pictures of apples and bananas and Miami palms—that was something different. And her mother's shelves of trophies and photos from her youth, silk ribbons, and crowns with genuine stones in the tiaras. Linda's mother had been a beauty queen, and hence Linda, by association, was some kind of princess.

And so I packed my little Nike bag. Toothbrush, whitening toothpaste, makeup remover, lip balm, facial toner, night cream, cosmetics bag, underpants, a bra, a panty liner. And Anne Frank's diary. I had already read it three times during the summer, but I was reading it again because I was going to give a report on it for a history class. Linda didn't know who Anne Frank was; she knew only about Paul Frank's super-expensive monkey shirts. She had bought them in Miami, and she gave me a cute hooded jacket with a smiling, wide-cheeked monkey on the back.

And a nightgown. Gownie, like Mother always said. On my nightgown there were figures of Snow White and the seven dwarfs who stood in a circle around Snow White. A Christmas present from Mother.

That one, like so many of Mother's recent presents, belonged in the category of the Girls' House. Many other things also belonged in that series: horseback riding, piano lessons, pearly nail polish, quilted vests, Swatch watches, and Viola—and Tony too, even though he was a boy.

Linda had lots of her own things. She slept naked. She used a shaving gel that always smelled the same. She never drank orange juice. She only wrote with mechanical pencils because she hated pencil shavings and eraser debris. And so on.

At a Starbucks in Miami, she had seen Brad Pitt and Angelina Jolie and had asked for their autographs. That had been a super wow and near-fainting moment.

She had gotten a piece of tooth jewelry at the hottest freak store on Lincoln Road. It glittered every time she laughed, and she laughed a lot; click, click, click, twinkled the tooth jewel. And, of course, Linda laughed at the nightgown Mother had given me for Christmas. There were lots of reasons to laugh. See, I didn't use G-strings either—I wore regular underwear. Linda *could not live* without G-strings. Or toe rings. And Sade's voice. Linda thought that Sade was cool. But for the history composition Linda was going to write about her sister. Sister, you know, was true *history*.

The teacher read Linda's composition aloud, and wiped her tears. The class listened in complete silence. Olivia Rossi had committed suicide; she had hanged herself at the age of twenty. She left behind a letter that said only that there was no sense in living any more since *adulthood is a drying river bed, a rose that has dropped its petals, a state of not dreaming about anything anymore, a state of not daring to do anything*.

Olivia's favorite bird was a flamingo, the color of the setting sun; and she believed her soul would transform into this, wrote Linda, at the end of her composition, which she dedicated to Olivia.

With a tear-streaked face, the teacher handed the paper back to Linda. The whole class was swallowing tears. Coughs, sniffles. Everyone was looking at Linda, who took the paper from the teacher with a humble nod. White teeth, tanned slender limbs, a short ragged jeans skirt, with sun-bleached, honey-red hair down her back.

In the hall after class, I took Linda's hand and squeezed it hard. Why didn't you tell me? And I thought I was the only one who had sorrow in her life!

To my surprise, Linda roared with laughter. She tore the paper, which the teacher had given an A+, into pieces. No, Olivia didn't die on the noose of a rope! Besides, she was actually her half-wit cousin, who was run over by a bus during morning rush hour!

2.

The world of middle-aged women is funny, like a cream cake that has mustard filling instead of jam, and salt instead of sugar. It's full of hopes that are also fears, full of inhibitions that are spoken of brazenly, full of all kinds of prejudices and beliefs.

Will I be like that some day?

After we had gone through Linda's mother's belongings several times, it was my mother's turn. In the middle of a particularly dull school day, we decided to go to my house. Mother had many more locked cabinets and closets than Linda's mother, and Linda was surprisingly good at picking those locks as well.

What do girls look for in their mothers' hiding places? Everything they hoped they wouldn't find. Strange things. Lies. The forbidden. The scary. Revelations. At the bottom of Linda's mother's nightstand drawer they found a bag of marshmallows, a white gold diamond ring engraved "To Anita from Arthur, July 1, 1960," three issues of *Penthouse*, Valium, Cipramil, caffeine pills, geisha balls of various sizes, and lubrication gel.

Sometimes I had caught a glimpse of a porn magazine in Fred's closet, stuck in a rubber boot. And in Uncle Saku's kitchen closet, under the vacuum cleaner bags, was a pile of magazines with men romping each other. I never opened those.

We never found anything *really* exciting or special in my mother's room, unless you count the pictures of female genitals in Mother's books and files.

3.

Every now and then, Linda skipped school for a few days without telling anyone. After school, I'd ring Linda's doorbell just to make sure, even though I knew she wasn't at home; or if she were, she wouldn't open the door, for one reason or another. On those days, I made reluctant visits to my former life: I went to the Sports Arena to watch my old gang rehearsing their program for competition, and a few times I even went to hang at the Girls' House.

The cheerleaders seemed to be nauseatingly childish in their hustle, as if the most important thing in the world was going to a few competitions to scream, wave pom-poms, and build human pyramids. The girls looked suspiciously at me in my street clothes and whispered until I walked out, leaving the familiar Sports Arena smells of sweat and rosin behind me.

The atmosphere at the Girls' House was always socially conscious; every corner had a circle discussing the melting of the polar ice caps, the world's clean water problems, or bullying at school. Even Astana Yoga, which I had started in the beginning of autumn, felt the same: sun salutations and windmills, bare feet, the puff-puff-puff breathing technique that I had never learned.

When Mother asked what was wrong with me, I slammed my bedroom door so hard that the keys and coins in the glass bowl jingled on the antique table in our hallway.

I tried to hang around in various chat rooms, but without Linda even that wasn't the same. I started a couple of juicy fights: I claimed that my girlfriends' posed pictures with their puckered lips were childish, and I told all the boys hanging out on those pages that they were four-legged slime.

After she returned to school from her do-it-yourself vacations, carrying the strong scent of tobacco and a who-knows-what sweet substance, Linda told amazing stories of guys, one more handsome than the other, and fine apartments where she had participated in all-day parties, sampling various alcoholic beverages and smoking pot. Linda had become acquainted with some unbelievably wonderful people—some were *Cosmo* models—and with them absolutely anything could happen. Like what? They, for instance, had sex together. It was so exciting to watch an entire group of people making out, Linda said, and I tried to imagine, but I think I really couldn't. I could never imagine kissing a girl. Had Linda done something like that?

I was watching Linda and admiring how beautiful she was, even after partying hard. Hickies on her neck, with Donald Duck Band-Aids covering them as exclamation marks. Otherwise she was completely without makeup, pale.

Of course, I wanted to take part in Linda's school-skipping adventures, but she never asked me. So I decided to try even harder.

Every day after school I spent some time—chilled—at Linda's. We spent hours in chat rooms and on various webpages. Laughing, we wrote on the adult entertainment discussion boards, took wild pictures of each other, and uploaded them for fun—Candy Gallery and BabeSex pages.

A new site, The Girl Brigade, was looking for sexy pussycat models, and we decided to enter the contest. We were Chloe and Shakira. We put on makeup and oiled each other and took pictures of each other in our bikinis. The expression of the mouth is important, Linda said. Open, with puckered lips, but not too much. Like a bird being fed, a dim expression of surrender in the eyes. She laughed.

We downloaded new songs from the net to our MP3 players and danced like dervishes on Linda's bed. We pretended we had won auditions for a star contest on TV. Wow, wow, screamed Linda. We are "live sex!"

At times, Tony would call my cell phone and ask me to a concert or movie or wherever, but I'd tell him I was busy with cheerleading, or just wouldn't pick up the phone.

Linda's mother never noticed, even though we taxed her stocks of wine and beer. Besides, Linda told her how she had seen the maid snatching alcohol from the cabinet, and her mother frowned, Okay, alright, I should've guessed. The maids in Linda's family started to change often.

Sometimes we went to the video rental in the nearby shopping center and took a bagful of movies. That's right, we took them. Linda never had to pay for anything, and while I wondered about it, Linda's tooth jewel just glistened. Click. The men at the video rental were drooling over Linda, and maybe a bit over Linda's mother, too. Yep, Linda promised to say hi to her mother from them. Yep, the man was allowed to touch Linda's stomach, brush his finger against her navel ring. Sometimes we loaded so-called "psycho-physical couples therapy" movies from the shelves into our bag and watched the movies at home, smoking our ciggies quietly.

What does a golden shower mean? And DP? And FF? I asked Linda. I was reading text on the back of the movie's box. Linda almost choked in her laughter, *fuck babe*, I hope you at least know what the word *hardcore* means?

I nodded, blushed, and hoped that Linda would not ask me to explain what it meant exactly. I hated the fact that I blushed. I recalled that Mother had a doctor friend who cut off people's nerve connections, and by doing so managed to tone down his patients' facial coloring.

Oh-oh, said Linda, while we watched the movie. And in moment, wow, wow. Have you thought about trying that? she asked me.

I've thought about trying everything, I answered carelessly, and in a way it was true. I was such a ridiculous beginner in my sexual experiences. But where could I get more experience, and quickly? Not with Tony.

Linda was quick and slow simultaneously. All her movements were catty; she articulated slowly, paused, then all of a sudden quickly let out everything she had in her mind at the moment. Linda was also unbelievably quick in getting to know people. You saw that right away. By the time her first week in school was over, she had already spoken about stuff with all her classmates, and early on she also started talking to the kids in upper classes—and especially the boys wanted to get to know her better. From a group of boys, several hands stretched out to offer her cigarettes, and they kept asking her playfully about how much the little babe's Saturday night would cost. Aren't nights free of charge for humankind, Linda laughed. Or are you guys paying for the right to sleep? Who's talking about sleeping? the boys grinned, cupping their hands in front of them as air breasts.

I listened to them from the side. I was thinking about what Mother would say about Linda, Linda's cleavage, mini-skirts, and eye makeup. Or Linda's mother.

At home I told her only carefully-selected bits about our friendship. That Linda is a pretty good student. That Linda is happy and friendly, popular, and so on. And it was true, too, all of it. I also told her that Linda had traveled a lot. But I didn't tell Mother about Miami. Mother surely would have lectured me about drug-related crime and hurricanes. At least.

I drew palm trees in my diary. They looked strange next to pictures of Anne Frank. The teacher had already reminded me twice about the report. Yeah, I had said. Real soon. I'm almost finished writing it. Never before had I been late with my reports. In the diary, I drew bullets, after which there should have been drafted paragraphs, but I couldn't get enthusiastic about it. How had that book inspired me before, so much so that I slept with it under my pillow? A young girl, fear of death, an attic room, first love, fate.

Did you get your report back yet? How was cheerleading going? Are you still going to the Girls' House? Mother asked while she was opening the box of take-out pizza. Yeah, I have, all kinds of things, I answered my Mother-of-the-doorways, absent-mindedly. Let me do my homework in peace. I was wearing the *I don't give a fuck* T-shirt that I had gotten from Linda and that Mother had not seen yet. Linda thought the pink shirt looked good on me, but I knew what Mother would say about it.

I slammed the door shut in Mother's face.

Mother got mad and said that this kind of thing was not done in our house. Not before and not now.

What? I asked, angrily, while texting Linda. Yeah, yeah. In this house we don't do this and we don't do that.

Sometimes Mother looked at me absentmindedly across the breakfast table, her reading glasses on the tip of her nose, and asked me, Sweetie, where did you get this or that piece of jewelry or a blouse? I told her that Linda and I exchanged clothes and went to flea markets where you could get good clothes for real cheap.

Linda shoplifted clothes with unbelievable skill and had never been caught. After stealing my first belt from a boutique, I was still shaking an hour later. Even so, these shoplifting expeditions were exciting, and we started a habit of a couple of hours of shopping-shoplifting sprees after school on Fridays.

After shopping we stopped for hamburgers to go through our acquisitions and to watch the dark, foreign boys who hung around the hamburger place. Sometimes we met someone Linda knew and were able to go with them to stylish bars and rock clubs. Linda always took care of the cover charge, and I never consciously thought about it. You could ask if I was really so naïve to think that Linda had gone with the bouncers to the men's bathroom or the coat closet to have a nice chat. She was gone only for a moment and came back smelling like a breath mint.

Linda also got me a fake ID. One day she gave me a passport with a picture of a blonde girl whose face resembled mine a bit. Olivia Silva Rossi, I read in the passport.

Surprise again—a U-turn: Olivia Silva had been Linda's big sister after all. And as Linda had written in her composition, she had committed suicide at the age of twenty, when Linda had just turned nine. The sister had been found in her room, hanging from a lamp hook, but she had not left a note.

Don't worry, Olivia would be happy if she knew that she was useful to somebody, Linda said with a grin.

From that moment on, I used Olivia Silva Rossi's identity, and I used her shortened name, Olivia Silva, for fun sometimes, even online.

It was only during the spring after my disappearance that Mother found out about Anita's other daughter, who had also died. Linda was buried next to Olivia. Mother had asked Penalty Box to attend the funeral, and looking at the red granite gravestone with Olivia Silva Rossi in golden letters rang a bell in his head. He could not immediately connect it with anything, but he knew that the he had seen it recently.

Linda's mother later mentioned that the big sister had also liked online chat rooms, and Penalty Box figured he had seen some old pages with that name. But he never checked. Had he done so, he would have seen Linda's and my online dating ads. I always used Olivia Silva in them. Also, at the Wet Pet Club I sometimes went by the name Miss Olivia Silva.

For a few nights, Penalty Box sat at his desk, under the glow of his desk lamp, and thought about those names. He googled them, tried to find the pages, chat rooms, online porn, messages from men in the business where those names would show up. At that point, Penalty Box was quite certain that I had been kidnapped. By someone or some people, but for reasons that he couldn't yet figure out.

In the bars and music clubs downtown were young men who looked like justification for a rose butt tattoo. However, I never got any further with them than kissing and petting. Linda's friend, Irina, was almost always in the bars, and it seemed that she had already been with all of the best-looking men. She recommended some *specifically*. I listened closely to her and looked at her expensive accessories. She always wore designer brand name clothing, and the guys buzzed around her. I couldn't believe my ears when Linda told me that Irina wasn't even close to eighteen.

Let's come up with some cool things to do together, suggested Linda. Things that neither of us has done with other friends. Yeah, I was thinking about Merita and Viola. Also Tony, for a moment.

Let's eat cotton candy in the shower, Linda threw out.

Let's try to see which one of us can eat more licorice sticks? I suggested.

Let's watch three Brad Pitt movies in a row.

Or both the *Kill Bill*s.

Is there more than one?

Oh now, you *are* hopeless, Linda laughed.

Let's dye our hair platinum blonde.

Let's become band groupies and go around the whole world!

And let's make plaster casts of all the guys!

I didn't get it, as so often happened—I looked at Linda with surprise.

Cynthia Plaster Caster, you know. The world's most famous band groupie. She makes plaster copies of the dicks of all the rock stars and sells them on the internet!

And then we'll fly together to Miami.

Yes. Almost all the discussions eventually ended up with Miami. In speechless agreement we went to either Linda's or my computer and looked for pages with pictures of Ocean Drive and other popular club streets of Miami Beach.

Samuel was wonderful, and Bob; but Bob was too old, Linda remarked with a deep sigh. And I was trying to enter into the spirit; I imagined that somewhere in that pastel-colored scenery glowing with sunshine there might be a tall surf-haired boy with white teeth waiting for me, and he'd call me his sweetheart and honey, and his bronze skin would reek of Ambre Solair.

4.

I had given up cheerleading a long time ago and was carrying a half-empty duffel bag with me. The most troublesome thing was that the trainer had tried to call Mother a few times to ask why talented Jasmin had suddenly quit without explanation. I had told Mother that the trainer had been suffering mental problems and been fired from his job a long time ago, but kept making really strange phone calls to some of the girls.

Did he try to harass you? Should I do something about it? Mother asked, horrified. The papers have been full of such incidents recently.

Help.

All I had to do was steal Mother's cell phone for a couple of hours. I sent a text message to the trainer in Mother's name, explaining that we would be moving to Miami in the fall. That I'd have to quit cheerleading, unfortunately, and could thus never become a climber. And please send greetings to all her friends, and congratulations to Vanessa.

Instead of my exercise stuff, shoes, and tights, my duffel bag now contained cigarettes and sometimes beer or cider and various things shoplifted from stores. Mother didn't notice anything; she was busy at work, but occasionally did ask how cheerleading was going.

5.

At Linda's place things were always relaxed. Her mother was seldom home, and even if she was, she had friends or a male friend with whom she spent quality time at the other end of the apartment. Linda could stay on the computer as long as she wanted, and nobody came peeking over her shoulder to complain about what kinds of photos she was looking at. And Linda could watch TV or rented movies all night if she wanted to.

The coolest thing was just to hang around the city with Linda and plan next weekend's parties. Linda had a big group of friends, and there was always someone whose parents were gone. They were all easy-going party kids, who didn't care much about school; all of them smoked dope—a sweet smell hovered above the white sofas and swimming pools—and many had tiny pills with them, which they melted on top of their tongue studs. They laughed, and they accepted me with open arms into their *laissez-faire* world. Soon I felt I was my own self only in Linda's company.

It's true that Mother occasionally wondered about my increased practice schedule, but she accepted it all, believing me when I said that before the competitions I had to practice all the time.

It was always exciting when Linda told me about Miami Beach, about beach parties that lasted all night, about the shops and cafés, clubs, and the people on sandy beaches, about the perpetual feeling of summer parties. We'd go there together when we had enough money. We'd spend an entire year there!

6.

So, Mother never suspected anything. Not about school nor teachers nor skipping nor Linda. Mother was totally and completely out of it. Even our fights were ridiculous. About getting up early enough in the morning and about bathroom turns and clothes and makeup. Too late, too long, too early, too much.

I even argued with Tony. Tony wanted to know where in the world I spent my time since he can't get hold of me anymore. And he asked, Why was I so cold and unfriendly? Are we still together? How could I take constantly hanging out with a bimbo like Linda? And so on. I laughed in his face.

The only people I never heard fighting were Muma and Papsi. Sometimes it was only Muma's voice that could calm me.

When I spent a night at Muma and Papsi's, they never asked where I was coming from and where I was going. Sometimes Mother wondered a bit when I was so eager to spend a weekend with the grandparents or go there during Mother's business trips. On the other hand, she was happy about it, of course.

On one point Mother was, quite accidentally, right. She hit the nail on the head when she said that we were spending too much money nowadays. Indeed, with Linda I was spending more money than ever before. We spent money on cosmetics, movies, and clothes despite the fact that our shoplifting sprees had reached phenomenal proportions.

The monthly allowance I got from Mother didn't go very far. Father had always been so stingy that I didn't even bother to ask him, and Hannah reminded me that the new child in their family also needed money. Jason still played ice hockey four times a week, and Father complained about that costing way too much. I had money that I inherited from Mikael in the bank, which of course I shouldn't have touched, but after I started, I couldn't stop. The account was soon drained. Sometimes I even went to bum money from Tony, who gave me some when I explained I had left my wallet at home.

Muma and Papsi gave me rather large amounts at times—for candy and movies—and they made me swear not to tell Mother. But that money also ran out fast. What I got on Sunday was gone as early as Wednesday. And the weekend, with all its goodies, as Linda always said, was still ahead of us.

All of a sudden, Linda disappeared again. She was absent from school, nowhere to be found. I looked for her in all the bars and cafés, but nobody had seen her.

That week felt really long, and the worst was that I thought Linda had gotten a heap of money from somewhere and gone alone to Miami.

But could Linda have left me alone? Could she have found a friend who was more fun, more beautiful, more bold? Someone who's as experienced as she is with guys—or even more so?

When Tony called again, I went to the movies with him and then out for Chinese food, because I didn't want to stay at home, either. But, I couldn't focus on anything he said; I answered absentmindedly. I didn't want to go home with him at the end of the evening to kiss. I was only thinking about Linda.

On Monday morning, I almost cried when out of the classroom window I saw Linda walking across the schoolyard toward the entrance. She saw me in the window and stuck out her tongue. Click clack. She really had gotten a tongue stud, even though her mother had—oddly enough—been totally against it.

Now I know how we get to spend Christmas at Miami Beach, whispered Linda to me after class.

The White Room

The room into which I was led after that horrible initial solitary confinement was white—a white bed, white furniture. After the windowless seclusion, the sight of the white room made me dizzy. It was as if I had entered a painting. Miss Frank blended perfectly into the white room's white carpet, where I had placed her, taking her off my lap while I looked around, squinting after all the darkness.

Let there be light, the Baptist said. I had not seen him for a few days, and I had almost forgotten what a big man he was. At that point he only wanted to see my first reaction, and he left me in the room to rub my eyes.

The lock snapped behind me, and Esther, who had led me to the room, was gone. When I tried the door, it was, as I had already guessed, locked from the outside.

There were white clothes in the closets. White flowers in a vase. Wherever I looked, whatever I touched, I saw only white. Satan hates the color white, the Baptist had said. Satan is afraid of the color white. White makes the Enemy of the Soul sick.

All right then.

I sat on the white bed with Miss Frank and asked her if she was having the same dream I was. Maybe so. At least her ears were flat along her sides, like wings.

Time went by. There was no clock in the room, and from the window I could see only a slice of garden surrounded by high walls and filled with unfamiliar trees and flowers. For a long time, I didn't know who else lived in the big house. I would see only the Baptist, sometimes Rebecca, and sometimes the deaf-mute Esther. When I asked where everybody else was, the

Baptist pretended not to hear. He punished me with "invisibility." That was almost the worst. I quickly learned the limits for my questions, the boundaries for my comments, the threshold for irritation. At times I heard that I was an impertinent little whore. A pitiful excuse for a slut. And so on. And then there was the issue of getting used to the leather belt. Once at school I had heard about chastity belts; now I had to use one. I had to wear it whenever the Baptist was gone, and, occasionally, just to suit the Baptist's whims.

I've forgotten the following days and weeks; I don't remember more than narrow slices of them. In the beginning, when I was alone in the room, I talked to myself, and always in the *we*-form. *We've landed in a situation that we must survive without any acknowledgement of the meaning of an inner life*, à la some Robert A. Johnson or Steven B. Dawson. I wonder what they, or people like them, know about the sort of existence in which I lived, as if there no longer existed a realm for the soul. Only objects, schedules, circumstances, or rather: one circumstance only.

In the beginning, the Baptist came to see me every morning and every evening, and I swore I'd escape whenever I had a chance. I didn't want to eat; I stained the mattress during my period; I lay at the foot of the bed and wanted to die.

From the window I saw how he sped through the gate in his long white car, and I watched how the gates closed slowly. Soon I learned to recognize from afar the sound of the engine of that 1960s Chevrolet. The Baptist came and went; sometimes he was gone for a few hours, sometimes for a week. He had regular habits that were easy to learn. Every morning he woke up with the songbirds. He went for his long runs, sometimes as often as three times a day, with a white sweatband around his forehead, in white shorts and a shirt. His best ideas came to him while he was running, or so he said. It was scary, threatening. What did he see when he was running? I had no idea what it was like outside the walls.

Esther led me through the halls and corridors. We looked at African sculptures, shields, spears, war helmets. Oversized paintings and miniatures, vases, Gobelin tapestries, graphics. In one small hall there were only a couple of shelves on which someone had aligned glass jars in a row. They contained aborted female fetuses—from a gynecological hospital—that Baptist had bought for the sake of curiosity. With dramatic gestures, Esther warned me not to touch anything, since even the smallest disturbance of the bottles would cause the fetuses to disappear without a trace. All that would remain would be cloudy water. How could I have touched anything? My hands were tied behind my back. During the first months, whenever the Baptist left, that's what he did.

Once Esther showed me her own room. Blushing, she opened the curtain. Her window sill was full of bonsai trees. They looked so perfect in all their shrunken ridiculousness that I started to cry and laugh at the same time. I remembered Mother's paper birds, and I wished that I myself could have folded one teeny-weeny nightingale and placed it on one of the tree branches.

For the first time since I had arrived—no, for the first time in a really long time, I felt my soul.

The Year of the Peacock

✳

Lido said that Randi didn't have to participate in anything special at the Wet Pet Club. It was enough that the games were kept running, videos and refreshments were available, and the Pet Shop Girls were in good spirits. And why wouldn't they be in good spirits, in easy-going, light-hearted moods? There were plenty of ways to achieve that.

Protecting and guarding and being in fucking charge of the situation, said Lido. No reason to think about it any more than that.

But what about not being able to fall asleep at night? There were plenty of ways to cure that too. Randi knew, and he had already tried them.

But still. Some teenage girl walks into the shop to pet the guinea pigs and gerbils, and within a couple of months, she's working full throttle in the back rooms. And in another two months, she's circulating on the Raped While Sleeping Young Pets webpages; she's wearing a curly red wig, and her name is Poppy or Rosy or Candy Cane.

Ringo thinks it's great. The girls are amazing. Unbelievable talent. Everything is just unfucking-believable. Honey heaven! Meringue paradise!

You talk like Lido, too, Randi told his brother. Like a mockingbird.

Of course, Randi liked to watch the young girls. Maybe more so every day, and that was okay. He liked them most on weekday afternoons when they came rushing in through the entrance door out of breath and looking like very ordinary schoolgirls, giggling, and jumping around. Besides, they took really good care of the animals in the shop.

A female customer, who had come to buy kitty litter, wondered why this particular pet shop had so many male customers. Is it because the parking garage is so close? she asked. Are there exotic or dangerous animals in the back of the shop, because customers keep disappearing there every so often? The shell curtains just tinkled. Or has pet photography suddenly become so popular? Who knows about all these new trends! And why do all the girls who take care of the pets in the shop always wear the same T-shirt, each with a different number on the back? And why are all the girls so very beautiful, and always wearing so much makeup? But maybe this is how middle-aged women always feel when they look at young girls, and these looked so awfully young. Ha-haa, the woman laughed. Ha-haa, the whole world has changed so much; every time you open your mouth, you sound like a pathetic fossil. Nothing is like before, she sighed as she paid for her purchase. The door slammed shut behind her, and the bell tinkled.

Pet Shop Girls

The pet shop was located on the ground floor of the shopping center. It was a spacious store, its windows decorated with pictures of various animals, and on each was written, "Hiring now. Two girls needed."

We were those two girls. Jasmin Martin and Linda Rossi. Laughing, we stepped inside.

The bell above the door rang. We jumped, and started to giggle.

A few girls were busy alongside the aquariums and small cages. They turned around to look at us.

Linda had called the Pet Shop in advance. Some of her friends already worked there taking care of the animals. Irina, whom we knew from the bars, was really excited. They had a variety of exotic animals, too, and you could care for them as much as you wanted. Plus the money was good; we'd heard it was completely, totally good. And in connection with the shop there was also a very popular studio where customers could have their pictures taken together with their cats and dogs.

From the back room of the shop, a blonde woman came to greet us. Her clothes were so stylish that Linda and I gave each other that those-aren't-replicas glance. The woman gave us a friendly smile and tilted her head as she looked at us. How can we help? she said, smiling. When we asked for work, the woman asked us our ages, and we responded just as we had practiced. She introduced herself as Liv and said, Well, why not, and had us fill out a few forms, after which she would introduce the animals to us. So, we can start right away? We're hired? Yes, certainly. And those papers aren't all that important. Really? We sighed and squeezed each other's hands.

My name is Liv, you can call me Lillan, the woman said. It's good for us if you can start right away. It's a big store, lots of animals, plenty of work, lots of helpers.

We'll work hard. We're hard-working girls, Linda said quickly. I stopped to look at the bunnies right away. The chinchilla had had kits, and among the little ones, there was one who had cute, dark circles around its eyes. Miss Frank, love at first sight.

Linda liked lizards and aquariums. I began by taking care of small rodents. Don't get attached to them, Lillan kept reminding us, as we cooed and whispered to the animals. This is a business and not an animal shelter. One day they'll be sold. One day all will be sold.

Monday

by Sara Martin

Before I ask anything else of the two young women sitting in front of me, I ask if they know the following piece. Then I start to sing and tap the side of the table with the blood pressure monitor pump.

The young women look at me. Neither of them says anything. One shakes her head, the other raises a finger and says, “Could it be ‘Manic Monday’?”

“And the singer?” I ask, and the women glance at each other.

The one who raised her finger thinks about it.

“Go ahead and say it, if you know,” I encourage her.

“Susanna something,” the woman guesses. “That’s all I can think of now.”

“Correct,” I say with a smile. This was my favorite song when I was a student. After the weekend-long final exam study groups that smelled of rubbing alcohol, we used to sing “Manic Monday,” tell anatomy jokes and recount legends about what-was-forgotten-in-the-stomach-of-the-patient-during-the-operation, take blood pressures and measure sugar levels, and compare our plans for specialization. For the longest time I felt that I wanted to be a sleep doctor, that is, an anesthesiologist, just like my own mother had planned to be in her time, before choosing eyes.

Six o’clock already I was just in the middle of a dream
I was kissin’ Valentino by a crystal blue Italian stream
But I can’t be late ’cause then I guess I just won’t get paid

These are the days when you wish your bed was already made
It's just another manic Monday
I wish it was Sunday
'Cause that's my Funday

"How can I help you?" I ask after I've finished the song and wakened into a half-finished thought: What if my daughter is indeed a lesbian and has run away with Linda?

The female couple's first words get by me because I get an irresistible urge to call Anita Rossi right away. Do we really know our children? Does the mother know her daughter? And the daughter her mother?

I examine the vaginal walls of a middle-aged woman who has come to see me because of problems with intercourse; and at the same time, I'm thinking about the trip to the Louvre with Mikael, which turned out to be our last trip together, and I'm also thinking about the afternoon of mother-daughter shopping a couple of weeks ago.

With the help of mirrors, I examine the sore mucous membranes. Wound marks, abrasions. The future, I think. Now is the time for mourning.

Mom-mmy, Jasmin had called from the boutique's fitting room, and when I peeked through the curtains, I was surprised. What had caused that surprise? Something in the girl had changed. But what? The curtain was half open, and Jasmin was posing in front of the mirror, her hip askew, in her tiny skin-tight top.

"Now that hurts," the woman says, and I pull my finger out slowly.

Isn't this wonderful? Jasmin had said, looking at the lacy top and herself, rocking on her toes.

"Why is it," laughs the client as she gets up, "that when you've just started to understand something about the whole song-and-dance, you feel like sawdust down there, and it's tender and painful, and you just hope that it'll be over soon?"

I smile and ask the woman to carefully step down from the examination table. Just then I hear the lowest of the low voices whisper in my ear: Somebody just walked over your grave.

I step to the side and stumble over something, fall to the floor, and hit my chin on the base of the examination table. The pain pierces through me.

"Oh my," says the patient and helps me get up. "Are you hurt?"

"No, I'm not," I say, and rub my chin and cheek. At least not yet.

Paula Pauliina knocks on the door and asks if everything is okay. I awake from my thoughts. I press a towel against my chin; I feel like drinking a glass of red wine, slamming the entire glass. And then another.

Or, going to stand in the park across the street and screaming as loudly as I can.

Or, calling the overnight guest, who left his business card, to tell him that the daughter whom I had casually mentioned to him was missing. Lost.

Regarding the man, he is married, has children, a wife, all safe. Of course.

"Your sister is on the line," Paula Pauliina says, staring at me through her thick glasses. She is steady as she stands, her feet inside her prescription shoes with the wooden soles. How can anyone have such round eyes? I say that I'll call her back later.

Paula Pauliina appears to be exceptionally absentminded, sluggish. She's puzzled by that big fire; one of her earlier crushes must have been a firefighter. In between her work, Paula Pauliina always follows the news, and recently she's gotten interested in the internet. Sometimes I've tried to find a common denominator in all of her bustle. She always gets her work done, too; she rarely calls in sick; she rarely asks for a day off. My first receptionist kept arriving late, she used the work phone for private conversations, was brusque with clients, would polish her fingernails. When Paula Pauliina suggested that she could start working as a receptionist, I was hesitant at first. I didn't know how much education she, my maid, had had. Then I realized that, after all, she had taken care of Jasmin when she was a baby. And that's how it started.

I think about my receptionist for a moment, and my thoughts find their old ruts. And, since no new ruts are found, I have to admit that I've never met a more predictable or punctual person.

What changed? I keep thinking, while a regular patient, a stylishly-dressed fifty-eight-year-old lady is undressing behind the curtain. The woman's guide dog sits at the door and attentively watches her owner. And me. My forehead. My chin. My hands. My ankles. What could it see? And smell? Dogs always make me insecure. Sometimes outside the stores, I notice that some giant crouching thing, tied to a bike rack, is staring at me. Well, what is it? I ask aloud. What do you see in me? And they never answer.

I always liked to watch Jasmin getting dressed. In the mornings, the girl stood in front of the large hallway mirror, and I stood next to her. But what changed? And when did it take place? Only now do I really think about it. Something new, a chill, biting breath of wind, and, for the first time, in that boutique's fitting room. In the movement of her hip? In the expression of her mouth? In her smile? In her voice?

I help the woman to the examination table. Her hands are cold. Luckily, she's wearing thick socks. Sometimes it bothers me when my arm touches a woman's ice-cold ankle.

The woman is a widow. Her vagina is small; it appears untouched, like the vagina of a young girl. Must've reverted to its former state, I think. The woman is beautiful, well taken care of, like some soft-skinned fruit. Or maybe I get this impression from the scent of her skin cream—clean, fresh Nivea or a softer LdB.

All of a sudden I feel like confiding in the woman. Dear ma'am, do you ever experience moments when you must solve an issue in your life right now, today? Clarify, analyze? Set your feelings apart in a row of pairs; invite them in from recess like a teacher at the schoolhouse door; spend time with them, teach them a bit of addition and subtraction, listening comprehension, reading skills, opening the voice?

Next. A woman is lying on the examination table chewing gum, with her hands straight along her sides; she bends her knees, as if that's all she ever does. Unlike nearly all other women, she does not tense her body.

I ask the woman to scoot a bit further down the table, and she jolts her hips downwards. She's humming at the same time.

She has shaved her whole vulva. There is a surgical-steel ring in her clitoris. This always complicates the examination. I'm holding the ring up with my pinkie while pushing the instruments inside her. The ring reminds me of things I'm too weary to think about now. Diseases, often serious ones. Injuries, defects, accidents. Should I have become a scientist, working in a lab, out in the world, in research groups—that would have been a different life. Then there might not have been a Jasmin. Or Jason, of course. The pain grates me again when I think about Jason. For the whole day, I've thought only of my daughter. My son, after all, exists, lives, is breathing, is present.

Or is he? I get the urge to call Jason's cell phone, and I speed up the exam.

A clean bill of health, I think to myself, relieved. I had been prejudiced against my client because of the obvious way she makes her living.

"Now this may pinch a bit," I warn, as I take the Pap smear from her cervix.

"Go right ahead," says the woman.

I glance at my cell phone, which flashes a message from Anita: "No news. How about there?"

I type in a "no" for Anita, then write on a Post-it note: a missing person is not dead. I attach it to the monitor of my computer, among other yellow Post-it notes.

When Seela calls about the Tupperware party that evening, I have to sit down and stare at the calendar on my office desk until the letters and numbers on it gain some meaning. Yes, it's true, for Monday night, at 7:30 p.m., it shows a party at Seela's. In Seela's spacious living room, which has white and burgundy leather couches, glass tables, and always plenty of fresh flowers in vases. Mostly tulips. Seela especially likes tulips. As I probably do. I have to think for a bit whether tulips are really my favorite flowers.

When Seela asks if everything is okay, I ask her if she knows where her daughter, Miriam, is. And when Seela answers with a faint smile in her voice, saying that at this time of day, the girl is where all children of her age are, in school, I ask if she knows that with absolute certainty.

When Muma calls, I put the phone on silent and stare at the screen: Mother is calling.

"And how are you doing? What brought you here today?"

The woman wants a stronger estrogen pad and a better lubricating gel. The gel from the pharmacy burns.

The products from the health store don't help. She has tried old wives' remedies, even butter, and virgin oil, hahahaa. I examine the woman but can barely insert any of my arsenal. Her mucous membranes are swollen and blistered. I try to examine her gently. The woman breathes heavily, and before I have time to formulate my question, she tells me that her husband wants it very often. What does "very often" mean? I ask quietly, my tone of voice as professional as possible. The woman is so tense that my fingers are in danger of becoming stuck in the dry vaginal hole.

"Very often is very often," the woman answers with a short laugh, and then immediately gives a yelp of pain as I pull the instruments out.

I ask how the woman feels, what she wants, but she says she wants the same thing as the man wants. See, otherwise the man will leave. I check her date of birth in my papers, and I sigh. I prescribe the woman continued hormone treatment and suggest some lubricant. I think for a few moments, write down the names of other over-the-counter lubricants that come to mind, and I wish her well.

I glance at the clock, press the button on the buzzer, and wait for an elderly woman to walk in. She is my former, now retired, Ob/Gyn instructor, whose cancer I diagnosed some five years ago. The woman was operated on promptly, and she's been handling her treatments well.

Because the woman is fifteen minutes late, I open the door to the waiting room and ask Paula Pauliina if the woman has come. Paula Pauliina is watching the fire, which is still on TV. She turns around as if caught doing something worse, blushes all the way up to her ears, and apologizes for the fact that she had forgotten to mention that the woman's daughter had called this morning and said that her mother had died on Sunday evening. Paula Pauliina doesn't notice my reaction; she continues by saying that, instead, in the bathroom there's another woman who had just arrived—a new patient requesting an emergency appointment.

"Tell her to wait another moment," I blurt out. I retreat, my legs rigid, and close the door. I stand for a moment with my forehead against the door. I have both a humbling and overwhelming feeling that I will never see my daughter again. The feeling seeps into me slowly, from the top of my head, and eventually fills me up completely.

I pull myself together and press the buzzer. On the other side of the door, a green light turns on. Someone will soon stand in front of me to tell me her most pressing issues.

"My child is dead, I am sure that my child is dead," says the woman. She pulls her coat more tightly around her stomach. "How many months are you?" I ask her, while looking at her thin midriff, trying to estimate. "Four, or a bit more," she answers with tears in her eyes. "I know it is dead. I can't feel it any more."

"Why didn't you go directly to the emergency room? Is this your first child?" I ask while setting up the examination table for her. I hope she doesn't notice how my hands are shaking. She continues to stand at the door, pressing her palms to her stomach. "Let's check it out right away," I say, and show her the space behind the curtain.

I spread gel on the woman's round naked stomach. I apologize for the fact that it might feel cold. I set up the ultrasound and start to slide the instrument slowly across the woman's stomach. I look for the contours of a child—more slowly than usual. I turned the monitor so the woman can follow the picture, and every now and then I glance at her pale face.

The child is here, I think. Good. The child is safe. But during the following seconds and minutes, closer scrutiny reveals that the young woman is right. The child's heart no longer beats. I verify the difficult diagnosis again and again.

I'm looking for someone else's child, and I don't know where my own child might be. Is her heart beating? I help people for a living, but now I can't do anything but panic.

After the young woman has left, aided out by Paula Pauliina, and with a referral in her hand, I go directly into the waiting room toilet and throw up. What comes out is not much. After all, I haven't been able to eat anything all day. I kneel down, holding on to the rim of the toilet bowl. I flush. I vomit more. Through my heaving, I hear my cell phone ring. I get up lightning fast and rush to the phone sitting on my office table. Spit still hangs from my mouth as I answer.

It's the Girls' House. The woman apologizes that she is only now returning my call, but she wants to let me know that Jasmin has not been to the House in weeks. It also seems that the fee for yoga has not been paid. I thank her and promise to pay right away. I wonder for a moment if I should call the police immediately or go home first, to Jasmin's room. Instead, I dial my parents' number.

The Big White Noise

1.

Darkness. How is it that I've never before noticed how enjoyable it is to be in the dark, writes Mother. She takes a shower without the lights on, she cooks food without the range lights beaming, she watches TV—the little that she can stand to watch—by candlelight. Her electric bills are ridiculously low. The same thing with food bills. Mother had bought Nordic walking poles and in the evening exercises with them along the streets and walking trails. She's not afraid of anyone following her or of gangs she might encounter. Mother's in a state of mind called I-couldn't-care-less and finds enjoyment only in hearing the sharp picks of the poles on the asphalt.

Muma and Papsi call Mother several times a day. They go to the grocery store for her and try to make her eat. Other relatives come to visit. Saku's boyfriend, Ramon, brings Mother some sushi he has prepared himself. He brings her houseplants with big leaves, talks about feng shui, keeps moving furniture, and changing around the decor. He's not allowed to touch my room. Saku and Ramon are both quite taken with Penalty Box's athletic physique. Penalty Box is interested in Saku's area of research—shame. It's a motive for many things, Penalty Box notes.

After a long time, Seidi finally visits her elder sister. Her down-to-earth talkativeness feels good to Mother. They sit on the couch and eat popcorn. Mother has always liked the smell of freshly-made popcorn. She looks at her long-legged sister, who talks about horses and golf courses and about her shoulder, which has been dislocated for the third time, and about the upcoming surgery. Mother lets her sister change the topic at will.

Alone, Mother visits Mikael's grave. She tells Mikael that I have disappeared. She calls Fred and asks how he is doing. She also asks how Fred's parents are, even though she hasn't done that for a long time. My parents have lunch together downtown. They talk about me—what kind of child I was. They reminisce about their trips abroad together. Mother talks to Father too about Penalty Box, how she trusts that the former star player will solve the case. Just see that you don't fall in love with the lead investigator; that wouldn't be appropriate, Father warns her, softly. They find a way to get along with each other, and no longer end all their meetings in a quarrel or sullen silence.

How can something like this happen here, in this country? Mother writes.

My picture is in the school yearbook. The picture with my head tilted. The last picture taken of me, a head-and-shoulders shot. I'm beautiful, gifted, and popular, as are all the girls on that page, and I'm also a helpful and generous friend. For some inconceivable reason, I've declared that I will be an oceanographer when I grow up, a dream I've held onto since I was ten. "How neat" has been listed as my favorite saying. Alternatively, "Real cool."

Mother goes through everything, over and over again. She stares at the school yearbook, searches the faces of the girls and boys, all of whom resemble each other. What if one of the classmates is behind it all—jealousy, revenge? Mother looks for some clue, a revelation, something she could get a hold of, something that would explain how a thing like this could have happened here, in this country. Should she call Penalty

Box? Has he thought about classmates, teachers, school employees? Has he investigated their backgrounds? And then, after a moment, the whole idea seems laughable. Mother looks at the faces in the yearbook again and apologizes to each of them, quietly.

And then this. Mother sees how her ex-husband—the one who knows more about everything, who can do everything better, who is sensible, thorny, cynical—falls apart. This is new, this is unprecedented, and it disturbs Mother even more.

My father, Fred, who had started seeing a therapist, eventually becomes disappointed with Penalty Box and the lack of results from the police investigation; and so, with the passing of time, he hires a private eye to investigate my disappearance. And all of a sudden, Mother feels a deep gratitude and tenderness toward Fred, even though she doesn't believe that the private eye can bring anything else to the case but greater expense.

Over the next few years, people are reminded of me in a variety of ways. When a Finnish cheerleading team does well at the world championships, when my favorite yogurt, cinnamon apple, is withdrawn from the market, when a tsunami hits the Southwest Asian shores a few years later.

Then, too, my parents think about me first; I had always been interested in surge waves and earthquakes. As a little girl, I read everything about Krakatau and Santorini. During our trips abroad I always wanted to talk about the ocean. I listened to the shells' white noise, with devotion.

2.

The Baptist often says, Do not think that you know anything about anything. In the beginning I thought it was horrendously provocative, and I always argued with him. The Baptist kept calling me an unsophisticated brat and a teenage idiot, and that really made me mad.

You took my senior high school away from me, I yelled at him.

You took my favorite teachers and my favorite foods! My plans for the future, my taste in clothes, my food, my friends!

Miss Frank watched me from her cage and pressed her ears against her side. She—like the Baptist—did not like raised voices.

I've never been afraid of the Baptist.

I knew he wouldn't do anything really bad to me.

All that he did was, eventually, good.

Right now I don't want to say anything more.

Except that the Baptist was right, in a way. What happened was that when Father and Hannah divorced a few years after my disappearance, and their mutual child, Luka, stayed with his mother, Jason wanted to move back with Mother.

It was good for Mother. Then she could concentrate on being a mother for her son, in a totally different way. Jason redecorated his own room and, after school days, often sat around in my room. He organized my clothes closet, my old toys, and my photo albums. Mother, of course, had not wanted to throw anything away. Jason talked to me, told me about his school days and about some crazy fat boy, who called Jason B.O.T.D.O., Brother Of The Disappeared One. Sometimes he secretly smoked a cigarette, his body hanging out the window, and he whispered into space, Hi there. What in the world happened to Jasmin and Linda? Gradually, football and ice hockey and surfing on the internet were put aside, and Jason started to read books. That is, really read books. He started to devour all kinds of books, without discrimination: novels and textbooks, books about astronomy and mathematics. Nobody could have expected that.

The Peacock Crows

*

Ringo knew how to approach girls, at first with curiosity and politeness, and then more and more seductively. He knew how to give them the exact right amount of alcohol or other substances so they became suitably lively and uninhibited. They would want to experiment and agreed to anything.

The girls who had been found in the city's bars and cafés became, with just a little persuasion, new pet girls. No more online ads were needed. And they were more than enthusiastic about the photo sessions. All this, of course, couldn't have pleased Lido more. The fewer questions from the outside, the better. That's what Lido always emphasized. No talk, no noise, just a little fucking peace and quiet to get the job done, privacy protection and epicurean enjoyment. Lido liked these sophisticated words he had adopted from his clients.

During the fall, Ringo began to spend night after night away from home. Sometimes he wasn't even seen during the day, and Randi would be left alone for hours at a time in the Pet Shop, especially in the morning when neither Madame Liv nor any of Lido's countless girls were there. On weekends, Randi pursued his own interests by fishing with a group of fishermen just below the nearby rapids, occasionally even catching a trout.

Ringo had started to spend his time at various downtown girl clubs, and through those places he drifted into all kinds of circles for buying and selling. As he liked to say, his businesses were mega-successful. Even Lido didn't fucking understand as much about internet commerce as Ringo and his new friends.

Behind Lido's back? Randi sometimes asked, trying to clear his confusion.

Stop being afraid of everything, or else you'll end up like Uncle Chanu, Ringo said. He laughed and left, again with a young girl on his arm. He didn't stay for dinner, even though Randi had fixed saffron fish that could have passed for Mother Lalla's cooking. In the market, Randi had befriended the owner of a spice stand who sold saffron that you could actually use for cooking. Typically, the bright yellow powder here in the north was so mild it couldn't have made you sneeze even if you had sniffed the whole bottle.

Randi ate his own portion of fish, left his brother's portion on the stove, and got absorbed in his textbook.

Long laughter will turn into tears. If there are two, there will be a third. An accident does not come with a bell around its neck. If you got it by singing, you'll lose it in a whistle. The teacher had had to explain and re-explain the last one, and Randi was still not sure about what situation would be appropriate for a saying like that. Randi practiced the sentences aloud. Occasionally, he stood in front of the mirror to see how he looked when he spoke a foreign language.

*

It's true that Randi, too, gradually started going out to the bars at night with the Pet Shop girls. He preferred to take them to clubs where they could listen to live music. Preferably something soft, swaying, quiet. There actually were places like that in the city. Real musicians, and people who listened and spoke to each other quietly.

Randi's dream was to ask out the blondest girl in the Pet Shop. Most often she hung around with her friend who had reddish hair. Something in the blonde girl had caught Randi's eye right from the beginning. Randi couldn't say exactly what that characteristic or feature was, but it calmed his mind. The girl was different from the other Pet Shop girls in the sense that she was difficult to approach, or at least Randi found it difficult to approach her. It was as if there were some invisible aura around her that made Randi insecure and caused words to stick in his throat. So Randi never got around to asking the blonde girl to go to the clubs with him. The others certainly came, happily.

Randi kept telling the girls about his home country, about the seasons—five of them instead of four—about the various animals, and the foods that were prepared and seasoned in a unique way. Randi believed that the Pet Shop girls listened to him and liked to talk to him. Randi, in return, listened to them talk about their families, their siblings, their favorite movies, their clothes and cosmetics, about their first boyfriends. They needed to talk about their former lives, and they seemed to forget that Randi was one of Lido's men.

And it *was* Randi's job to befriend the girls, to be interested in their concerns, to develop their trust, to lure them to work at Lido's club, and then to have them stay and keep silent about things that should never be mentioned on the outside. As autumn turned into winter, Randi gradually understood that he too, was a bird, a decoy.

*

Randi watched his brother use the powder for the first time as early as late spring. Ringo used it only occasionally, and he didn't seem to be all that dependent on the substance. He claimed that alcohol was much worse, causing problems and addiction, whereas these clean powders simply gave him days-worth of energy, helped keep him feeling good and positive, and allowed him physically to do what had to be done. Fuck, they weren't much stronger than the caffeine pills that even Randi sometimes popped.

During the fall, Randi saw his brother snort powder up his nose from the Pet Shop counter in the middle of the day, so that any client looking for a dog collar—it could have been a police officer—would have seen it. At that time, Randi didn't say anything. Ringo was irritable and busy, and more and more often ordered his impertinent little brother to mind his own business.

Lido himself used coke regularly, and the young girls at the Wet Pet Club were given it all the time, especially for longer and more daring film sessions or weekend parties. And, admittedly, Randi had tried it a few times, and it helped him forget what he was doing and why. When Lido mixed the white powder into whiskey, it was a manly gift, and it had to be accepted.

*

At the beginning of autumn, at the Wet Pet Club, Randi had a threesome with two young girls, even though he couldn't remember much about it the next morning. His dick was sore, which meant, of course, that the girls had been young, maybe even virgins.

Lido said that being with the girls—testing the girls—was part of Randi's company benefits package. When he wanted, Randi could choose any of them. And with Randi's looks, they were easy to get, really easy.

Lido guarded some of the girls more strictly than others. They were classified as *Lido's virgins*. Often they'd be offered as first-timers, and the older men didn't have the sense to feel the girls out with much attention to detail. With those girls, Lido made much more money than with the others.

*

One night Randi was sitting at the computer, watching a movie that had been shot the previous night at the Pet Shop. Two men enter the shop and wish to purchase a bunny. A girl with dreadlocks, with her head tilted, asks what kind of bunny the gentlemen would like. Something small, tight, smooth, pure-white, the men say, watching the girl. The girl wears a sleeveless blouse and a very, very short skirt. The men watch how she walks to the other end of the pet shop.

When the girl bends over to pick up the bunny, both men dig out their cocks, and, to the accompaniment of rock music, they quickly grab the girl.

Randi got excited by what he saw and felt embarrassed, since one of the men was Ringo, and he recognized the girl too.

*

One day Ringo showed Randi some recent pictures of the new blonde girl and her friend. May I introduce Vanilla Bebe and Pink Cream. Guess which is which?

Ringo enjoyed the situation. He may have noticed how Randi had been watching the blonde girl. And he thought it was fun to show the *before* and *after* pictures next to each other. The Pet Shop's little helper and the Wet Pet Club's little slut. Ringo told him that Lido, too, had noticed the new pair of girls—sweet little packages—and in addition to the pictures for the website, they had already been introduced at the club.

What did they do there? Randi asked.

Blowjobs, lap jobs, dancing nude, yum yum—for now, his brother answered. Lido wants to keep them a little bit special for now, you know.

Randi tried to hold back any reaction. The blonde girl was even more slender than she looked with clothes on. Ringo had already tried the other one, the honey-haired girl, but hadn't been with the blonde girl yet.

The following night, Randi couldn't sleep, thinking about the girl. About how one evening, when Randi had lit a cigarette after closing time, the girl had handed him a glass ash tray across the Pet Shop counter. That small gesture had made Randi so happy he hadn't been able to get to sleep then, either.

Just as he did now, Randi had thought that night about the river back home, where they could swim together. Would the girl have fun in rushing water? Had she ever danced in falling rain? Did she know what warm almond milk tasted like? Those were the things Randi thought about in his small room, barely larger than a bed, with his arms behind his neck, eyes closed. That's where the girl was completely his, that's where she looked him in the eye, talked to him, touched his arm. There, under Randi's closed eyelids, they had each other.

Even Randi couldn't estimate how much in love he was with this pale girl—or, was it just homesickness, a longing for girls playing in the monsoon showers back home?

*

Now, this is not quite how I imagined it would be. But what is it, really? Sometimes Randi tried to ask Ringo his opinion about the kinds of people he considered heroes and those he considered cowards, and if what they were doing was somehow bad or ugly, even though everyone knew it was done all around the world, despite the fact it was an old custom. But Ringo burst out laughing. Ask your bowl, Ringo suggested. Write a letter to the spirits. Or confide in Mother if you imagine that it could be useful somehow!

Ringo had dark blue circles around his eyes. He barely slept. He just kept handling the young female figures all night long and sniffing the white powder he received from Lido's bodyguards or his own contacts. Ringo was amused by one piece of news that he kept telling everyone who wasn't tired of listening. He had found out that Lido sent money to his old mother. He made his couriers take the money right to her so that the old man she'd been married to couldn't snatch the money and pour it down his throat. However, his mother couldn't help but give him the money, and that's where it all went—down the old geezer's throat. That's how Lido, without thinking about it too much, kept the backdoor open to the junk city of the cement factory, where, years later, he would return because it was easy to disappear there. There, no official or unofficial bloodhounds could find someone like him.

*

Randi tried to think about the Year of the Peacock, about manhood, and about not giving in, about natural strength. Something that could be called will and honor, like Father had talked about in his time. That everyone had to have that feeling next to his heart, even a spice dealer, and a spice dealer's son.

Ringo had a different mindset. He thought that some ugly things were just as exciting as beautiful ones. Ringo thought that naked girls, who provided certain services to fat old men and danced in their laps like monkeys, were enchanting in a very special way. Ringo also thought that blood and pain were beautiful.

*

It's true that somehow Randi was captivated by those visions. Although he didn't take part in the girls' services or the orgies at the club, he watched. And if you watched one night, you had to watch the next night too.

It would have been impossible to explain something like that to Mother. Even though Mother, also, had gotten caught up in a TV series the same way, a soap opera that she had to watch every afternoon at half past four.

The girls infiltrated his dreams, too. For a long time, Randi had been sleeping poorly. In addition to the blonde girl who snuck behind his eyelids every night as if into some velvet-and-silk lined love nook, Randi kept thinking also about the other girls. Some Pet Shop girls had black-and-blue bruises that were visible during the day. Fresh scars. Yet, they didn't want to quit. At home, they said they had gotten the bruises during PE class, aerobics, or kick-boxing.

There were many kinds of men. More and more often, some had asked for Randi's price, too, and for services he couldn't even imagine. Randi had never asked Ringo if he had offered his services to Lido's customers. He just couldn't bring himself to ask.

*

Toward the end of autumn, the weekend parties at the Wet Pet Club became wilder and wilder. In the midst of the carefully-selected customers, outsiders appeared, or at least that's how Lido regarded some of the men. He accused some people in his immediate circle of accepting bribes and talking too much. What if some fucking spies filter in, or blackmailers? What if the police show up?

At some point, Lido started to get nervous. The first real problem arose when one of the customers was unnecessarily heavy-handed with Lido's then favorite pet, Raisa. The girl got scared and wanted to quit the Pet Shop on the spot. Lido offered her money and lots of other nice things, but this dreadlocked girl—who had spent a couple of weeks in Lido's private club—wanted to go home to Mom and Dad, now.

To Mom and Dad! Lido mocked. Mom and Dad had boozed themselves into institutions long ago. You've lived with your old crony grandma all your life and you dare give me a mouthful of fuckin' lies!

Randi saw Lido hit Raisa in the backroom of the club. The girl screamed hysterically, and Lido hit her again, this time so hard that she fell to the ground, limp.

After that, Randi never saw the dreadlocked girl. And none of the other girls said anything more about her. It was as if she, Raisa, had never existed.

The "I want to go home now" syndrome hit almost all the Pet Shop girls sooner or later. Some were satisfied with the money and the clothes and vague promises of a glamorous future. At the least, the rest were silenced by various degrees of threats should they dare tell anyone about what they had seen or experienced.

It worked. No one spoke.

Undeniably, Lido and his bodyguards were intimidating, and no further talk occurred. Randi sometimes wondered about the kind of life the girls returned to, wherever home was. What did they tell their families, their mothers and fathers, their siblings?

*

Randi kept thinking about the blonde girl. One afternoon, a little before closing, he mustered his nerve and asked the girl to go to the backroom of the Pet Shop with him. After a long break, the two girlfriends were again working on the shop side of the business. The one with the reddish hair, who had been cleaning the aquarium, gave the blonde one an insinuating look and turned away with a smile.

Would you come right now? asked Randi, feeling how much he was blushing.

Okay then. The blonde girl finished up what she had been doing at the rabbit cages, took a piece of gum out of her mouth, and stuck it under the rim of the table. She came with Randi. As they entered the backroom, the curtain rattled against Randi's face. Small, dried-up oyster and mussel shells, far away from the sea.

For a moment, they stood facing each other in the dim room. Randi wanted to tell the girl how beautiful and nice she was. When the girl let out a deep sigh, knelt down, and started to open Randi's pants, he lifted her back up, pulled her up in front of him, and looked her in the eye.

In genuine astonishment, the girl looked at Randi for a second with her blue-gray eyes. She pulled away from Randi's hold and ran through the door.

*

That same day, Lido came to the Pet Shop, grabbed Randi by his arm, and told him to fucking watch his brother more carefully. Lido smiled angrily. *Your brother is fucking skimming off the top. Your brother is not fucking supposed to be skimming off the top.*

Around that same time, a wild bacchanal was planned at the club. Word had gotten around that a group was renting the Wet Pet Club for the entire weekend. A private party. The blonde girl and her friend, who was prone to laughing, would be part of the fresh group of girls provided to that party. Lido advertised them as top-of-the-line girls, crème-de-la-crème asses.

*

It became obvious that Ringo was more and more involved in his own deals. Many times, Randi had tried to talk to his brother. He had a feeling that someone was watching their apartment, and he was certain that

Lido was well informed about all of Ringo's little side deals.

Ringo put too much trust in Lido's smile; he failed to take sufficient precaution. He called himself Lido's *club manager* and *trusted man*. Ringo would not fare well in the game if he were called to account for his dealings. And maybe there was still somebody above Lido—someone who should be feared even more. Occasionally, Randi thought he would tell it all to Uncle Chanu, but he didn't dare.

*

Almost always girls and men were in their apartment when Randi returned home, at any time of day. Movies were on TV, and the screen of the computer Ringo had brought in was filled with naked skin. Half-empty glasses and powder residue littered the tables. It was such a mess it took all his strength just to think about cleaning it up.

Upon leaving, the men left Ringo a pile of bills. The girls dressed quickly and left the apartment with dulled eyes, without even glancing at Randi.

One time, the blonde girl and her friend with the reddish hair were in the group. When the girls were leaving, Randi handed the blonde one a letter he had been carrying in his pocket for a reason. The blonde girl glanced at the letter and at Randi, and for a moment he imagined that the girl had gotten the message, but then she dropped the letter behind her on the hallway floor like a meaningless advertisement, a candy wrapper, or a piece of trash.

After Ringo left with the last ones of the group, humming and restlessly primping himself, Randi had gone to his own room. He just looked at the messy bed and the DVDs on the floor.

Ringo was in some of the movies; in others, there were the men and girls Randi knew from the Wet Pet Club. While he was taking care of the girls, his brother's face was flushed and his eyes shone with excitement. Ringo was obviously king of the movies. He got the best-looking girls and was often with more than one at a time. His muscular brown body set itself apart from everybody else's.

*

And then Ringo disappeared. He didn't show up at the Pet Shop during the day, and he didn't come home at night. A new young man started at the Wet Pet Club in the evenings. He videotaped the action in the booths and in the backrooms. When Randi asked, it turned out that nobody had seen Ringo for days, and Randi knew what that meant.

Randi still went to work as usual. He stood behind the Pet Shop counter and watched the Pet Shop girls come and go. The aquarium glass was cleaned, the guinea pigs' sawdust was freshened, and the shell curtain kept rattling. In the afternoons, Randi let Conrad out of his cage. Randi followed Conrad flapping about on top of the shelves. That horrible creature should be killed, said Madam Liv, leaning on the doorframe, watching the bird. It doesn't give joy to anyone. *So what*? mumbled Randi, lifting the bird back into his cage.

Randi didn't ask anyone about Ringo, but just waited. He had patient genes, and he knew it was just best to wait. He took walks in the reeds on the ocean shore and listened to the wind. He followed the moon's phases, which looked quite different from the moon at home. In the evenings he made himself a pot of tea and browsed through Ringo's internet pages and an enormous amount of correspondence. Ringo had clients from all over Europe. If Randi's calculations were correct, his brother had been offering photos and movies of underage girls to more than a thousand clients in the last few months.

On the first day of December, Randi wrote a letter to his mother. At the end of the letter he mentioned that the Year of the Peacock, which was soon to end, had been—as his big brother Karim had predicted—a time of enormous changes.

The Pet Studio

1.

I wonder if your vaccinations are up to date? Mother said. I guess the animals have all been checked and are healthy so you can't catch any exotic diseases. A doctor friend of Mother's once contracted dengue fever during a conference trip and was in really bad shape, and Mother always reminded me of this. Another colleague did research on the foot-and-mouth disease epidemic. Mother had plenty of acquaintances with cautionary tales; and she had examples for each disease and every accident.

By the end of our first week at work, it seemed as though we had always been there. *Work*. It didn't even feel like work: feeding little rabbits and guinea pigs and golden hamsters and taking them out of their cages for exercise. Even cleaning the nymph-parakeet's cage or the wheat snake's terrarium didn't seem repulsive, let alone cleaning the aquariums.

After the work day, we both held little rabbits, one after another, in our laps. We petted them and combed their fur. They dug themselves into our armpits and trembled. Miss Frank was especially sweet. Her fur smelled of vanilla and her pads like freshly-made popcorn.

Sometimes Lillan asked us to clean the studio. It was a fairly small room with bare brick walls that had been painted white, a few differently-colored cardboard rolls leaning against the wall. In one corner there was a burgundy sofa that resembled a divan, and on its backrest were a couple of white pelts. A large, brown leather armchair and two high stools stood in the other corner. At the back wall was a fancy computer with a webcam. Next to a television was a small shelf of videocassettes and DVDs.

We had agreed to work at the Pet Shop on Mondays, Thursdays, and Fridays for three hours a day, from five to eight, which was closing time. However, soon we were going there every day. And Lillan had no problem with our presence. On the contrary. We could care for the animals as much as we wished, but we couldn't feed them too much. Nobody liked the fat ones.

And we laughed. Yeah, true.

Some of the other Pet Shop girls frequently visited the Pet Wholesale nearby, where they bought food for the animals, sawdust for their pens and cages, and other supplies. Once we heard from Irina that at the Pet Wholesale you could earn some extra money if you did extra special little jobs. Warehouse jobs? I wondered. We can't operate forklifts. And we're too weak to lift bales of hay. Irina laughed. You need to be invited for these jobs; you wouldn't apply for them yourselves. In other words, you'll get these jobs if you get these jobs.

2.

The man we assumed to be the actual owner of the Pet Shop was a muscular guy with a ponytail. We first saw him when he parked his car in front of the shopping center. A Jaguar, said Linda, as we watched the man talking on his cell phone. He wore a well-fitted gray suit, a bolo tie around his neck, and dark glasses, despite the fact that it was cloudy outside and drizzling.

Can anyone become rich like that in the pet business? I wondered. I thought about the pet store somewhere downtown where we had bought Diana a long time ago and its owner who always walked around in a faded cardigan with an aquarium net hanging from a string around his neck.

In addition to the Pet Shop, the man with the ponytail owned a bar, or a club, or, at least, a fashionable party place, and he also brought various performance groups, bands, and other entertainers into the country for gigs. Linda had heard it from somebody, who had heard from somebody else, and so on, and so forth. Linda believed that the man was famous, some kind of a celebrity, who was guaranteed access to whatever and wherever he wanted. The man, no doubt, looked like it. He walked with wide steps, his chest held high, and he never came alone; he was always accompanied by men in leather jackets, who looked like bodyguards, even when he came to the Pet Shop.

He once introduced his girlfriends to us, two at one time. He spoke with a foreign accent, and the girls laughed when the man said: May I present to you Sofi and Ebba?

The girls were not much older than us. Linda and I held out our arms to shake their hands, but they just laughed. We saw them in the shop every now and then, and when we asked why they didn't take care of the animals at all, Lillan said that they had been hired to work as studio assistants.

3.

We had certainly heard about the *protectors*; some co-workers had told us. And one day, at the back of the store behind the long checkout desk, stood one of them, a dark-skinned man we had not seen before.

We had heard that they both were friends of the owner. And at least some of the girls had gone out with them. Dated them. It somehow seemed to be part of the arrangement. And that's what we, or at least I, wondered about; these were already older men, especially the taller one. Even though they actually belonged in the category worthy of the rose butt tattoo.

The tall, dark one watched us, eyes smiling as midnight highways, as we stepped inside the store.

Hi, Jasmin. Hi, Linda, he said, his voice soft. The strange accent suited it well. My name is Ringo.

Yeah, we know, Linda said, laughing, her voice low. She glanced at me. Wow.

The man's hands rested on the table top as if on piano keys. He had exceptionally long and skinny fingers, like those of a lizard, and beautiful pink oval-shaped fingernails, like those of a woman. There was something strange about his hands, but I couldn't immediately decide what. It seemed as if they somehow glowed.

And that over there is my little brother Randi, the handsome one continued, his manner calm.

The little brother kept glancing at us, leaning toward the other end of the counter. Wow, wow, relayed Linda with her eyes. I had never before seen such a beautiful man. He nodded in an almost shy manner and lifted one hand. He never talked much, he seemed to be primarily intent on caring for the shop's decrepit parakeet.

Other girls told us that these *protectors* were a bit like security guards. There were a lot of robberies and petty crime at the shopping center. Maybe so. We accepted the explanations at face value. At least, these two didn't resemble Lido's bodyguards, who barely had enough room to turn around in the Pet Shop aquarium aisle. We were always afraid they would break something

One night when we were about to leave the Pet Shop, Ringo was waiting for us outside the store. He asked if we would like to earn a little extra money, or actually quite a bit more money. Wow, answered Linda. Wowwowwow.

Monday

by Sara Martin

I lie down on the examination table and look at the ceiling. I place the stethoscope in its place and listen to my own heart. I recall my own first visit to a gynecologist, a secret kept from Mother. I wanted to have my "downstairs" inspected, and absolutely by a male doctor. As the man was approaching my lower quarters with the speculum, I watched his expression intently, and thus I was gradually convinced that there was nothing odd about me after all, since his expression never changed, but stayed formal, throughout the exam.

I pull the stethoscope off my ears. I can hear the sounds of a shopping channel from the waiting room. Christmas presents are already being shoved at people, of course. Paula Pauliina keeps ordering items, trying them out, and then returning them. On occasion, I've bought an unused pedometer, a milkshake machine, and a set of knives from Paula Pauliina, and then donated them as presents or given them to the doctors' charity auctions.

Paula Pauliina. Couldn't her parents decide which name to give her? Or did it somehow become more endearing when repeated in the diminutive form?

In any case, Paula Pauliina is an unmarried middle-aged woman; in fact she's only a few years older than I am, childless, one of those who do their Christmas shopping on Christmas Eve morning, unless they get stuck at a bingo hall.

Thinking about Christmas seems impossible.

Jasmin opening the soft presents.

Jasmin sitting on the dark parquet of the living room floor in the red woolen socks knitted by Muma.
Jasmin existing.

Anita is sitting on the waiting room chair, looking at old magazines through her lilac-tinted glasses. Paula Pauliina has already gone home, and the TV is still on. Every now and then, Anita glances at the news and fails to notice that I'm watching her through the open door. Here and there in the magazines you still can find the models and beauty queens who are her age. Some are involved in the fashion industry, some have found work on television, some have married well. One, an alcoholic, told all the magazines how she found religion.

Just as Anita checks the time on her cell phone, I push the door wide open and invite her in. She slides her glasses on top of her head and stares at me for a moment as if staring at a doctor. We shake each other's hand and then hug each other awkwardly. Anita glances around, mildly confused. It seems as though she's been crying.

I can't help the fact that I'm outright staring at this flawlessly beautiful woman who stands in front of me in a fur coat that reaches nearly to the floor. The last time we saw each other was in passing at some PTA meeting at the beginning of fall, where everyone was staring at this ex-beauty queen.

"It's been awfully busy at work," says Anita. "The Christmas party season is the worst. There are so many customers that, even with five women working, our days stretch late into the evening."

"But that's a good thing, isn't it, in a way," I observe. I point Anita to a chair next to the window. "My office doesn't really feel the effect of the Christmas party season," I reply, and Anita looks at me, amused. Then Anita says that she hasn't eaten anything all day. She has no appetite because of this thing, and she even skipped her afternoon pilates session.

"Maybe we could go out and have dinner somewhere?" I suggest and wonder if she can smell the recently regurgitated food on my breath. "I mean later, when we've come up with a plan of action and have gone to the police," I continue, trying to inhale while talking.

Plan of action.

Here we are, sitting opposite each other, two women who've lost their children, with a plastic uterus between us.

Who actually made that uterus? I find myself thinking, for the first time in my life. For the first time in my entire career, I'm thinking that somebody, somewhere, manufactures plastic uteri for a living. Large uteri of Western women. Is it a small woman in China or Thailand, a young girl?

I'm thinking that right there, between us, could also be a makeup head. In Anita's world, there would be a makeup head. In my world, there's a woman's reproductive organ.

"I've had two abortions," Anita says quickly, "and also one miscarriage, five years ago. I then thought I was going to die."

I don't know what to say. I have nothing to contribute to such a revelation. Anita is not my patient. I don't intend to examine her equipment. Actually, I don't want to know anything about her. I want to find my daughter.

"Let's make a plan of action," I say.

"Let's," answers Anita.

"I would never have believed that something like this could ever happen," I say, looking at her.

"Neither would I. I still don't believe this is happening, but should we go first to the police station to file a report?" she asks, checking her expensive cell phone again. "So that we can both understand exactly where we stand right now."

There are certainly more pleasant ways to spend a slushy Monday evening than sitting in the waiting room of a police station. I look at the other people there, reporting who knows what kinds of things. I hold a number in my hand, still nauseous. I've already been to the police station restroom once, and I don't feel like going again. On top of everything else, there's a young woman behind the reception desk who's looking at Anita with intense curiosity. I'm struck by an instinctive reaction: I don't want to explain our situation to this person.

Moth-err, can I go to Linda's to do my homework? Moth-err, can I spend the night at Linda's since we're studying late for a test? Moth-err, can I please go to Linda's for the whole weekend 'cause we're baking and cooking food for home ec?

"We'll be fine." Anita puts her hands on my shoulders. Her fur tickles my face, classic perfume wafts around her, pure sophistication.

We're not the first ones to come this Monday evening for the same reason.

"Oh really?" I ask the young woman, who's searching for the right form in her drawer. I'd like to be able to choose the person to whom I report our situation.

Our daughters are now officially transferred to the missing persons list. "When did we see our children last? Is it likely they're still on the go together?" Plenty of questions, lots of information: heights and weights. Descriptions and distinguishing characteristics. I have to give that some thought. I don't think Jasmin has any distinguishing characteristics; at least I can't think of any. Anita, however, can list many: a tooth jewel, tongue piercing, navel ring, and that fresh tattoo—a rose on her left buttock.

I watch Anita as she lists the distinguishing characteristics acquired by her child. She reads from a sheet of paper. Over the course of the day, she has written everything down: navel ring, tongue piercing, tooth jewel, lists Anita. "Did I already mention the navel ring? And four piercings in both ear lobes."

My goodness, I think to myself. Jasmin seems so untouched, so pure. She has only her blue eyes, her blonde hair, her medium height, her slenderness. Neither Anita nor I can be too sure about the clothing. "What might be missing from the closets?"

"Could we come back tomorrow to fill in this information? That is, if the girls haven't returned home in the meantime!"

"So, you don't know exactly what they were wearing?" repeats the woman, raising her eyebrows.

"No, we don't. We last saw them eight days ago! We haven't checked the clothes closets yet! We haven't had time! We've been at work!"

Are we bad mothers, many times over?

We step out of the police station and walk slowly to Anita's car. Both of us have folded our copies of the missing person's report into our respective shoulder bags. We've been told that approximately ninety-nine percent of all these types of disappearances are solved, and that consoles us somewhat.

The weather is turning wetter, and the streets are slippery. There's still a smell of smoke in the air. Even in the police waiting room the TV had coverage of the firefighting efforts in the eastern industrial district. A massive fire, a large industrial building, such-and-such number of fire departments deployed, and the fire rescue work plus the clearing up in the aftermath will continue till tomorrow.

We've been told of other disappearances, we've been asked how the girls were doing in school, about their use of the internet, about new hobbies or new friends, boyfriends, jobs, medicine, bank accounts.

Did the girls have secrets?

Did they spend a lot of time on the internet?

Have the mothers ever looked at certain kinds of internet pages?

Have the mothers noticed any unusual changes in the girls during the fall? In the way they dressed, the way they behaved? In anything, even small things? If nothing comes up in the next few days, the police will visit the girls' homes. The police will take a DNA sample from a hairbrush or a toothbrush; they'll look things over, trace the locations of the girls' cell phones, if possible.

And then they'll talk to friends and teachers and cliques, and then check hospitals and so on. And only then will they ask for help from the public; only then will they extend the search to the media, place pictures in the papers, et cetera.

Quietly, we listened.

I had sex last night for the first time in a long time, and already it seems to have been an eternity ago. I would like to ask God if this is punishment for it, for sleeping with a married man, but I don't have this God to whom I could ask that question. My worldview is a scientific one, so I don't have anyone to talk to. I'd kick the dirt on the ground if the ground weren't covered with frost; I'd ask the stars if the sky weren't behind a gray cloud.

In the parking lot, I say, "What are we going to do now?"

"We'll wait," says Anita.

We'll wait, I repeat to myself. We'll wait. We'll fill out the next form, one degree grimmer, which will be forwarded to the Violent Crimes Unit. Dental records, Xrays, medications. Secrets? How can you know if someone else has secrets, and how can you know if they're light secrets or dark secrets? The spring comes. The window is left ajar. A fly buzzes between the window panes and cannot escape. We're waiting. We might just as well wake up. The world could look different. Eventually we're old and wrinkled, despite all the modern trickery. Our vaginas atrophy, and eventually we're left alone, completely in peace. We freeze in the forest, fall to the asphalt, sink in the cold water, are forgotten at home, are covered by earth.

"While we're waiting, let's go and have a beer," suggests Anita, and she flicks on the headlights of her car.

The Pets

1.

Sofi and Ebba explained to us the "dos" and "don'ts." We watched a few times through a peephole in the studio wall.

If—and most often when—the client wanted only a quick after-work blowjob or a vigorous handjob, he was led to the employee's lounge adjacent to the small kitchen. There you could find a wash basin, some soap, mouthwash, paper towels, air freshener. You could, of course, lock the door from the inside.

The studio had been reserved for the other customers. There it was possible to enjoy a lap dance, a quick fuck, film both, and then watch it. You could do it all online, too.

You were to welcome the clients with a friendly smile, speak in a whisper, and ask for special requests: Would they, for instance, want the girls to be completely naked or only partially nude?

Linda was immediately of the opinion that, Hey, why not? You could and should experiment with everything, and besides, *Remember Miami*.

Sometime earlier, we had, indeed, wondered about the men who looked as if they were coming straight from work and who walked right past the Pet Shop desk into the studio or the adjacent employee's lounge, and who returned after a moment with glowing cheeks.

This is how it went: Yummy, yummy, said the man, as he inserted his organ into my mouth in the dim employee's lounge. He held the back of my head in his hands. I heard the ticking of the man's watch. I tried to think about palm trees and warm sand, the sounds of an ocean.

The first time, I almost choked. It was the same feeling as once when, after a fight, Jason had tried to push his sweaty hockey sock down my throat.

Fortunately, the first client was a man who didn't smell like anything in particular and who was in a big hurry. I didn't quite remember what all I had to do—lick, suck, nibble, bite, but it didn't really matter, since the man came almost immediately.

What if somebody we know shows up, like a teacher? I whispered to Linda, as we were brushing our teeth in front of a toilet sink and gurgling with the strongest antiseptic mouthwash sold without a prescription. I felt like vomiting, but I couldn't make anything come out. I had been so nervous that I hadn't had any breakfast or anything after that either, except for a couple of chocolate bars. Mother thought I had lost some weight, and she started telling me I wasn't eating enough for breakfast. She wondered if perhaps I was doing too much of that cheerleading stuff. A few times she thought she had caught a whiff of cigarette smoke in my clothes, but I explained that some of my friends smoked—what can I do about it? Which ones have such a habit? Mother then asked, amazed.

Do you think our teachers or relatives visit a place like this? asked Linda with a puff, staring at me in the bathroom mirror. Her tongue ring piercing was bleeding, and she kept spitting the blood into the sink. I had a small abrasion on the roof of my mouth.

Who are these people then? I whispered.

Hey, *little working girls*, don't think too much, Sofi and Ebba advised us, laughing. After the first few days, they had noticed our confusion. This is just like any other job. Cleaning the toilets, emptying the trash. Do the job, take the money, and have dinner at a Mexican place. *And don't forget, lots of chili*.

After our first week as working girls, Irina asked us, in an almost motherly fashion, how we were doing and what we thought about all of this. Had we only done lollipop jobs or had there been some other kind of fun? It would be a good idea to get checked by a dentist, and, of course, to take care of contraception diligently. At that point, I had already started taking Linda's birth control pills, and I think I was less afraid of getting pregnant than of Mother finding them in my handbag.

Irina was a forerunner. From the dimness of the employees' lounge, she had already moved on to the next stage, the Pet Wholesale, or Wet Pet Club. But we won't talk about that job now—you'll see it later, said Irina. She pretended her lips were an imaginary zipper that she closed.

Amir, Rolf, Reko. Some of the men introduced themselves, which was odd and somehow unpleasant. I didn't want to know anything about them, not even a name. I always hoped they wouldn't come back, but some of them did. And then they became more familiar and tried to talk to me. I never answered. I just nodded, shook my head, or murmured.

And then a man in a wheelchair—he didn't introduce himself—asked me how much it would cost for penetration. When I stated a randomly large sum, which he agreed to pay, there was no going back. Lillan held on to him as he pushed himself into me. It didn't feel like anything. The man collapsed back into his chair, panting heavily. I didn't even bleed.

At the time, I washed my hands constantly. At home I used so much toothpaste and mouthwash that Mother wondered about it. Sometimes even in the middle of a school day I'd take a shower in the locker room, because I suspected there were strange smells floating around me.

2.

One day Ringo had news. He said that Lido's personal photographer was insisting taking on pictures of us for his new internet gallery.

Pictures of us? Linda and I looked at each other.

Yes, you are so fucking sexy! Ringo smiled and revealed a bright, white, even set of teeth. No wonder nearly all the Pet Shop girls had already slept with him. He was unbelievably good looking. As he talked, he kept glancing at his brother, who stood with his back toward us, feeding a molting, scraggly bird. Once again his brother had brought a bowl of water with rose buds floating in it to the shop counter. It actually seemed kind of sweet, though Lillan always sighed and said, This ain't no feed store.

Nooo? Ringo stretched and flexed his hips, once, so loosely that we were forced to stare. We had always wondered what he had been doing before coming to work for Lido. Dancer? Waiter?

Lido's personal photographer wanted pictures, especially of blonde girls. And the two of us were blonde, very blonde. The blondest girls in the Pet Shop. Besides, he had seen our pictures on other sites. Sextet? Sweet Sixteens?

I'll give you usernames and passwords so you can visit the Wet Pet Club pages, said Lillan. She showed us some pictures of girls we knew from the Pet Shop, downloaded from the website. We barely recognized them. I blushed, and Linda laughed.

3.

Naked. Being without clothes. Posing sexily. *Poseting*, as Irina said. For a couple of years already it had become something of a must. All the girls did it; it was normal and fun. See for yourselves: pictures of skimpily-dressed girls travel around on the various youth sites, open to everybody. Scandal Point was the most popular; all the girls wanted to show off their pictures there.

That was exactly the reason why taking pictures at the Pet Shop didn't seem like a big deal. It didn't feel bad to take off your clothes in front of strange men, and it didn't feel bad to include little animals in the pictures. I preferred Miss Frank, of course. As a matter of fact, it was thrilling. Animal stuff was nice. It was fun to learn to pose properly, to lie with a bunny in my lap on the couch, and to imagine I was a totally different person. Sexy Babe, 69 Kitten, Miss Rain, Cute Face, Kinky Angel. Good girl, girl of many good names, smiled our black-skinned photographer. He was the one who came up with the names while looking at the finished pictures.

Soon after our first photo sessions, Lido asked us to come and visit him at Pet Wholesale, the Wet Pet Club. You must've taken all kinds of fucking dance lessons, trained for dance shows or something? Do you know the basics of waiting tables? To take and give from the right, et cetera? asked Lido, chewing a piece of gum and tapping his fingers on a harmonica.

Pole dancing and lap dancing would be easy jobs for us. Little clothing, plenty of attitude. We'd receive free sessions in the solarium and the outfits as extra pay. On weekends, there would be fun client events, in which all the Pet Shop dancers could take part. Most importantly, the pay would be good.

That Kind of a Year of the Peacock

*

Everything sucks, mumbled Randi to himself from the window seat in row fourteen on the airplane. The metal ringing bowl was in a small red bag somewhere down in the bowels of the plane. He hadn't counted how many tiny navel jewels there had been. Many, that's for sure, and they really looked like little larva, something that ancient relatives might have collected from leaves and ate. Raw. Fucking hell. Everything sucks. Ringo was skimming off the top, and Lido hadn't put up with it. That's why his brother's luck had run out, but Randi wasn't ready yet to think through it all, not quite yet, even though it was the reason he couldn't take it anymore.

Actually, Randi had been taking more shit than he could handle. It was also because of that last night and those girls that Randi's shit-absorbing capacity—if he even had one—had overflowed. That blonde girl's reddish-haired friend had fallen down some stairs in the middle of the party. There she lay, moaning, on the stone floor of the warehouse. The music thundered. Everyone was totally messed up. At some point, Randi suggested it might be a good idea to call a doctor, and Lido had become furious and started to drag the fallen girl back up the staircase. She was completely limp, unconscious. That's when the other girls got nervous. They seemed like birds that had gotten loose, too small yet and still unable to fly, birds flapping around back and forth, crying for Mother, and making horrible noise.

The result was complete chaos, and Lido's bodyguards, with their arms folded, waited for instructions.

✳

The ringing bowl that Mother had given him bulged from the little red travel bag. Randi had washed it carefully in the airport men's room before packing it in the bag. At some point, Ringo had taken it for himself; used it to annoy Randi because he knew his little brother would be offended.

The bowl had smelled horrible. Someone had urinated into it, and thrown used condoms in it. Dirty paper towels. Cigarette stubs. The girls had spat into it. Who knows what else? It was disgusting. At the very last moment, Randi had run to look for the bowl. He had rushed past the threatening bodyguards and was afraid that the bowl had been taken somewhere.

When he left, Randi looked around one more time. He saw the Wet Pet Club burning.

✳

Why such an impulse? What could cause such an act? Maybe Ringo's disappearance, maybe the blonde girl and her friend, maybe Lido's arrogance, which had become unbearable. Only a few nights earlier, some of the girls had been shoved into snowdrifts, without any clothes on. That had been for fun—some young man's bachelor party; Lido had recently found a great market for those. The girls were forced to dig their clothes out of the snowdrifts. Randi didn't want to think about it anymore.

✳

Randi had planned everything in advance—precisely, to the smallest detail.

He had gone to say goodbye to Uncle Chanu. He told him that Lalla's sons would be returning home. He needn't worry; this phase of his life lasted only for a year. Randi wished the laundry success, gave Chanu the loaf of bread he had baked himself—the last one baked in that country and in that small oven. It should've been called a pancake since it didn't look right; not *naan* and not *chapati* but something between a tortilla and flatbread.

Chanu bowed and hugged his nephew, his eyes moist. Give my greetings to everyone at home. He handed Randi a pink hyacinth. A piece of a northern Christmas.

Looking at the hyacinth, lying awake in bed with his hands behind his head, Randi planned it all. He waited for the right moment; and then it came, after the girl with reddish hair had fallen down the staircase.

Nothing could go wrong.

Randi was absolutely certain at the time that there were no more girls or clients on the upper floor. In the general confusion, the club had emptied out. One of Lido's bodyguards had carried the limp girl with the light-reddish hair outside to a car, and when the man did not return, Randi decided that they had, after all, taken her to a hospital for treatment.

Lido and three other men had stayed behind and sat in one of the upstairs "meeting rooms." Their voices were muffled, talking in Lido's native language.

Randi hadn't seen the blonde-haired girl anywhere in the chaos of the emptying club. He was disappointed, and missed seeing her one last time. He wanted to touch the girl; not Vanilla Bebe nor Olivia Silva, but the slender blonde girl who had eyes the color of blue-gray water and the world's most beautiful smile. Randi wanted to hand her his thick sweater, set it on her shoulders, and while doing so, touch her arm, and the hollow at the nape of her neck.

Randi lit the match. That's how simple it was. The hamsters' sawdust and the rabbits' hay burned with a joyful cracking sound. In the flames, all the colors of his home country: henna-red, emerald-green, indigo-blue, and glowing saffron. And soon the whole big building was in flames; Lido, with his clattering boots and overstuffed bags, rushing downstairs and outside through the smoke. Lido's barked commands: Fuck! Go get the rest of the shit! What are you fucking standing there for? Expressions of surprise in the glow of the flames. Goodbye, Lido.

What Anne Frank Didn't Have Time to Find Out

1.

If I had still been writing my diary on that Sunday night in December, what would I have written?

Maybe something like: How can I help you? Mouth, breasts, vagina, anus, armpits. Yes, we take most credit cards.

Or, maybe: A lap dance is a dance among other dances. To be a human vine on the altar of men.

Or: I'm fucking stupid. But fuck, I'm very good at it.

I might have written that some men were chinchillas, some were turtles, or praying mantises. There were a lot of snakes and lizards out at night. Birds were fewer in number. Mollusks crawled across the skin from some moist darkness. They left a slimy path behind them on the stomach. Some had cold and sleek fur; some were a dark cavalcade of wolves.

But the Baptist was different.

When the Baptist first saw me dancing at the Wet Pet Club, I was high. A pink shower of stars was going round and round in my head. I was holding Miss Frank, even as I was dancing.

What do I, in the end, remember of that long weekend? The club was full, the music was pounding, the lights were flashing on the windowless walls. Laughter and the jangle of glasses. Some wanted to watch movies, some were bustling about in groups. I danced with many and for many. Jelena and Mirza served more and more rounds of Pink Stars. The room floated in darkness, heavenly debris, icebergs, flying bunnies, escaping whales. The Baptist took me into his lap. He talked about Satan and sex and salvation; he stroked my head—that I remember. I talked to him about the heavenly debris and the whales. I was messed up. He said he was my salvation. He told me he had chosen me from all the girls. Your mother betrayed you, your father defiled you, your friend seduced you.

Somewhere a ways from the burning building, two people stood by as the Baptist carried me to his car. A homeless couple who were interviewed on the morning TV shows and pictured in the newspaper. The couple watched the flames, which had already pierced the ceiling of the industrial hall. The couple didn't mention a word about us to anyone.

Rumors of the forbidden surrounded us. We stepped into the intermediate state between water and ice. Into another world.

2.

Who did the dirty work? Who put Linda in sweatpants, carried her that slushy December night to the construction site, dumped her body, and covered her with dirt and debris?

Nothing was discovered, nobody named. It was as if the club had never existed. Everything that hadn't burned was destroyed quickly, razed to the ground.

Rumors about the fire and the Pet Shop at the shopping center circulated for a while around our school, until they eventually subsided and dissolved into the ordinary discussion around quizzes, dating, relationships, and matriculation exams. The rumors turned into fictional stories, myths, legends, and then died away.

The Pet Shop was searched after our disappearance; a second time, even more thoroughly, after Linda was found; and yet again, after Tony's last questioning. The police tried to connect the shop to our disappearance, but nothing that could have led to any charges could be squeezed out, even from the regular clients. Penalty Box was persistent, though. He had always thought that pet owners, especially those who had dogs and walked them, were most helpful to the police.

Many girls had worked in the shop during the fall. But that's always the case in a pet store. None of the employees contacted by the police could tell them anything all that unusual. The same thing with regular clients.

Nothing significant was found in the store's backroom either, of course. Only piles of rubber bones for dogs, sand for cats, and a well-kept little photo studio. Even the fire inspector gave the place a clean bill of health. The owner of the store, a handsome middle-aged woman, who also owned a flower shop in the same shopping center, felt sorry for the fate of the disappeared girls. She had, of course, read everything about it in the newspapers.

Penalty Box wondered about the woman, and went to see her a couple more times. He leaned against the store counter—under which there were a few pieces of my bubble gum—and asked about this and that. What kind of girls made the best workers and what sort of wages did she pay them? The majority of the girls had been underage and, hence, could not work the cash register. Had that caused problems? How did she divide her time between animals and flowers? Wasn't it difficult to manage two businesses? Penalty Box asked if the woman visited a solarium or tanning booth regularly or had she recently gone on a vacation. And so on. But Penalty Box couldn't catch her in anything. Time to blow the whistle, he said. Call a time-out.

The Pet Shop seemed like a run-of-the mill animal store. It looked well taken care of. All the documents were in order.

Linda was found on the construction site of a new residential neighborhood when contaminated soil was being removed from the children's future playground. The site was blocked off, construction halted. The police immediately launched a wide search.

They searched for me in the same area with the help of cadaver dogs, and, because of Linda and me, people had to wait before they could move into their new homes. Some cancelled their purchases, partly because of the contamination and partly because the corpse of a girl had been found there. Owners of the new development gnashed their teeth, but what can you do? Penalty Box was strict. Just think if that were your own child. That worked.

Linda had a flawless set of teeth, which meant that the forensic identification took some time. Penalty Box called my mother and gave her the news before contacting Anita. In addition to Penalty Box and my mother, a police chaplain was also present when Anita was given the news.

My mother accompanied Anita to the Office of the Medical Examiner to identify Linda. It was a sunny spring day, and painfully bright to eyes already raw from crying. Jason wanted to come along, but Mother wouldn't let him. Sulking, he didn't want to go to school that day. So instead, he sat in my room, looked through the photo albums, and wrote me by hand the first long letter of his life. It started: I'm absolutely certain you're alive, you bitch! Everybody's just faking it—you too!

Linda's death occupied the minds of the police for a long time, and it still does every couple of years. Linda was wearing an Adidas jogging outfit that Anita had never seen before on her daughter. Her body had mild bruises here and there. It seemed as if she had fallen somewhere; a few broken bones supported that hypothesis. There were no signs of sexual violence, and no alcohol or drugs in her system. It seemed as if she had been run over, and the driver, who had fled the scene, was behind the deed. Every clue was thoroughly investigated—in vain. At this point, the case is a total mystery, noted Penalty Box to a journalist who interviewed him. And the other girl remains missing, another journalist reminded him. We are more than painfully aware of that, responded Penalty Box.

Lido had already become Arseni Vitali by then. Or Mustafa Raban. Someone beyond my country's borders. Ringo would be found a couple of years later; or rather, parts of him would be found: the hands that had been cut off were found at the bottom of a freezer in a raided restaurant. Those hands would end up in the unsolved files of the Office of the Medical Examiner. Palms that glowed in their plastic bags. Palms like lit-up starfish. Many pathologists and police investigators examined them, studied them. Eventually, they were used for instructional purposes. Ringo became a puzzle, the parts named Glowing Right Palm and Glowing Left Palm. In the years to follow, when isolated bones or parts of a male body were found—parts of a body that didn't seem to belong to the native population—they were always first matched against Ringo. Would this fit with Glowing Palms? What a pity. Many wanted to solve the puzzle.

3.

After my disappearance, slowly over time, Muma stopped speaking. It happened within a couple of years and in such a stealthy manner that nobody really noticed at first. She didn't want to meet her friends any more; she no longer wished to play bridge or watch TV. She did not foster any hope. She was absolutely certain that I was dead, by an act of violence, and that it was first and foremost her fault, because she had believed in me and allowed me to go.

In the beginning, Muma took care of my mother, as if she were a small child. She brought her Mother's favorite foods that she herself had cooked. She kept the kitchen clean, sorted the mail, and called daily to ask how she was doing. Papsi tried to comfort Mother in his own way. He brought her books that he thought appropriate. When spring came, he brought her small bags of seeds for kitchen herbs. He showed her some of his most interesting new stamps: Monaco and the picture of the Princess, Pakistan, and the cobra de capello.

From the very start, Mother tried to convince Muma and Papsi that she didn't blame them for anything. The same thing might have happened even if Mother had been at home that week.

Muma was a wise person, even though she swallowed my lies hook, line, and sinker. She always wanted to believe me, even though I constantly asked her for money for the same things. When I forgot my earlier lies and was embarrassingly caught in another, I came up with new white lies.

Muma and Papsi were complicit in my schemes. They wanted to please me. It was actually quite touching, to the point of being sickening, but it fit our plans, Linda's and mine, better than well.

And oh how I had been waiting for that one weekend at the end of fall, with Mother abroad and all that freedom available!

There's a time for everything, says Papsi and laughs. I can hear his voice all the way here. No longer does he reminisce about the weddings and funerals. He wouldn't recognize me now, even if I were to return. He no longer recognizes his wife and his children either.

Everything is familiar and strange. Muma takes pills so she'll forget, and Papsi takes pills to remember.

4.

Paula Pauliina liked to read stories to me when she was putting me to bed. When a nice little girl dies, read Paula Pauliina in her monotone voice from a book of Hans Christian Andersen's fairy tales, she flies with an angel over her dear, old places to bid them farewell, one at a time. She has wide, white wings on her back, and in her hand she carries a bunch of flowers, a gift to God.

I remember that fairy tale whenever I look online at satellite images of my hometown, an aerial map; it's as if I'm flying above the houses and parks. The trees in the schoolyard have grown; new asphalt roads are everywhere; houses have been torn down and new ones built in their stead; I see plenty of parking places and modern shopping centers.

Sometimes I imagine I can see Mother in the window looking out on the street. I wave with my index finger.

I'm not spoken of often any more. My name doesn't get mentioned weekly. Sometimes, in the middle of the night, I wake up hearing Tony's voice—as I remember it, soft, the voice of a choir boy. He's whispering my name—Jasmin, Jasmin. Sometimes, between our tender kisses, he calls me Jade. In fact, I've always hoped that Tony would track me down somehow, that one day he'd stand at the electric gate with his head tilted, and I'd be watching him in the kitchen monitors. My restless moonlight knight in his shining armor!

Sometimes I float above the house where Muma and Papsi used to live. I see the berry bushes and rows of carrots. Papsi had a green thumb. He understood all kinds of seeds, when they should be sown, and when not. Papsi followed the moon's cycles, and he could feel the best planting times in his knees, or so he always claimed. A human body is useful for many things, he said, laughing, when I asked about it. I've got soulful knees.

Not all plants get along with each other, just like people, he told me. The tubers push each other; they smother their competitors. And sometimes, seeds haphazardly thrown on the ground will grow happily in all directions, without a care for anyone else.

5.

Then there was the phase when Mother wanted desperately to forget it all. She thought about adopting a girl my age from China or India, or about taking a teenage foster child to live with her and Jason.

For some time, Mother couldn't read any articles about crime in the newspapers. After me, dozens of girls, boys, young adults, and old people disappeared; there were hundreds of robberies, sex crimes, murders, executions, all kinds of problems typical of today's urban culture. But Mother wanted only to hear about the bright side of life—concerts, art exhibits, ballet, Eurovision song contests, elections, apartments for sale, travel ads. Although Mother sometimes took antidepressants, she never seriously thought about taking her own life. She eagerly wanted to live—that's what she thought—until I was found. That gave her life meaning.

Neither did Mother ever seriously plan to move away. During the first few years after my disappearance, you couldn't convince her to travel out of the country, since she was absolutely certain the moment the plane left the ground, I'd be found somewhere, and she'd be far away.

The search for the perpetrator will never end, Penalty Box said to Mother. That was his way of comforting her.

And neither will my pain, thought Mother.

6.

Longing for love, for the sensual, for the joyous, for the thrill. For pain too, hard pain. Horrid, terrifying, contradictory, illusive, tolerable, pleasurable. Why was it so wonderful? Why was it so tempting?

I'm in a family counseling center, and I let it out. I give my account, I shake, I cry. The child psychiatrist and the school counselor, Mother and Father.

I try to remember things I've forgotten.

They're making a good girl out of me again.

Jasmin Victoria Martin is being updated. Neat, cool, simple.

I still wake up to the familiar nightmare. Mother and Father and Mikael are around me. In the background, the voices of Jason, Muma, Papsi. Tony, Merita, Viola.

Here I am. Instead of causes, I've been looking for consequences, and there are plenty of those, many, too many to count.

Monday

by Sara Martin

Today—was it only this morning that I opened my office door, like any weekday morning, and heard the cell phone ringing in my purse? Paula Pauliina had turned on the TV, which was showing coverage of a fire on the morning news show, and the first client was already waiting in the chair with a women's magazine in her hand.

I drive back to my office and, without turning on the lights, walk to the reception room. It feels as if I've forgotten something here. I look at myself in the mirror. I look until tears begin to flow. Was it today, on Monday, when a young woman and a young man came into the room, out of breath and full of laughter, right away wanting an ultrasound picture of their future child. Was it today the doctor let out a laugh and said it might be a bit too early still; nothing could be seen yet.

Was it early or was it late?

I browse through my appointments calendar. Names, arrows, exclamation points. The police suggested I take a few days off. They'd be in touch. As soon as they heard something. And even if they didn't. I was given the name of a contact person and a phone number, a crisis helpline. If it seemed necessary. And even if it didn't. Maybe after a couple of days. Unless the girl had already returned by then. I could, of course, write myself a prescription for Cipramil. If it seemed necessary. And even if it didn't.

The Smell of Smoke

*

Randi did return home. He went directly to his room with his bags. For two weeks he slept under a mosquito net, didn't want to talk to anyone, and refused to meet anybody.

Ringo will definitely come back later, he whispered to Anil when he had opened his eyes a little. Ringo still has things to do. You have to keep striking while the iron is hot, but he'll definitely return. And Anil believed. And Mother Lalla believed when Anil told her what her youngest child had said.

Mother Lalla sniffed Randi's hair and inhaled a slight whiff of smoke. With her eyes closed, she breathed deeply the foreign smells her younger son had brought home with him. She hoped they would soon evaporate. And they did—the smells reverted to the old smells; but the boy, from then on, was different.

They waited patiently. Many rains, many house cleanings, arrivals and departures of many young male relatives. Anil followed one to the station and returned with another, continued to live with her mother, work in the office, prepare food, wash the laundry, and in the evenings still find time to take classes.

And on the hallway wall, in their small glass cases, were the butterflies whose yellowish wings were like pieces of old maps.

*

Often, years after all of this, Randi thinks about the blonde girl and her friend. He imagines different fates for each of them, just as he does for the large bird that nobody wanted to buy at the pet store. He's already told his son about the bird. His son's question always is: Oh, was it one of those dodo birds? Father's stories are all about prehistoric times.

That's how Randi himself sometimes feels about that year of his youth in the north. Occasionally, his wife asks questions. She mourns the fate of big brother Karim. Randi has tried to discover the whereabouts of Karim Suraweera; he's sent messages and inquiries to various places in the world. It's possible that his brother is still alive somewhere, isn't it? And maybe the blonde girl and her friend now live somewhere with their families and their children, trying to forget a certain period of time, in the same way that Doctor Randi Suraweera has tried to forget, almost completely. And his wife, Chanda, doesn't ask. She lets the memories be, just like that round metal bowl on the hallway table in front of the mirror, the one where Randi insists on keeping his eyeglasses. He won't allow the bowl to be moved, and won't put his glasses in a case. Chanda lets her husband think about the snow-covered paths where the crushed mountain ash berries looked just like blood. She lets him remember the early morning fishing trips to the bank of the rapids, the spotted salmon whose writhing bodies at the bottom of the bag made him long for the riverbank back home.

Randi's third child and his first daughter is named Jasmin. It's a name that his wife happily accepts. Doctor Randi Suraweera, with a specialization in gynecology, attaches his nameplate on the door of the Tanhai clinic. He's starting to reach the age when the afternoon sun's heat stings his arms and tires his body. And he's no longer reluctant when he lines up the worn photos of relatives, chosen by his wife and faded by the sun, in a row on his desk. Generations, flaps of butterfly wings, Father's travels to the mountains, and Mother's lullabies—even the one where a little star dies out, and in different place, simultaneously, another small star lights up. So travels time in light, so travels light in time.

In the afternoons, the smell of smoke rises from the willows on the canal bank or from the lane at the end of which the street kitchens are warming their pots. And with that smell of smoke, a picture always develops in Randi's mind—a picture of a pale girl, an adventurous one, things you can't mention to your wife or at the clinic or over the dinner table. Yet that world existed, *when your heart's on fire, you must realize, smoke gets in your eyes*. In order to stave off a certain memory, Randi lights a cigarette and inhales the first puffs as deeply as he can. And every now and then it feels as if somebody, somewhere, were handing him an ashtray, a light breath of wind, a pale hand, such a very narrow wrist.

Before, Now, If

1.

The room is ready. My own room is finally ready.

Recently, I've been busily renovating. I've repaired the gardener's cottage, which with time has become my favorite place. I've decorated it pink and white. From the windows, I can see the sea and the part of the garden where my namesake flowers grow. Various fragrant bushes meander across the top of the wall. Never, even in an English garden magazine, have I ever seen anything like the pillar roses that the Baptist planted.

I remember when I was first allowed to walk freely in the garden of those meticulous nuns, and I saw the marble tombstones that were worn smooth, the names and years faded away. I thought that I, too, would die here, and that I would eventually take my place among these unknown devout sisters. I looked at the decorative bushes, with their shapes still resembling animal forms, and I admired the arbor formed by lime trees. In their day, the nunnery and the hospital were built to protect the inhabitants against the Devil who had become flesh. That's what the Baptist told me. And so it was truly ironic that a couple centuries later the dilapidated house functioned as a bordello for soldiers on leave. I wouldn't have believed that once again I would stand and watch this scene, full of tenderness towards all those who had lived, healed, suffered, rejoiced, made love within the house, full of tenderness towards the unknown and the nameless.

Yesterday I cut my hair and, after a long time, looked at myself in the mirror I found in the Baptist's desk drawer. He told me he had gotten rid of all the mirrors in the house, but he hadn't, after all. I turned my head from side to side, and it felt odd not to have my hair brush across my cheeks.

Every day I study the various works of art: paintings, vases, crowns, jewelry, statues. I walk along the corridors, ascend to the second and third floors, and hear the Baptist's voice over my shoulder: No brunettes among the Madonna pictures of Florence. See the piousness of the little girl's expression—her devotion, the power of her judgment. Pay attention to Mr. Historian of Jurisprudence's hand position. Mrs. So-and-So has become enamored with her portrait painter, and the painter's narcissism again is displayed in the way he's painted the forbidden glow in Madam's eyes. A monkey named Tobruk was a gift from a friend—take a careful look at the animal's left ring finger: lo and behold, there's a coat of arms on it. And next, let's look at three court paintings from the seventeenth century; all of them portray fireworks. And next, the amphorae, and after those it's time for Egyptian art...

I barely watch TV, but if I do, I pull out some VHS tape of a series, most often British, that the Baptist recorded for me. And then I feel as if he were still present. We sit next to each other on the sofa in the green parlor, facing the same direction, and watch.

At times, I listen to music, mostly flamenco and classical, which the Baptist loved. Sometimes, I play the piano myself, and diligently change the glass of champagne under the lid of the grand piano, just like the Baptist taught. I ride Bianca regularly, and I feed the stray cats that climb over the wall, as well as the peacocks that stomp about in the yard. The mail still brings me my magazines. I'm familiar with the most recent news about the ozone layer, the floods, the avalanches, and the long periods of heat and drought. I know what should be thought about the new U.S.

president, and I know about the speech the newly-elected Russian head of state recently gave in the Duma. I follow the internal strife within the European Union, and I know that fighting continues in the Gaza Strip.

I never graduated from high school, but I've studied several languages, and the Baptist has told me more about history and nature than I probably would have absorbed in school. I know everything about Dutch light and Vermeer. I've also become such a skillful curator that, for instance, yesterday an art collector, asked me, now known as the Baptist's nephew Martin Huber, to check out the crack in a small onyx statue. Right now, I'm evaluating a Mondrian owned by one of the Baptist's longtime customers. It's bright and hard, with a glaring white background, and, unfortunately, I have to tell the owner that it's a fake.

2.

For a few years after my disappearance, Mother didn't observe Christmas. When she and Father got back together, Christmas returned to their calendar. Along with that, they started going to church and rejoined the parish.

These days, Jason has a crush on the school librarian. For years, he hasn't touched a soccer ball, and he gave all his sports equipment to his stepbrother, Luka. Mother and Father's "evening star" Victoria, or Vicki, is now seven years old. She just started elementary school, and, unfortunately, I've only seen two pictures of her—one when she was a baby and one as a kindergartner.

Mother has concentrated first and foremost on being a mother, at least for now, and hasn't thought about returning to being a doctor, even though Father, to her big surprise, encouraged her to reopen her practice.

Today people have more money at their disposal than ever before, and they're happy to spend it on themselves, observed the one-time world reformer.

Since *Monday*, Mother has written a couple of nonfiction books about women's self care and natural medicine, and about menopause. Every now and then, she visits various nursing homes to cut patients' hair and teach origami to those interested in learning.

I do know that Vicki was baptized in church. The recently-retired Penalty Box was invited to be her godfather, and during the reception following the baptism, after a long time, they talked about me and my case. Penalty Box expressed regret that he was still wearing a beard on his chin. He would've been so happy to shave it off in my honor. He told Mother that he would still return to his office every now and then, simply to delve back into my files once more. The journey to a nearby place may sometimes be long, but a player must never give up, and the game must go on.

Ultimate causes can't always be determined. And you can't google everything. Even though I can upload an image of my face and ask a program to search for the closest match among movie stars, no website in the world can find the Jasmin that I might have become.

What are all the things that Mother and I would have bickered about? How many times has Jason escaped a scolding because of me? Which prospective boyfriends would Father Fred have disapproved?

Sometimes I wake up hearing Linda's voice. Wake up, Jasmin! she shrieks, pounding my face with a pillow. Get your ass up, Jasmin! I catch a whiff of her scent, just as I caught it for the first time when she sat down next to me at school.

I keep my eyes closed until I've mustered enough strength to open them and see that my friend isn't there. Nor the Linda she could have become.

Last summer, once again, I thought I saw her. I was running errands for the Baptist in town, dressed as Martin, as I usually did when we were out together. A tall blonde woman pushed a baby carriage directly into my stomach. With a quick motion, she pulled the carriage back and continued to walk past me as if nothing had happened. I breathed sharply and curled over in pain. I looked up at her from knee level. Honey blonde hair swaying, safari shorts, rhinestone sneakers. Absolutely and certainly Linda. But why didn't she recognize me? Was it my short brown hair? The glasses I started wearing a few years ago?

My stomach hurt for a long time after that. I imagined there was a child in there; that I would accompany the woman who looked like Linda; that I would soon be a mother who, in crowds, would be shoving her baby into people's laps.

What kind of mothers would we have been? Never, ever, did we talk about such things. Motherhood was not a part of any plan for our future. We both abhorred younger children and graded their hideousness: Tony's little sister got an A-plus, and Jason straight Cs.

I think about Merita and the games we played together in kindergarten. During roll call, we'd flee and share a hiding place under the stairs. That was a land of almonds and raisins, our secret girl country, and we believed that nobody could see us there. I think about my first kiss from a boy whose name I simply can't remember. Tony's caresses on his parents' bed. The day my classmates graduated from high school and left for college to pursue their dreams. Some are already fathers and mothers. Some have already had several years of married bliss.

My world is comprised of three components. Before. Now. If.

What if I say that the Baptist's wife and young daughter died in a shipwreck a long time ago, and the Baptist was supposed to have been with them, but had to cancel at the last moment due to an emergency at work? What if I reveal that he lived with his mother, and that she abused him, occasionally tying him up for days without food or drink in a four-poster bed in the attic? What if I recount how his fanatically religious parents, along with their like-minded friends, threw him from the end of a pier into the water, time after time, as part of some strange water ritual?

Or maybe the Baptist really was Mr. Dakota, who, in addition to his top academic job, did business in a wide variety of countries, through middlemen, bribes, and errand boys. Or maybe the truth is that I, Jasmin Victoria Martin, asked him to take me with him. That it was I who persuaded him to take me along.

Monday
by Sara Martin

The light in the stairwell dies out just as I open the door to my apartment. I collect Monday's mail from the hallway floor—bills, an invitation to the medical center Christmas party, an invitation to another conference, another invitation: to the opening of the art exhibit of Mikael's niece, and junk mail.

A piece of glass still glitters on the hallway floor. Why didn't I notice it this morning? Such a big piece, from the crystal bowl. Somebody could've stepped on it. Somebody who? I pick up the piece of glass and place it on the hallway table. The light turns on, the light turns off. My head hurts, a sharp pain, and I grasp the hallway table with both hands.

In the beginning of December the city is at its ugliest, gray and slushy, windy, full of secrets. People are mulling over divorce, people are quarreling in doorways, promises are being broken at Christmas parties, some won't return home.

I had gone to a farewell dinner with my foreign colleagues. That was followed by the goodbye rituals, a well-known rite at all the conferences: the exchange of business cards; hugs at the airport restaurant, bags bulging with your own and others' most recent studies; thin laptop cases; waves of goodbye and well-wishes; and then the last flight home. It was already well beyond midnight when we arrived at my place—that is, the night guest, who at the last moment had rearranged his flights, and me. After the man had fallen asleep next to me post-intercourse, I kept thinking about Mikael, once again. I had carefully opened the drawer of my nightstand and looked at the picture of a blond man with curly hair. Had I loved him too much, at the expense of everything else?

Suddenly I feel like making a phone call. To whom? To Ella.

Ella answers the phone in exactly the same manner as thirty-five years ago.

"Ella speaking. Hello, who is calling?"

I listen to her for a moment and then say, "Sorry, wrong number."

Ella had frizzy hair. What else do I remember? I go to my dresser and pull out a bright red album. Class pictures are stuffed between the pages, mostly loose. It takes a while before I find her. The frizzy-haired girl in the back row, large front teeth, dimples, charming.

Jasmin Victoria Martin disappeared during the first week of December in the City of O. The last eyewitness account of her was made in the stairwell of her friend's apartment building on Friday, December first, around six-thirty p.m. The same night, a girl who resembled Jasmin Martin was observed at a nearby store, the shopping center, on a bus, and in the metro. At the time of her disappearance, Jasmin Martin was wearing tight faded jeans, a white T-shirt, and a hooded pink sweatshirt with the face of a laughing black monkey on the back. Around her neck she wore silver-colored chains and in her ears pearl earrings and silver hoops. She was carrying a turquoise backpack and possibly a small, blue-and-white duffel bag.

Good evening. Tonight on Police TV, among other things, we'll discuss the case of Jasmin Martin, who disappeared a year ago.

Good evening. Tonight Police TV revisits a missing persons case from two years ago.

At the time of her disappearance, Jasmin Martin was five feet six-and-a-half inches tall and of slender build. She had straight blonde hair that fell to her shoulders. Her eyes were bluish gray.

The police said that they suspect foul play in the case, and are conducting a criminal investigation.

I can't live anymore, I said, first to one psychiatrist and then to another, but nevertheless, I could.

I didn't cry at Linda's memorial service, nor did I cry at Anita's funeral.

Jasmin, the Runaway. Jasmin, the Prodigal Daughter. Be what you are, but come back home, I pleaded in all the magazine interviews. One who has disappeared has not been lost.

Accusation. Defeat. Revenge. How do you take revenge against someone who is never coming back? By forgetting? By burning her possessions, one after another? By killing the one who is longing for, that is, yourself? No! Soon it's another Christmas again. Soon it's another New Year. And now we are approaching Easter. Through His death He destroyed the power of death.

Jasmin walks in the front door, opens the car door, descends the steps from a train with a bunny in her arms, climbs in through the balcony, through the window, the bathroom, arises from a lake, wades from the sea wearing a diving mask and a snorkel hanging from her neck, just like that. The diving took a bit longer than I thought. Sorry, Mom. Jasmin calls one summer day. From somewhere. On a Monday. In the background I can hear the sounds of a botanical garden—water gurgles and birds whistle.

Goodness, Jasmin, where are you?

Fuck you, you stinking old bitch.

Who is it?

Spring. The window is left ajar for a day. A fly buzzes between the glass panes, can't escape.

Hi, Mom!

Jasmin hollers from her room. There's a turquoise backpack on the hallway floor. Next to it, she's kicked off her sneakers. A long pink scarf and a white quilted sweatshirt with pink fur around the edges of the hood.

Oh, you're home already! Did you remember to reheat your dinner?

Yeah, of course, and I'm done with my homework. Be quiet, I'm on the computer!

Baptism

Did Laura masturbate? Did Beatrice achieve vaginal orgasms? Did Julia have sex dreams? Joan of Arc, God's nymphomaniac! Cut her hair and burn her at the stake! Was Milena a whore? What about Siri von Essen? And Rosa Luxembourg, that Commie coquette. Ulrike Meinhof, that terrorist bitch who slept with everyone, just for the cause.

Did Emile Zola just stop by? I'm absolutely certain I saw Vladimir Nabokov yesterday. Henry Miller hasn't left the place for a month, right? He's even writing here, isn't he? Is that Fidel's beard peeping from the doorway? Or Hemingway's? Did he tell you about his catch this time?

I've seen all the most beautiful beach children of Barbados. Saithon, Malai, Sawittree, where are you? I saved them too. Welcome Suleika, Debora, Hagar. I rebaptized them. They were expected to receive one thousand men, and only then would there be negotiations about tickets for the boat and the return of their passports. I saved them from Satan himself. I saved children from refugee camps, children ravaged by war, abused by both their own and the enemy's soldiers, and eventually even by the peacekeepers. They, too, were Satan's camouflaged underlings. My name is the Baptist. I am the Savior. Hallelujah. Amen.

Are you there?

I'm here.

As I write these lines, the Baptist is already dead. It's early in the morning. It's that time when the bartender's jokes become lame, the dance pole is sticky; when people keep dozing off on corner couches, when everyone's too tired to start anything.

The vaulted room is dim and cool, a puzzle, like the man who recently died and with whom I've lived the past twelve years. On the walls around me are broken pieces of mosaic, found under lava; frescos from bordellos, where everyone is smiling and laughing while making merry. On the floor, against the wall, is a piece from a cave supported in a frame, and a painting from somewhere in the Sahara that portrays people floating in water—the most valuable of the artifacts the Baptist owns. According to his own words, he bought and sold things whose purchase price, or sales price, for that matter, could not be determined. He asked me to put the cave painting diagonally opposite his bed so he could see it. It took me two days to move the block of stone.

There are still dark plums and grapes on the table, his last supper. When I noticed the bread crumbling in his shaking hands and the soup growing cold on the tray, I peeled the plums and grapes in my mouth with my teeth, and then pushed the meat of the fruit into his mouth with my tongue. Then I rinsed it down his throat with a swallow of green tea from his glass. With a little sound of thanks from him, I knew he was still conscious. He smiled. A caterpillar on his shoulder.

He told me that my skin is sonnets and ice cream. He told me that I'm a statuesque child, transparent like an alabaster maiden or an ice sculpture from my home country. He promised to whittle sin away from me, and selfishness, and the halter top superficiality. He would make me even brighter.

His hands. His blue eyes. His hair that smelled of date pipe tobacco. He was a cypress, dark and sharp, not resembling anyone else. I don't hate him. I don't miss him. I don't regret my attempts to flee, my pouting silences, my fake illnesses. I bit him in many places. I crushed his thumb. I stuck a fork into his knuckles. I knew his body better than that of my mother's. I learned the full color spectrum of bruises from bluish-black to rusty red to saffron yellow, on my own skin as well as on his. I could draw his heraldic emblem in my sleep: a crown, with buds sprouting from its points. During his trips, I rummaged through his stuff when Esther wasn't looking. I became skillful at picking locks. I was especially interested in the large, locked glass cabinet where he kept binders labeled *Sexualia*, with different sets of dates.

For a long time, I called him Jim Thompson even though I knew it wasn't his real name. I loathe, hate, despise you; I pity you; I will kill you as soon as I can!

He ignored my cries. He told me about a Phoenician king, who killed a dragon and buried its teeth in a field. Later, soldiers and heroes grew in the field.

I already miss his voice: You're making a racket as if you were the Whore of Babylon!

I long for his instruction. If *Luxuria* means lasciviousness, how should one truthfully understand *luxurious*? the Baptist lectured as he showed me the tricks of gilding.

His name was Bruno Max Huber, and he was a scholar. He wrote several books and traveled around the world. He had a diamond in his earlobe. He had dimples. He knew everything about phallic sacrifice, orchids, and lap dancing. His wine cellar remains without comparison. He died before he could finish writing his latest book; I disappeared before finishing my last school essay. Even now I can hear the Baptist's laughter. He liked my childish sense of humor. He liked everything childish about me. Sometimes, when I said something especially funny, he slapped me on my cheek—not so that it would hurt, but so that a warm feeling would linger on my cheek for a long time.

I've washed his body for the last time. When I was pouring water on his pale forehead, I remembered how he cleansed me for the first time: rinsed me clean of sin, gave me the name Ruth in baptism twelve years ago, and I can't imagine another name for myself anymore.

I've combed his hair and parted it carefully down the middle, just as he himself used to do. I've cut one gray lock from the nape of his neck to keep, I've clothed him, tucked him in, followed all of his wishes to the very end. His grave will be next to Rebekah, Esther, and Miss Frank.

When Paula Pauliina called and asked me in my native language if it was Jasmin speaking, it took me a moment, only a moment, before I chose another language and answered as if I hadn't heard anything: Hello? Who's there? Who are you trying to reach? I can't understand you.

Paula Pauliina let out an apprehensive laugh and said, Don't you try to pull my leg, little lady. I recognized your voice right away.

Little lady. Pull my leg. She used phrases like that. They hit me like meteors from the sky; they burned a hole in my soul—yes, in what is left of it.

She coughed and sniffed. We were quiet. The telephone line cracked and hissed.

I sensed her confusion, which hadn't quite dared yet to become satisfaction. She had gone through a lot of trouble to break through my many levels of security. Hacker Pauliina. I almost felt like smiling. Evidently she had been taking IT classes recently. She must have worked her way through some brand-new service provider and eventually identified where in the world my messages had been sent from. She had been tracking me on the internet for two years. Never had she lacked patience, never! She had finally connected me from various sources, combed through my topic areas, collected my pseudonyms, the online personas I used. She had followed forums on tsunamis, active volcanoes, and earthquakes. She had monitored several Anne Frank discussion boards. Eventually, she connected the pseudonyms and the themes. She realized that the writer was one and the same. And bingo! Finally, through a new spyware program, which Téa Kantor had loaded onto her computer, she had found me.

Paula Pauliina had not mentioned anything to either Mother or Penalty Box, yet. The situation was almost too much for her to bear. She sounded agitated, and she half-hoped she was mistaken. I almost felt her sweat mixing with the smell of her perfume.

After our parents' divorce, Jason and I always tried to guess if Mother would come back or not. Are we going to stay with Father? What will happen? When Mother eventually returned and took us to Mikael's place, I didn't know if I was happy, or if Mother had actually returned or not.

Soon my mother will open the door and step into my room. The others are already asleep. She moves quietly. Instead of turning the lights on, she touches the candle wick with a match and waits until the flickering light rises to her shoulders, as if cloaking her in the atmosphere of this timeless room. Mother sits in my chair in the dark, sets her teacup on the table next to the candle, and turns on my computer, which she hasn't had the heart to give up, with its screensaver that pictures me and with the world of my girlhood on its hard drive.

Next to the old computer is a small new laptop. Mother thinks it's almost too fast. She feeds it a few words as bait, slings the words out there as if feeding a beast, keeps tossing evening snacks to the little barracuda. It swallows the snacks greedily, expecting to get a new bite right away.

I've been declared dead, but Mother won't quit feeding the computer. She won't quit searching. Still, she occasionally writes herself a prescription and takes a few pills for this melancholy, as she herself thinks of it—a melancholy that has become a part of life. Mother has not quit hoping.

And I haven't quit wondering what my purpose actually is. What is it that I would like to proclaim in this life?

For years, I thought about how I'd explain to you why things went as they did.

For years, I tried to create parables, take as points of comparison stories from the Bible, legends, fairy tales that I heard as a child.

For years, I wondered about my childhood, sought explanations there. I wrote down the poems I'd read, the pop songs I'd heard, even the nursery rhymes.

Hey Mother, sometimes tame birds go mad. They fly against windows, they rip off clothes from clotheslines, they dive through thorn bushes creating dust whirls. After these attacks, complete silence. In the end, even the final feather floats to the ground. A big axle grinds. And then everything continues, just like before.

Once again, the computer monitor fills up with material Mother never would have encountered and never would have known about had I spent all these years at home. In the evenings, she actually enjoys looking at the pages that pop up before her as they will: one picture is live, the next one is pulsating, naked skin glows, passwords are required, memberships, commitments, a credit card. Sometimes Mother's computer catches a virus from the skin pages, and she has to get herself and the little barracuda a new course of drug treatments, another antivirus program.

Hey, hey. Little Jasmin sits in Father's lap and swings her bunny.

That picture will not disappear. It's a perfectly complete composition. A day in the life of little Jasmin. In the city of O., years ago.

Pictures, websites, forums, galleries, catalogues, menus dash before Mother's eyes. Every now and then she lets out a sigh, shakes her head slightly, and takes a sip a tea from her cup. Sometimes there's a smell of smoke in her nostrils. She glances at the candle, which burns calmly in the draftless room.

At the end, Mother opens her personal e-mail account, which also has a name: Tuesday. Has the longed-for message finally arrived?

Epilogue

1.

Before Jasmin and Linda, there were Sheila and Anna; before Sheila and Anna, there were Nanao and Runa; before Nanao and Runa, there were Liza and Marianne; before Liza and Marianne, there was Aisha; before Aisha, there was Hannele; before Hannele, there was Kibra; before Kibra, there was Marie; before Marie, Ursula; before Ursula, Merle; before Merle, Tina; before Tina, Dira; before Dira, Lenka; before Lenka, Despinia. The list continues. Tomorrow it will be Carina; the day after tomorrow, Marta, Katerina, Iida, and Eila.

The Pet Shop is as real and universal as Benetton, Boss, McDonald's, the Tattoo House, and Nokia.

All those girls—children actually—are difficult-to-interpret, shy, bold, curious, full of teenage wildness, lacking pretense, greedy for experience. They're kittens whose eyes haven't yet opened, and when they do, they'll always be blue, always.

But the irises of the missing children found on milk cartons, cereal boxes, lamp posts, wooden fences, and brick walls are of many colors: gray, green, hazel, brown. Where are you, Katarina? Has anyone seen our Oksana, Anna Livia, Chita, Noulmook? Do you know anything about a girl who looks like this? Could you call the number below, or ask her to come back home? A reward. A sparkle of hope. A morsel of knowledge. A lead. Explain. Why.

2.

During biblical times, and long before, there were holy girls living in the temples of Sumer, Babylon, and Canaan, priestesses of a Goddess, making love to men and having come to the temple to honor the Goddess.

Among these nations, sexuality was sacred and highly valued, and the sexual act was a rite. It was a sacrifice offered together, in mutual corporality. Pleasure was a way to the holiest place.

These sacred sexual customs did not disappear by themselves. They were consciously rooted up. The male priests of the new rising religion that was based on male divinity, together with their supporters, systematically destroyed the belief in the Goddess and her worship.

And soon from the brothels of Pompeii you could hear the howling of the *lupas*. And old *meretrices* in front of the gates of Vesuvius in Necropolis offered their services behind tombstones to beggars and the dying. A profit-driven, secular prostitution had been born.

Within Western culture, prostitution has existed for 5,000 years. The Akkadian cuneiforms from 4,000 years ago have references to prostitution. The patriarchal society is estimated to be approximately as old.

The roots for actual brothel activities are found in ancient Greece. The philosopher and statesman Solon established the first brothel in Athens. The brothels were soon ordered to be taxed, and this increased their number because the profit from taxes benefited both the state and the tax-collecting authorities.

Within the Christian church there have been bishops who have owned girl houses. They justified it by the income to the church and protecting respectable women.

Among the ancient prostitutes, the highest caste was the courtesans. In addition to their physical virtues, they also had to be able to carry on a conversation. For an upper-class Greek man, a courtesan was an elegant companion at a party where an honorable wife could not be taken. Unlike most women of the classical period, courtesans could acquire fairly large amount of wealth, which they controlled independently. It was only the very richest men who could afford to keep a courtesan as their lover.

However, a large portion of the prostitutes in the classical period were slaves. Indeed, some slave traders took into custody girls who had been abandoned or taken as booty, and raised them as prostitutes. The distinction between a slave trader and a pimp is not clear.

In the Greco-Roman world, prostitution was a legal business, and a large seaport might have several slave brothels. In the brothels of Pompeii, there were slave girls from all around the Mediterranean. The men of the city could, if they so wished, experience the exotic, while those who had traveled from abroad could be offered women of their own country to alleviate homesickness.

In Rome, there was a register of prostitutes, and they were taxed heavily. The high taxation was not a result of social unacceptability of prostitution, but rather the fact that it was such a profitable business that the pimps and the brothel owners could afford to pay high taxes.

In the ancient world, there was no disgrace associated with the use of a prostitute's services. It was quite common for men with families to regularly visit a brothel, or for groups of men to rent prostitutes as entertainment during festivals. Men from all different social classes visited brothels or used prostitutes. It is said that some men of noble birth established their own brothels for the slaves they owned.

The brothels of the classical period were tight in their quarters, dirty, and dim. The pimps were shameless in their efforts to make the prostitutes look better. In a textual fragment that remains from the works of the comedy writer Alexis, he describes a variety of ways to make a prostitute seem more enticing. He tells us how short women used shoes with cork bottoms, whereas the tall women had to walk with a stoop in thin-soled shoes. Eyebrows were blackened with soot and cheeks were colored red with henna. If a girl with beautiful teeth did not smile, a thin piece of wood was placed under her lip to force her to hold her mouth open.

Even though brothel life was not easy for the slave girl, in the Greco-Roman world there were prostitutes who suffered even worse conditions. Extreme poverty could lead a woman into prostitution. An expensive courtesan may have been able to choose her company, and the slave prostitute who was confined to a brothel at least had a roof over her head and a space wherein to practice her profession. But a free woman turned prostitute usually did not have the protection provided by a brothel or a pimp.

Free, poor prostitutes sought their customers in the streets and marketplaces. These women were of the lowest caste among prostitutes of the classical period; they were women of the streets in the literal meaning of the phrase. In fact, one reason why it was not suitable for respectable women to walk down the street too often was that they could be confused with indecent gutter girls.

Mary Magdalene may be the best-known prostitute mentioned in the Bible, even though new interpretations have been presented about her profession and relationship to Jesus of Nazareth. In the Gospels, prostitutes are mentioned only twice; they are sinful women and whores, who are discussed as bad examples. In the New Testament, the apostle Paul's letters warn the Corinthians who worship the goddess of love. Paul also underscored the difference between the sacred and sexuality. Combining these two was considered sinful.

At the end of the Middle Ages, prostitution flourished in Western Europe, especially in the cities. With time, plenty of unmarried men came together in cities: young merchants, artisans' apprentices and journeymen, and clergymen.

The prostitutes were thought to serve the sexual needs of young unmarried men. It was not considered proper for married men or clergymen to visit joy houses. Nonbelievers, that is, Jews, weren't allowed to visit "Christian" brothels, and thus Jews had their own brothels. However, the reality did not reflect the principle. In addition to young men, married men, monks, priests, and even bishops and cardinals used the services provided by prostitutes.

Toward the end of the Middle Ages, in official texts, the terms *meretrix* and *meretrix publica* were used for prostitutes and loose women. The common people, however, used their own terms such as *beautiful women*, *common girls* and *common women*, *public women*, *strumpets*, *whores*, and *sluts*. The French had *belles filles*, *bonnes dames*, *filles joyeuses*, and *filles publiques*—expressed more crudely as *bagassa*, *garce*, and *putain*.

The range of appellations was large. Only a few writers bothered to define a prostitute or prostitution as a phenomenon. In the Middle Ages, prostitution was regarded as a moral rather than a professional choice. Or it was considered as a sinful state of mind, which made the woman behave badly.

The term *meretrix* was applied to any sexually active woman, not just to those who practiced commercial sex. Mistresses were also regarded as sinful women, who had loose morals. Many men in society who were well off had unwed concubines. High-ranking clergy might also have children with their mistresses.

The representatives of canon law took a position that rejected mistresses and prostitutes even more so. They believed that these two groups of women were to be separated from each other. Prostitutes, who slept with anybody, were even more sinful than mistresses.

A prostitute who managed to become rich and to be respected by men rose above the ordinary prostitute. She could choose her customers and dedicate her services as a lover or concubine only to a few men. Courtesans such as this were rare even during the fourteenth and fifteenth centuries. Their actual period of ascendancy did not come until modern times.

The most notable theologian of the Middle Ages, Thomas Aquinas, regarded prostitutes as fallen women and called prostitution "a smaller evil" and "a necessary evil." In his opinion, prostitution was a safety valve for men's sexuality, and it protected honorable women from seduction and rape. He also understood that prostitution could guide men away from sodomy, homosexuality that is.

The Church's position toward prostitution was controversial. In principle, the phenomenon was not accepted; however, in practice it was tolerated, because forbidding it would have caused an even greater evil. This attitude goes back to the church father Augustine, who was of the opinion that conventional heterosexual practices would be endangered if prostitution did not exist.

Tolerating prostitution also meant that men's premarital and extramarital sexual relations were tolerated. This, however, did not mean that prostitutes were accepted. Both law and public opinion labeled prostitutes as immoral.

Women from various backgrounds ended up as prostitutes during the Middle Ages. There were poor girls, who were left completely unprotected when families were dispersed. There were widows, who had no livelihood after their spouses died. There were rape victims, who became objects of shame and who felt that they themselves were guilty. Young women who had been raped lost their chances for an honorable marriage, and many husbands abandoned their wives after they had been raped. For these women, prostitution was the only means of earning a living.

During the Middle Ages, the career of a prostitute was usually a short one, and they did not have many opportunities in their later lives. A few of the "retired" prostitutes could continue as brothel hostesses. The Church, on the other hand, offered these women repentance and a cure: it encouraged prostitutes to join an order or to get married.

In 1224, the first order of repenting nuns was founded for harlots who had repented. Cloisters of the Order of Saint Mary Magdalene were established in many cities. Because the sisters used white clothes, they were called White Ladies.

Marriage was the other option, which clergymen suggested for former prostitutes. Pope Innocent III praised those men who took prostitutes to be their wives or their servants in order to save them. From this beautiful thought, however, the road to an actual marriage was long. In reality, it was not easy for prostitutes to find employment as servants even with the help of their former customers, who worked for courts of law or for the Church.

During the Middle Ages, there were also women in towns who practiced the sex trade by themselves and who found their clients on the street and in market places, inns, and ale houses. The number of these secret and occasional prostitutes always grew larger when people flooded the cities during times of markets, church events, and other holidays.

Mostly, prostitution was practiced in small private brothels, which were managed by madams. These madams had under their protection two or three girls, who lived either under the same roof or in the immediate vicinity. In some cases, small brothels were run by widows of artisans, for instance bakers, carpenters, or barrel makers.

"Free" prostitution was tolerated up until the fifteenth century, but gradually there were efforts to regulate it and, eventually, prostitution became institutionalized. The towns of southern and western France, Italy, southern Germany, and England started to establish publicly-owned brothels.

Usually, the citizens of the town rented the brothels out to a madam, an abbess, who in theory had a monopoly on the local sex trade. She acquired the girls, oversaw their activities, followed the regulations, and reported to the official regarding everything that anonymous customers told her. From the point of view of the town, the abbess was an important person: she provided the town with money as well as valuable information.

Instead of a large house, some towns had several places that had been reserved for public prostitution. Some were buildings with several rooms surrounding a courtyard, and others had entire streets lined by public houses and brothels. All these places were under official protection and were dedicated to the practice of so-called permissible fornication.

The first public brothels in France were established in the 1370s and 1380s. During the first decades of the ensuing century, many towns bought a communal girl house or had it built. Italian towns had adopted the custom a little bit earlier.

Despite regulations, bath houses, which existed in every relatively large town, also developed into brothels. They usually included several rooms reserved for sexual activities. For instance, around 1470, Avignon had six, and Lyons and Dijon seven, *joyful bath houses*, in addition to their regular brothels.

As early as in the beginning of the thirteenth century, Jacques de Vitry wrote that in Paris, prostitutes are "everywhere." He may have exaggerated the issue somewhat; however, even before the establishment of official brothels, it was evident that towns had to start restricting the areas where prostitutes could look for and receive their clients. Generally, prostitutes were forbidden to appear near churches, cloisters, and cemeteries. A certain street or area inside or outside the town walls was marked off-limits for brothels. Many French cities, such as Toulouse, Carcassone, and Pamier, ordered their prostitutes to live outside the city walls.

Starting from the end of the thirteenth century, cities in France established official red-lantern districts. In 1285, Montpellier in southern France gave permission to a red-lights district, a "hot street," where prostitutes had to live. The prostitutes were allowed to live and appear in only areas designated solely for them. Corporal punishment and confiscation of clothes were used to enforce the rules.

Also in the German-language areas of continental Europe, as well as in England, prostitutes were forced outside the city walls. In England, both the crown and the cities tried to regulate the practice of prostitutes. King Edward I—who also expelled the Jews from the country in 1292—ordered in 1285 that all London prostitutes must move outside the walls or be imprisoned. The order did not seem to be effective because it was renewed several times. Also Leicester and Cambridge expelled their prostitutes.

Because the prostitutes continued to drift into the cities, both the crown and city councils kept passing new laws against them. In 1345, Edward III lumped whores together with lepers and ordered both groups to wear a visible sign, forbidding lepers from living within city limits and the prostitutes from living inside the walls. When these bans proved ineffective in practice, London ended up reserving certain areas within the city for prostitutes.

During the Black Death, European cities lost a great number of their inhabitants. Houses within the cities became vacant in a large scale, and people—including prostitutes—from suburban areas flocked into them. Hence, at the end of the fourteenth century and the beginning of the fifteenth century brothels reappeared in the cities.

When a street had been assigned to be used by prostitutes, the stigma of a whore street remained for centuries, despite the fact that the brothels had moved on. Old street names still tell the story of their former inhabitants: Paris has Rue Froidmantel, la Court Robert, Rue Charon, Rue Tyron, and Champs Fleury, and German towns have Frauengasse Strasse, Frauenporte Strasse, and Frauenfleck Strasse. Regardless of language, street names that include the word "rose" have originally been prostitute streets.

City officials controlled the hiring of women to work in publicly-owned brothels, as well as the visibility of prostitutes in towns. Officials dictated not only the prices, but also what kind of clients could be allowed into the brothels. They drafted regulations in order to protect prostitutes from assaults and oppression from brothel keepers and others.

Officials also determined the opening hours of the brothels, and the days when it was permissible to entertain guests. The purpose of these specific brothel regulations was to retain the prostitutes as a commodity, belonging to the city rather than just existing within city limits.

As part of the means to isolate the prostitutes and to emphasize their lowly status was also the fact that a low-status official, for instance an executioner, was appointed to be their supervisor. In many French towns the supervisor was called "the king of the lewd."

Prostitutes, therefore, were clearly distinguished from the practitioners of other professions, who were less regulated and supervised by a more respected official. As early as during the first part of the fifteenth century, the post of "the king of the lewd" was, however, discontinued. After this, a woman—an "abbess," "queen," "headmistress"—controlled the brothels.

In 1439, the city of Florence founded a corresponding post *ufficiale di notte*, officer of the night. The person appointed to this post was to oversee the compliance with luxury laws and prostitution regulations, and to keep an eye on possible homosexual offenses. The job was not enticing, and it was difficult to hire people for that post.

Over time, there have been regulations regarding the appearance of prostitutes, as well as of their clothing and jewelry. The purpose of these regulations make them easily recognizable and distinguish them from the broader population.

There were three kinds of regulations concerning prostitutes: prohibitions, permissions, and various signs and labels.

Prostitutes were forbidden certain types of garments, but were allowed to use some fashionable clothes. Various pieces of clothing and patterns acted as signs or labels indicating that a woman was a prostitute at first glance. Despite the fact that people did not always care about these so-called luxury orders, they were an important part of the discussion through which the prostitute's identity was built and through which a line was drawn between "good" and "bad" girls.

Most towns did not allow prostitutes to wear clothes, jewelry, or decorations that were regarded as fitting for respectable women. The whores of Arles were not allowed to wear a veil because that was a piece of clothing for married women. Anyone seeing an immoral woman wearing a veil on her head was allowed to strip her of it. Actually, it was an unequivocal duty to do so.

In 1243, the regulations in Avignon forbade the prostitutes to wear a cape, which also was a garment for respectable women. Regulations in Marseilles listed those pieces of clothing that only honorable women could wear.

The symbolic meaning of the veil was also exhibited by the fact that in Dijon stripping a woman of her headgear was an accusation of the woman's sexual immorality.

Regulations also limited the anonymity that a head cover could offer to a woman. The city of Siena forbade women from hiding their faces behind a veil in such a manner that they could not be identified; however, prostitutes were allowed to wear such veils. A cape could be worn as long as it was held by hand and not used to cover the face. In Lucca, only widows were allowed to cover their heads with a cape when it was not raining. On the other hand, in many German towns prostitutes could not be seen without their heads covered for the reason that unrestrained hair was a sign of virginity.

The city fathers in London became concerned as local prostitutes adopted too many dress customs from women of higher social ranks. In 1351 they gave an ordinance regarding the dress of "common women." According to the ordinance, no lewd woman was allowed to wear clothing lined or decorated by the fur of ermine, badger, squirrel, or sheep. Neither could they have clothes that were lined by silk or some other expensive fabric. Should they violate the order, the clothes would be confiscated. This ordinance was meant to prevent prostitutes from dressing as "good and noble ladies and maids." However, since prostitutes of noble birth also existed, the ordinance did not apply to those.

In Paris several ordinances were given in order to separate prostitutes from honorable women. In 1360, prostitutes were forbidden from wearing embroidered or otherwise decorated hoods. In 1426, prostitutes were deprived of wearing "honorable women's decoration." Between these two ordinances, in 1415, prostitutes were ordered not to have gold or silver in their hoods or capes. Neither could they wear golden or gilded belts, dresses lined by gray squirrel skin or other "respectable" fur. Silver shoe buckles were also banned.

A few towns did not adopt restrictions. Rather, they encouraged and prompted the prostitutes to wear luxurious clothes and decorations. The city of Perpignan in France excluded prostitutes from all dressing restrictions. Hence, a woman who did not follow the sumptuary regulation was identified as a whore. Also in Toulouse, prostitutes were allowed to dress however they wanted to, provided that they wore a quite unnoticeable badge of their profession on their sleeve.

During the fourteenth century, some Italian towns tried to persuade virtuous women to dress in a simple manner; at the same time, prostitutes were permitted to wear luxurious clothes. Some towns allowed prostitutes to wear tinkling jewelry and other fine accessories, in the hopes that respectable women refrain from wearing them. In 1335, Florence permitted its prostitutes to wear any clothes as they pleased.

With the same purpose in mind, in 1343 Siena gave its prostitutes the permission to wear dresses made of silk and golden fabrics, as well as platform shoes, which the sumptuary laws forbade respectable women from wearing. The same regulation granted prostitutes the use of clothes sewn of fabrics decorated with painted tree, flower, fruit, and animal motifs.

In 1215, the Fourth Lateran Council of the Catholic Church demanded that Jews, Muslims, and heretics wear a sign on their clothes that would allow for their identification. This regulation was gradually extended to prostitutes as well.

All over Europe prostitutes were forced to use some kind of an identifying sign during the fourteenth and the fifteenth centuries. There was no general, uniform identification badge; the signs varied from town to town and from country to country.

The first recording of the sign of a whore is found in Languedoc, in the city ordinance of Castelnaudary, in 1333: all prostitutes were required to wear a cord belt. Later on, a striped dress came to be sign of a whore.

The court of Nîmes passed the first sumptuary law regarding prostitutes in 1350. A decision of an obligatory marker was made in 1353. Their dresses must have one sleeve made of different color and different fabric. At the same time in Paris people were busily drafting regulations regarding the clothing of prostitutes. Several small towns also started to regulate their dress code. In many places in the kingdom of France a tied colorful cord, hanging from the woman's shoulder, functioned as "the sign of shame." Also a man's hat, a red belt, a striped tunic, a white ribbon of the width of a woman's palm, or a white cap could have this same function.

In England, the usual identifying sign of a prostitute was a hood. In London, old regulations forced prostitutes to wear a striped hood together with a simple dress. The town of Hull even provided its whores with hoods.

In Italy, prostitutes were labeled with some piece of clothing, label, or color. In Pisa they had to wear a yellow ribbon. During the following century, in large towns this label could be gloves, a yellow or green scarf, a white cape, a black coat, or a red hood with tinkling bells, so that everyone could see and hear the person wearing this garment.

In German-speaking towns, the prostitutes were required to wear various labeling pieces of clothing: a yellow scarf, a red cap, a red-and-white or black-and-white conical hat, and a yellow coat.

Note that the labeling color for prostitutes was never blue—the color of the Virgin Mary's cape. When traveling, "respectable" women had to carefully find out what kinds of symbols prostitutes wore in each town, in order to avoid ending up, against their will, as targets of sexual harassment by men.

It has been argued that prostitutes were being identified so that respectable women would not be mistaken for lewd women, and men would not make improper advances to them. The real purpose of the identification was by no means to prevent respectable women from ending up in embarrassing situations, but to save men from these situations. If a man was able to recognize a prostitute from afar, he would not inadvertently reveal his lecherous intentions to a respectable woman.

The segregation of prostitutes at the end of the Middle Ages and even later can foremost be regarded as an issue of power. Earning money by providing sexual services gave the prostitutes a degree of economic independence that they otherwise would not have had. Because they had no families, and because they did not belong to any religious order, they were operating outside of the male system of power. Hence, the authorities—who were all men—felt the need to control their behavior.

Many European towns closed their brothels in the mid-sixteenth century. Even those cities that had no public bordellos limited the practice of prostitution on one street or one area of town, or outside the town. It was not a matter of the intolerance from the Catholics or the Protestants, but a general moral shift that drove the change.

3.

During the classical period, slaves were usually of the same ethnicity as their owners. The New Age slavery started when Native Americans perished in masses, and America experienced a labor shortage. Someone had the bright idea that every pioneer should bring with him twelve black slaves. So started a centuries-long slave trade from Africa.

For more than three hundred years, fifteen million black slaves were transported from Africa to America. Complete industries—for instance the sugar in the West Indies and cotton in North America—were based solely on the use of slave labor.

But what impact has the abuse and trade of girls and women had over the last 4,000 years? When I write about the plunder of female bodies, about female sexuality as merchandise, I'm in fact writing about a certain type of a colony and about a kind of colonialism.

Many of the early opponents of racism and white slave trade were feminists. The women's movement questioned the myth of the woman's biological inferiority as compared to the man, and some went so far as to doubt the claims made that black slaves were biologically inferior to whites.

The debut work of Olive Schreiner, daughter of a South African missionary, titled *The Story of an African*

Farm, came out in 1883. It became an international best seller.

Schreiner resisted the image of a woman in her times, as well as the racial doctrines. There was no scientific proof of woman being biologically inferior to man, just as there was no proof for blacks, Jews, Boers, or other so-called "lower-class peoples" as biologically weaker than others.

The fact that certain groups of people, such as white men, at any specific period of time, were in a privileged position did not mean that their innate qualities were superior to those of others.

Poor Olive Schreiner. The British abhorred her because she sided with the Boers; the Boers abhorred her because she decided to defend the blacks. Men detested her because she was a feminist, and South African feminists detested her because she demanded voting rights for black women as well.

A black woman, Saartjie Baartman, was exhibited widely to white men around Europe at the beginning of the nineteenth century. Look at her bottom! What a clitoris! What labia! Born to be used, fucked—born for prostitution.

A woman with the name of Truganina was the last Tasmanian. She died in 1876, a few years after Darwin's *The Origin of Species* had been published. Truganina's skeleton is still displayed in a Tasmanian museum in Hobart. She is seen as a seductress in a display case, her hand bent in an invitation, her head tilted.

Just before the beginning of the twentieth century, Europe was possessed by its self-indulgent images of destruction. In the laboratory of colonialism, all possible tests were being carried out. Meetings of scientific societies were bustling affairs.

Colonial peoples had characteristics that Europeans did not have. Applause, bravo! In the colonies, women walked around practically naked, and they seemed to enjoy it. More applause. They had wide high buttocks and hips, and their breasts, which were hanging unrestrained, seemed to practically demand to be grabbed. It was no wonder the temptation was too great for a man traveling to the colonies.

The concept of "sexuality" came into use in the nineteenth century. Discussion of sexuality began thanks to venereal diseases, which had resulted, on one hand, from the susceptibility to temptation of men traveling in colonies, and, on the other hand, from the growth of prostitution in European towns.

In 1897, the concept of *Lebensraum* was born in Germany. As a concept, *Lebensraum* is grotesque if it is transported into the present time, into the world of my book, into interpersonal relations, into *Sexualia*. All over Europe, *Lebensraum* is being sought after night and day; in the brothels and paid rooms of cities, villages, backwoods, slums, and secret places.

During the time between the World Wars, people had been afraid that they would be bombed back into the Stone Age—into the age of hunger, filth, and rats. After the Second World War, however, primitive barbarity started to look enticing in the eyes of many men.

Apocalyptic images, threat of mass destruction, and fear of terrorism opened the doors for new kinds of masculine fantasies of the Wild West and the Foreign Legion. In many science fiction stories, a nuclear attack is an almost desired opportunity that allows people to break the rules and prohibitions of city life.

On a smaller scale, a moral state of emergency exists in Thailand, Cambodia, Vietnam, the slums of Rio de Janeiro, the Philippines, Sri Lanka, India, Africa, and the Caribbean. In a scale closer to home, the prohibitions of sexual ethics do a somersault, say, during meetings of political parties, at sports events, rock festivals, or tango competitions.

Conquerors have a need to legitimize their conquests. Whether it is pieces of land in North America, South America, southern Africa, Siberia, Australia, the Pacific Islands, or on a young girl's or woman's skin, in *Sexualia*. Conquerors have a need to legitimize the plundering of land and the destruction of the indigenous people—on religious grounds, on biological grounds, on grounds of entertainment—in order to dress cruelty in a false robe of acceptability.

The legal rules of war have at all times needed to respond to two questions: When is it legitimate to start a war? What is one allowed to do during a war?

The legal rules of war have always presented two contradictory answers to these questions, depending on who the enemy is. The rules protect enemies who belong to the same race, social class, and cultural circles.

Unknown and new enemies are left without protection by the laws of war. When can you wage a war against barbarians and the untamed? The answer: whenever. What is one allowed to do during a war waged against barbarians and the untamed? Whatever.

Abu Hanifa, a Persian-born legal scholar and the founder of Baghdad's legal academy, was the first to forbid the killing of women, children, the elderly, and the sick during wars. He also condemned rape, as well as the taking of hostages.

During the Middle Ages, war among Western Christians who belonged to the order of knighthood (*bellum hostile*) was distinguished from war against outsiders, infidels, barbarians, or rebellious peasants (*bellum romanum*).

Bellum hostile was conducted with polite formal manners, whereas *bellum romanum* was war without any legal restrictions.

In 1925, around the same time that Josephine Baker presented her famous banana dance at Revue Nègre, the international legal commission gathered at The Hague drafted an agreement that would regulate aerial warfare.

Two opposite proposals were offered. According to the Brits, bombing raids were to be allowed only against "military targets," a concept that was left without further definition. According to the Americans, bombing raids should be permitted only in the "theater of war," which was defined as the area where land forces were fighting.

According to Quincy Wright, an American political scientist, "The right of primitive races, in the same way as the right of primitive individuals, is not the right to be recognized as what they are not, but to acquire for themselves a guardian—in other words, acquire themselves some guidance, in order to be able to grow to their full potential, thus realizing their own special predispositions."

In October 1940, the British government decided to create areas in Germany that later, during the Vietnam War, were known as "free zone areas." These areas could be bombed freely when the location of military or industrial targets was difficult or impossible to pinpoint, because of weather or other circumstances.

In 1960, the United Nations General Assembly approved the declaration granting independence to colonial countries and peoples: "All peoples have the right to self-determination; by virtue of that right they may freely determine their political status and freely pursue their economic, social, and cultural development."

A few years later, when a forty-year-old East European whore called Viveka Vamp tumbled into the Spree Canal, the West Berlin policemen laughed, and the soldiers whistled, "Viveka Vamp, *auf wiedersehen*!" Mysterious blue angels exist only in movies, and you were indecently red. Crimson and coagulated. And too old. Worn out. Used up.

The so-called colonial declaration was accepted by all except the colonial powers, which refrained from voting. They held on until 1970, when they agreed to support the principle of the nations' equal "right to self-determination."

For a long time, slavery was considered to be natural and a necessity. Blood vengeance was once an absolute issue of honor. Both were institutions, buttresses whose roots were deep in shared history, memory, and soul. And still they changed with time to become abhorred, obsolete, and rejected.

It is said that the white slave trade ended in 1904. In fact, the human trade of females has never flourished as it does now, at the beginning of the new millennium. The declaration should read: "All women have the right to self-determination; by virtue of that right, they freely determine their political status and freely pursue their economic, social, cultural, and physical development."

The word *Europe* derives from a Semitic word, meaning darkness. A Greek lexicographer Hesykhios, who lived some time during the fifth century, defined the word *Europe* as "the region of the setting sun." When in modern time people come to Europe to pursue better opportunities, freedom, or a higher standard of living, they in fact arrive in *darkness*.

One could ask if the journey described by Joseph Conrad has turned upside down? Is the Congo after all in Europe? Are Tasmanians, Guanches in the north? Kurtz is today's Girlz—in hip-hop terminology.

Open borders, *Schengen*. Globalization is a blessing for today's prostitution, for human trade, for sexual colonialism. Everything is possible. Something for everyone. Business is good. Welcome to Bartholomew's Fair. Today a three-legged child, a King of India, a dwarf in a bird cage, a woman in continuous heat.

Global prostitution has many faces: schoolgirls along the side of the highway, on the gravel roads in parks, at the far end of an archway, on Falkland Road, the lanes of Sonagachhi, Reeberbahn, micro-shorts, a miniskirt, a blouse, lace, plastic, Lurex. The season is always the same, and the fashion styles do not change. In Bruno Max Huber's *Sexualia* there is only one season.

Once upon a time, there were three Graces and nine Muses. This is a trip from Ishtar's priestesses to the whores of Babylon, from the dancing girls of the Moulin Rouge to Sexy Suzy and Fucking Fiesta on the internet's teen pages.

In all the countries of Europe, five- and six-year-old children are used as porn models or peep show stars. In Thailand, tens of thousands of female children disappear annually. In Manila, there are more than 5,000 child prostitutes, two-thirds of whom are boys.

Some of the adult women who earn their living in the sex business and whom I interviewed introduced themselves as sex therapists, erotic dance artists, entrepreneurs of adult entertainment. Throughout Europe, sex work is already a half-accepted professional enterprise. There are unions, retirement funds, beautifully written obituaries. And that is nothing new per se: as early as the sixteenth century, Roman prostitutes paved Strada del Popolo at their own expense after getting tired of wading in the mud; at the beginning of the twentieth century, prostitutes in Berlin established a retirement fund with the help of Communists.

Joseph Conrad ran off to sea at the age of fifteen. He came back and later wrote *Heart of Darkness*. That presupposed coming back.

If one of the girls I mentioned in the beginning were to come back, no one knows what she would write. About what kind of darkness, what kinds of hearts, and what kinds of backroads of cruelty?

In 1897, the enigma of malaria was solved. So disappeared the indigenous people's best protection against white conquerors.

To reverse this: what if all the world's imprisoned and captured girls who have been enticed into the sex business would have some horrible bacterium, a virus, a disease they would pass on to their abusers—a miasma that would cause blackening of the face, bulging eyes, and loss of hair? What would our world look like tomorrow?

I repeat: what would our world look like tomorrow?

Thank You

To my family. To Jukka, Alma, and Elsa, who put up with me through all of this.

An author's thank you:

Several histories of colonialism have been written, and the history of racism draws today's researchers. People write about pornography, and it is analyzed from various perspectives. However, no comprehensive history of prostitution, or, more colloquially, no history of the sex trade, has yet been written.

I am grateful to all before me who have investigated this topic. My warm thanks to the Finns Anna Kontula, Kristel Nyberg, Leena Rossi, and Kaari Utrio; your talks and writings that have dealt with human trade, the sex business, and prostitution have inspired me over the years.

A special thank you to the researcher and theologian Kristel Nyberg; with your kind permission, I have been able in my epilogue to utilize your writings about prostitution in the classical world. For instance, the anthology *Heavenly Sex* includes your section, "Prostitution and the Ideal Woman in the World of the New Testament" (Ahola, Minna; Marjo-Riitta Antikainen; and Päivi Salmesvuori, eds., Helsinki: Tammi, 2006).

A sincere thank you to the cultural history researcher, Leena Rossi (Licentiate of Philology). In my epilogue, I've summarized your article "The Strategies of Shame, or How Prostitutes Were Distinguished from Respectable People during the Late Middle Ages" (*Ennen ja nyt* I/2005), and I suggest that those interested also acquaint themselves with your longer English version, "Keeping the Whores Recognizable: Segregating and Identifying Prostitutes in Late Medieval Europe" (Holmberg, Eva Johanna, and Tom Linkinen, eds., *Practices of Inclusion*, Turku: k&h, 2005).

A thank you and a bow to my colleague, writer Sven Lindqvist; I return again and again to your travel journals that deal with racism and colonialism. Without the third volume of the Sahara series, *Kill Those Bastards* (Pequot, 1996), I could not have written the preceding epilogue.

*

Thank you to detective sergeant and violent crime investigator Maria Vuento; I will always remember our discussions together. Without getting to know you and without learning from your wise thoughts, this novel would have been different.

Thank you to sex crime investigators Tuija Kivinen and Jonna Turunen; I admire your professional skills, your warm empathy, and the sensitivity you have managed to foster despite your difficult work.

Thank you to the head of the Violent Crimes Unit, Kari Tolvanen; there were no questions to which I did not get clear answers from you.

I also want to thank chief criminal inspector Lars Henriksson at the Finnish National Bureau of Investigation; nobody could have illuminated better than you the history of children's sexual abuse and its manifestations on the internet.

*

Thank you to Jaana Koistinen, Leena Majander, and Niina Miettinen for all your help along the way.

*

I thank the Finnish Cultural Foundation, Alfred Kordelin Foundation, the Uusimaa County Arts Commission, and the Library Grant Board for their support and confidence in me during the past three years.

*

Thank you to the girls and boys, women and men, whom I interviewed, and who work in one way or another in the area of adult entertainment and the sex business, and who wished to remain anonymous.

These interviewees suggested that I append a questionnaire here, at the end of the book.

In this questionnaire, there is no “Undecided” option, and you can’t respond with “I don’t know.” Therefore: yes or no.

Have you ever received money for intercourse or other sexual acts?

Has anyone ever offered payment to you?

Have you accepted gifts, trips, indulgence after sexual acts?

Or:

Have you ever paid for intercourse or other sexual acts?

Has anyone ever asked you for a payment?

Have you given gifts, trips, indulgence after sexual acts?

You might wish to know how a sexual act is defined. A look, a touch, an oral caress, penetration? Everything goes. A retired Finnish man once spent six months' worth of his pension in order to suck a teenage girl's nipple for five minutes, in a car, in a dark parking lot.

The last question is: Who is the victim?